Ayra of Darkwater Quarry

Jill Turner Claybrook

maple avenue

publishing

For Madie

PROLOGUE

THE two men stood on the sandy beach, surrounded by soldiers. Though they were well known to one another, their greeting was stiff like that of strangers. Across the restless waters, the sun hinted its arrival, and a salty wind soughed through the nearby trees. The taller of the two held out a pouch pinched between his ringed thumb and finger.

"Your one request," he said coldly.

The other man took a step toward him. A smile flickered on his face when the soldiers surrounding them twitched closer, gripping their swords. He took the offered pouch, loosened the drawstrings, and peered inside. A round, blue gem gleamed in the dim light.

"You made good on your word, Tobian. I half expected to find a viper. But why should I be surprised? Coward."

Tobian's face colored as he drew in a sharp breath. "You've been granted pardon from death yet remain full of insults. I will never understand you."

"Oh, I know that too well. You are incapable of seeing beyond the cushions in your palace and too sensitive to understand my ways."

"It is my *sensitivity* that has spared you, Covalt."

"Spoken like a fool. But I thank you for making comfortable accommodations for me."

"It was not your comfort I had in mind. Merely having you far from me but not out from under me." He wearily ran a cold hand over his bearded jaw. "Tie his hands. And his mouth. I no longer wish to hear him."

Three guards stepped out of ranks to do as they were bid. Covalt stood contently, as if he were being dressed for a gathering in his honor. His blue eyes never strayed from Tobian's face. After his hands and mouth were bound, the small pouch was tied to his belt. They stood facing each other a moment longer. With a wave of Tobian's hand, a troop of guards led the prisoner to a large rowboat.

As the oars cut through the choppy waves, stroking him out to sea, he continued to stare at the shore, but his eyes no longer focused on the armored horses and cluster of men. The pouch hung from his belt, heavy with promise.

1

THE sun abandoned the quarry for land beyond the hills, and the faint scent of boiled cabbage and onions wafted through the air. Quitting time. A persistent crow sailed over the camp, taunting the dusty workers as they slowly made their way to the mess house for supper.

Ayra dropped her pick in the dirt and surveyed the small pit she had been working on for days. She hadn't found anything of value, but that wasn't unusual for her. In her thirteen years, she had never had much luck finding what she was looking for.

"You coming or just going to stand out there until the sun comes up again?" yelled her younger brother, Kelton, from the outskirts of the quarry.

Ayra made a face and pulled herself out of the hole. The cool renewal season wind swirled past her, whipping her tangled, ash brown hair into her eyes. She brushed the dirt from her wool frock and glanced at the well-built structures on the other side of the main pit where the skilled workers of the village lived. For a moment she watched the houses behind an imaginary wall turn into homes as they filled with people and firelight for the evening.

Heaving an exaggerated sigh, Ayra picked her way toward the array of small, gray huts, knowing her pace would annoy her brother. Kelton never did anything slowly, which was probably why he was one of the most productive pit diggers, despite his small stature and only being ten years from birth.

"Took you long enough," Kelton said looking up at the wispy clouds in the dim sky. "It's going to rain tonight, I think."

Ayra felt the faint tickle in her fingers that sometimes preceded rainfall. "Yes, I think you're right."

With empty bellies, they turned their backs on Darkwater Quarry and trudged past the noisy mess house toward a hut on the far edge of the camp. As she walked across the gravelly earth, Ayra tried to pretend the pungent smell was not cabbage but something delicious. Something worth tasting.

It was harder to imagine than she hoped it would be, and instead of getting a skip in her step, she felt her shoulders droop.

When they reached their hut, she stepped inside and looked around at the only home she'd ever known. A small, wooden table with two rough benches almost filled the main room, and a short shelf, heavy with books, hung on the wall. Her grandmother, Tanna, stood over the makeshift cook-stove stirring the standard supper fare—cabbage and potato soup, rations from the kitchen. Her long, white braid swished across her stooped back as she moved about, finishing the meal preparations. Ayra dropped onto a bench.

Tanna glanced at them with her twinkling, green eyes. Her weathered face crinkled into a smile. "You two had better grab a bowl and eat before you wither away!" She lifted the pot from the stove and placed it on the table.

"Thank you, Nana," said Kelton, filling his stone bowl. "It smells like you cooked up something extra special tonight!"

It was the same joke they shared every night, but mealtime would not be complete without it.

Ayra ladled out a portion of soup into her own bowl, allowing the potatoes to drop with loud plops. Her stomach growled to be fed, but her tongue protested for something new, like the sweet pastries kids from the outside talked about or whatever created the savory smells that occasionally escaped from the village. She dropped herself onto the bench next to Kelton and stared at her bland soup.

"Not hungry tonight, Ayra?" asked Tanna quietly.

"Not really," she lied, watching the potatoes in her bowl bob up and down as she poked at them with her spoon. There was no hope for her supper—or her life—to change any time soon. Her family had been prisoners of the king's debtor camp for generations. The reason for their imprisonment now long forgotten. In the last ten years her family had dwindled from nine to three. She was keenly aware it could continue to dwindle. She looked up at her grandmother's expectant face. "But the cabbage is well cooked tonight, so it would be a shame to let it waste."

Tanna smiled and nodded her head approvingly as Ayra put a spoonful into her mouth. A rap on the door gave her an excuse to get away from the table and out from under Tanna's inspection. She opened the door to find her friend, Kara.

"I brought you some bread," Kara said pulling a hand-sized loaf out from under the folds of her red cloak. "It's not from the kitchen. Mother made it. It's a little dark since she still can't get our fire stove to heat right, but I like it anyway. It's wheat instead of that awful rye stuff."

"It is pretty dark," Ayra said examining the round, black-bottomed loaf in her friend's hands. A delicate cough came from behind her. "But it looks all right to me. Thank you." She took the hard loaf and handed it to Tanna to divide up.

Kara stepped inside, quickly greeted Tanna and Kelton, and turned to Ayra to talk about the events of her day. Ayra had decided early on in life it was easier to keep Kelton as her only playmate and had tried to keep her distance from the girl, but Kara insisted they be friends. Ayra felt certain the older girl was her friend only for the sake of her own loneliness.

Kara's father had been unable to pay his landlord rent he owed on farmland and elected to come work off the debt before the warm season began and crops needed to be planted. Typically, families separated, sending the men and older boys to the camp, but Kara and her mother had come with her father to work and pay the debt faster.

As Kara dramatically prattled on, Ayra tried to be interested—nodding her head and smiling or frowning when she thought she should. To her it was all everyday occurrences, but to Kara it was still new. Ayra most liked when Kara told her about the village she came from and about her trips to Midivard, the head city. When Kara mentioned her father, Ayra remembered he had cut his hand sharpening a blade.

"How is your father's hand?" she asked with a fleeting look at Tanna. Ayra felt a little stab of guilt knowing she only asked to please Tanna rather than out of genuine concern for the man.

"Oh, it's healing. The cut wasn't deep, and the healer doesn't think it will get an infection if he keeps it wrapped and clean. He's working a little slower right now but should pick up again soon. I think we only have another two weeks until we'll be released to go home!"

Ayra clenched her fists. "I'm happy for you," she said flatly, forcing a smile.

"Oh, Ayra, I'm sorry. That wasn't thoughtful of me." The girl self-consciously grabbed up her golden brown braid. "I will miss you when I go. Can't say I will miss this place though. I'm ready to have my flower garden to tend and raspberries to eat." She bit her lip before she brightened again. "Maybe I'll send you some berries when they ripen."

Kara stayed a few minutes more before awkwardly excusing herself to go back to her parents. As Ayra watched her cloaked figure disappear into the darkness, she wondered what it would be like to wear something red and soft. Her baggy, brown dress suddenly felt heavy and uncomfortable. A cool burning swelled in her chest.

"Ayra," Tanna said with a warning tone.

At once Ayra's simmering thoughts boiled out. "It isn't fair!" She stamped her foot. "How come other families get to come and go, but we stay trapped here? I'm tired of picking at dirt and being watched night and day by armed guards like a thief."

"The world is a dangerous place, Ayra. We have an important purpose, you and me. We are safe here."

"An *important* purpose? *Safe*? I pick at dirt all day—don't see much importance in that. I hate that I've never climbed a tree or seen water that isn't brown. Did you know water should not be brown? And we're surrounded by armed men waiting to stick an arrow through us if we get too close to the borders. What kind of safe place is this? I *hate* my ancestors for passing their punishment to me!"

Tanna pushed her bowl away and shut her eyes. Minutes passed in silence, and Ayra began to feel the room was too small for the three of them. Her temper burned quick, and the smoke of guilt always lingered when the flame died down.

Ayra felt her grandmother's eyes on her again. When she felt brave enough, she looked up to meet them.

After several breaths, Tanna spoke. "I have never seen those men stick an arrow through anyone. You are too young to understand everything. But I know from our ancestors the world outside our quarry is full of those who would cause us harm. We must never leave the safety of this valley. Never. This quarry may feel like a prison to you, but it is a sanctuary to me." She stood and put her bowl in the wash tub. "I'm going out for my walk."

Ayra stared at her hands, feeling as if a hot coal were lodged in her throat. She knew better than to speak as she had—to lash out in such a way. Frustration in her mind battled with the shame in her heart. She glanced at Kelton and read plainly the chastisement on his face. Without a word he stood and went into the sleeping room.

You're too old to act like such a child, she told herself and angrily swiped the tears welling in her eyes.

A half hour later, Ayra slipped into bed beside a sleeping Kelton. Droplets of water calmly pelted the thatched roof. The tingling in her hands gently increased as the rhythmless drumming grew louder and louder. She looked over to where her grandmother should be sleeping. She had not yet come in from her walk.

Ayra rolled over and tightened the rough blanket over her shoulders. She didn't want to think about her outburst anymore. With the fingers of one hand, she found the birthmark on her left shoulder and traced over it several times. She had been told many times since she was small to show it to no one. Tanna had one that matched exactly, a link that always made Ayra feel close to her grandmother. She tuned her ears to the pitter-patter whisper of the rain, letting it speak peace to her soul. Her heart slowed its pace, and her breaths steadied.

She would be better tomorrow.

2

THE next morning Ayra woke to find herself alone in the sleeping room. The scraping sound of spoons against stoneware, along with Kelton and Tanna's occasional soft murmurs, told her she was not alone in the hut. As she listened to their faint chatter, words from the evening before crept in on the calm that came with a heavy night's sleep.

She closed her eyes and felt the weight and warmth of her blanket, wishing it could protect her from the biting thoughts.

Within minutes, the clang of the first pounding hammer carried across the quarry to her little window. She drew in a deep breath and swiftly whipped the blanket off, knowing it was easier to do if done quickly. She sat up and realized she had slept in her dirty work clothes. At least she had taken off her boots.

Just as Ayra entered the main room, Tanna and Kelton were

stepping out the door.

"Wait!" They stopped and stared at her expectantly. She wanted to say the right words to clear the guilty feeling in her gut, but they wouldn't leave her mouth. "I…I hope you have a good day."

A warm smile formed on Tanna's face. "Thank you, Ayra. Now hurry up. You overslept." She pushed Kelton along, but before shutting the door, she poked her head back in. "And I accept your apology."

Ayra returned the smile, grateful her grandmother had seen the real meaning of her words—just as she always did—and was quick to forgive. She hoped someday they would share more traits than eye color and a birth mark.

She slid her feet into her worn boots and sat down at the table to eat her bowl of barley porridge, choking down heaping spoonfuls to finish before the guards began the morning count. Punishment for shirking in the quarry was usually issued in the form of adding to the debt. As her family was never given any sort of tally regarding what they owed, she didn't care a scrap if they did heap on more time. But rules were rules, and Tanna made it clear she was expected to obey.

When her bowl was empty, Ayra raced out the door and sprinted to the lineup. The laborers stood in five rows, each with a man in a brown tunic moving down the line. The fierce face of a bear on their chests, embroidered in red, signified their authority. She reached the end of the fifth line where her family stood just as the guard approached.

He stopped with his tablet and quill in hand and sneered, "Still here I see. You two children will be digging today, and you, Tanna, will be on water duty." He made a mark on his paper, glanced at the other lines to see his fellow guards finished, and called out in a self-important manner the workday had begun.

Ayra stuck out her tongue as he walked away and instantly flicked her eyes to Tanna. She was relieved to see her grandmother had already turned away from her and hadn't seen her impulsive face.

The other armed guards were already in position—twelve surrounding the camp, four in the tower, and eight interspersed with the people. They were all men recruited from the village and trained on site. Though some guards were certainly more pleasant than others, Ayra could remember few occasions when guards had exerted force.

With her feet firmly planted in place, she attempted to put off her work as long as possible by pretending to wait for the crowd to disperse. Darkwater was the largest of three debtor camps in Mihtengard, with more residents during late harvest season to early renewal season. There were fewer during the other portions of the year, as industries around the country were busier during that time. Creditors and other wronged citizens could submit requests to the Crown, that would in turn pay the debt and assume the creditor's position. Citizens who could not pay the debts or their taxes to the king, or who had minor infractions in conduct, were sent to a camp.

Everyone who came to Darkwater seemed to know their obligation. Digging. Sifting. Sharpening tools. Pulling carts. It was seen as a mercy to be given the opportunity to work and repay the Crown or to earn forgiveness. And leaving without paying one's debt meant banishment from the country.

When her procrastination became obvious, Ayra trudged to her own waist-deep hole and glanced around the quarry before throwing herself into its depths. The Darkwater settlement was located in a wide, winding canyon with tall hills on either side. In any direction she turned her head, she could see only rocks, brushy hillsides, or sky. The stone quarry pit was at the center of everything, separating the village, Doren, and the camp, and claiming the lower half of the eastern hillside. The land was known for the fine building stones it produced. It was also rich with the blue precious gem, safner, and traces of gold, all of which were owned by King Leofric. The ground was pock-marked with hand-dug pits and man-made caves. She was told several abandoned quarries, each with their own pockmark pits and village remnants, rested further up the canyon, but she had never seen them.

Ayra grabbed her pick and set to work. The surface dirt was damp from last night's rain and fell away in clumps that needed to be broken up. It was tedious work and time usually passed slowly. She looked forward to rest day at the end of each week. She could spend that day staring up at the clouds and thinking for as long as she wanted or reading the books her grandmother borrowed from others. Currently she was reading a book about a man lost at sea. She wondered what it would be like to float in a boat, waves pushing up and down and not a rock to be seen.

An irregular rumble echoed through the canyon. Ayra stood and glanced around, looking for any sign of disturbance. Near the base of the carved hillside, she saw a wagon on its side and a growing cluster of men rushing from their work. She scrambled out of her hole just as Kelton ran up next to her.

"I can't see Nana. Can you?"

She looked around again, this time at faces. A prickle swept down her neck. She grabbed his hand, and the two ran around the edge of the main pit. As they neared the cluster, Ayra could hear men shouting as they dug through rocks and dirt with their hands. A wagon that had been loaded with rubble had apparently slipped two wheels off the raised road and overturned.

"Someone must be under there for them to be digging like that," Kelton said shakily. "I can't see Nana."

Ayra searched the crowd again for her grandmother's face. Her heart began to race with the swift movements of the men digging. She pushed through the gathering to get a closer look.

"Here! She's here! I have her hand!" one shouted. Several men moved to join the man's effort as others backed away to make room. Within minutes Tanna was pulled free from under the rubble, unconscious but breathing.

The next two days passed with no happy change in Tanna's condition. The woman remained in a constant state of fitful sleep, her breathing ragged and shallow. Her chest and legs were covered in deep purple bruises and one arm was broken. The village healer had told Ayra and Kelton she would not wake again. They had been allowed to work alternating half shifts during the day, and Ayra stayed by her side through each night.

For the hundredth time, Ayra reached out her fingers and gingerly stroked the matted, white hair she had loved to play with as a child. She wanted to re-braid the untidy tresses but didn't dare move any part of the broken body. As she combed the ends with her fingers, she thought about all the nights she had nestled on Tanna's lap to listen to tales of fairy villages in forests and disguised princes traveling across deserts. She thought of how her grandmother had held her and whispered words of comfort when her mother passed away. There was no one with her to do that now.

The door creaked open and quietly closed. Kelton at home meant the workday had ended and supper was over. Ayra hadn't even noticed the sun had dimmed and the room was getting dark. He lit the lamp in the corner.

"Has she opened her eyes yet?" he asked, his own eyes red and anxious.

Ayra wished she could give her brother good news but had none to give. "No. I thought she was coming 'round earlier but nothing came of it."

"Do you think she will wake up soon, Ayra?"

Ayra said nothing.

Kelton laid himself down on the other cot and stared up at the ceiling. After a long pause, his quivering voice broke the silence. "Ayra, I'm scared. What if she doesn't wake up? What will become of us? Who will take care of us?"

It was unlike him to speak his thoughts in this way. She had seen other signs of her brother's anxiousness the last two days. The boy usually ate like a grown man but had hardly touched his food. And his pit had hardly grown.

"I don't know," she quietly replied, hating the words. She laid her head on her grandmother's arm and closed her eyes. Tanna would have known what to say to comfort him. She would have been able to soothe his aching heart. But Ayra did not know what to do for him. She didn't have enough hope of her own to give any away.

She had drifted off to sleep when a hand on her head startled her awake.

"Nana!" Ayra's voice came out in a rasp.

Ayra watched Tanna's chest rise and fall a few times before her breathing became so shallow Ayra wasn't sure it was moving.

"Nana? Please don't leave us." She grabbed her grandmother's hand and felt a slight grip of Tanna's fingers.

Kelton sat up. "Is she awake?" He leaped out of bed and knelt next to Ayra. "Ayra. Did she wake up? What happened?"

She couldn't answer him. She stared at Tanna's face, willing her eyes to open again. She strained to hear any words or sounds from Tanna's mouth. The grip on her hand loosened. Ayra continued to stare hoping Tanna would take another breath. That her heart continued to beat under her skin. That the warmth of life was not seeping out of her body. Minutes passed, but her chest did not rise.

* * *

Four weeks had passed since Tanna's body had returned to the earth. A rough stone marked her grave next to Ayra's parents and grandfather in the remote Doren cemetery.

Kara had not come to visit after Tanna's death. The only interaction Ayra had received from her friend was an awkward hug in the mess house. A few times she had heard others— villagers and debtors—whisper about her and Kelton. *Someone should take them in. Poor orphaned children. It's a shame their debt can't be paid.*

Each day Ayra picked and dug until her hands cramped and her eyes burned from the strain and dust. By the time she crawled into bed, her body was so exhausted she couldn't even roll over. But her mind would not let her sleep easily.

Like the rubble that had buried Tanna, worries piled on top of her, threatening to smother the spark of life inside her. And she watched helplessly as Kelton fell under his own wreckage.

She noticed the guards were more attentive to her, as if they sensed her grounding force had been lost. But within those four weeks her view of the prison had changed. Life outside the quarry didn't tempt her anymore. She knew her and Kelton's best chance of survival was to remain in Darkwater Quarry.

3

Four years later

"GET up!" Ayra poked her brother in the side with her finger. "If you want to get any porridge you had better get your lazy sack of bones moving."

Kelton jerked his body trying to escape her jabs. "Stop. Stop! All right, I'm getting up."

Ayra watched to make sure he really was getting out of bed. He slung his legs over the side and slid his feet into his boots that were two sizes too large. They had been left to him by a man who had lived in the neighboring hut for two months. Even though they did not fit well, they were better than the tight boots with holes they had replaced.

"When I went through the meal line, the pots were almost

empty. You better move faster than that."

"I don't care if I never have another bowl of that slop again."

"You didn't get any yesterday either. You talk big, but if you're going to keep your strength up, you have to eat."

"All right, *Mother*. You're such a nag."

"Out!" she snapped, grabbing their picks and pushing him out the door.

The mess house was almost cleared out by the time they walked in, and kitchen workers were carrying pots to the wash tubs. The food was gone. In the last few years, drought had plagued the country. From what Ayra understood, farms were struggling to keep up with the demand for food. Darkwater Quarry was last in line for traders and food suppliers, so food that had never been plentiful was becoming scarcer. The debtor camp should have been more crowded this time of year, but the drought was causing such a strain that the king had relented some of his demands to keep more farms and businesses working. The low numbers were fortunate for those still forced to come to the camp as it meant they wouldn't starve.

"Is there anything left?" Ayra asked one of the current kitchen boys, whose skinny legs, roundish chest, and small head gave him a bird-like appearance.

"Not a drop," he said, looking up with a scowl. "Maybe you should have come earlier."

Kitchen duty was not a favorite task for most of the people who came to the quarry. Few were pleasant while working their shift. Ayra always hated her turn.

"Maybe instead of standing there like a—" Ayra stopped herself short of saying 'slack, half-brained chicken' and evened her tone as best she could. "Maybe you could find something if you looked. Please."

The boy looked back and forth between the two of them, sighed, and went into the pantry grumbling. When he returned, he produced a hardened portion of rye bread and tossed it to Kelton. "Don't you know the rule? Morning meal is at sunrise. You should get up and eat like everyone else."

"Thank you," said Ayra, pushing Kelton toward the door and roughing up her tone again. "We'll try to remember that one. And there are still crumbs on the floor from last night's dinner. I'm sure you're anxious to peck them up."

She couldn't stand it when the other laborers spoke to her as if she had only been in the quarry for a week. At the same time, Tanna would never have let Kelton show such a lack of regard for the rules. Ayra knew she would be lost without her brother, but it was aggravating to have her lot tossed in with his and his mistakes be hers.

They had missed lineup, but one guard lingered with a roll tablet. After checking in, they walked together to the quarry, passing a few men surrounding one of the camp's wells. One of them emptied a bucket of mud into a cart and lowered the bucket back into the hole. A thick rope with one end tied to a post and the other dropped into the well told her someone was down there. If they were digging deeper, the well must have gone dry again.

She wondered how deep they would have to dig this time before reaching water.

When they came to Ayra's pit, they parted without a word. She watched Kelton amble to his own hole before she jumped down and set to work.

As she mindlessly scratched at the sandy dirt and swirled scoops of it in murky water, she used her thoughts to help her forget her busy hands. She never dreamed of trees and sea-faring travel anymore but focused on the world within her view.

First on her mind was Kelton. Was he getting enough food? What could she do about his lack of ambition? How could she get him to be more compliant? To be happier? When her mind tired of Kelton meandering through it, her thoughts turned to Tanna. Recalling memories brought her grandmother to life again. She retold the stories she had heard on Tanna's lap, pictured the long white braid, and even scolded herself for her follies, though less gently than Tanna would have.

"Ayra," a gruff voice called from overhead. She looked up, shielding her eyes from the sun, now in its midday phase. A guard stood over her hole. "Come with me."

The pit of her stomach began to churn. She had never been summoned by a guard before. He did not seem angry or agitated, but that did not keep her from needing to wipe her palms over her skirt. As she trailed him into the camp, she noticed a group of horses huddled near the mess house. Unlike the dusty, bulky horses that pulled wagons of supplies and debtors, these horses were sleek, athletic-looking creatures, each with a colorful blanket and leather saddle. They were horses of kings-men.

After her initial surprise at seeing the horses, she noticed the men gathered near them. Their tunics were a rich, rusty orange and bore a miniature of the red bear placed over the heart. As near as she could tell, all the men had swords sheathed at their sides. The only reason soldiers came to camp was to collect the fruits of the mining pits. But there was no armored wagon.

She glanced around to see if anyone else was observing the unusual sight. As she turned her head, her toe caught sharply on a rock. She cried out and put her hands forward as the ground flew toward her face. There was nothing she could do to save herself. When she hit the ground, pebbles dug into her hands and a stabbing pain rooted in her knee climbed up her leg.

The guard she had been walking with stood over her briefly before he curtly asked, "You all right? Can you get up?"

"I'm fine," she muttered, pulling herself to her feet. Her cheeks burned, and she could hear peals of laughter. She told herself it was not in response to her clumsiness but did not dare raise her eyes to make sure.

Just before she walked through the mess house door, one of the soldiers shouted, "That was graceful, Pit Girl." She flicked her eyes in the group's direction hoping to hush the heckler with one nasty look. Her eyes fell on a young man with a bow slung across his shoulder and hair two shades darker than the rest.

His grin spread wider in the heat of her glare, and he added, "I wouldn't look away from where I was going, if I were you."

New waves of laughter pushed her quickly through the door. Safely inside the mess house, she lifted her skirt a little to check her right knee. She thought she could feel blood running down her leg, and she was right. A small split in her skin oozed red.

"That does not look well," said an unfamiliar voice. Ayra's head snapped up in surprise. A handsome young man—she guessed a few years older than her—with ear-length, curly hair came toward her. "Rooney, get some water and clean linen and tend to our friend here."

"No, I'm fine. Just a scrape," she stammered.

"Looks to be more than a scrape. Come, let us take care of it properly." He took her arm and walked her to a bench to sit down.

A slender man with a long, thin nose and smooth shoulder-length hair knelt in front of her. Her muscles tensed in response to his strange hands touching her leg. It felt silly to be fussed over for such a minor wound, and she tried to find somewhere else to look. Her eyes first went to the young man, but when she found his eyes were already on her, she quickly looked up at the rafters. Under his unwanted gaze she began racking her brain for a reason why she was there.

When the wound was expertly wrapped and her skirt hem again covering her ankles, she gave the thin man a stiff nod as he returned to his place, then stole another look at the curly-haired one before throwing her stare down at the floor.

Her lower lip tucked in between her teeth, and she placed her hand on the side of her face for a second before dropping it to recross her arms. Were they waiting for someone else? After agonizing seconds that felt like hours, she brought herself to look at the young man again. He smiled blankly at her, and Ayra was afraid she would have to speak first. Then as if he only just remembered he was the one who had initiated contact, he cleared his throat.

"Forgive my manners. My name is Gibsen. I am pleased to finally meet you, Ayra."

Finally meet her? She wondered what he meant by that. And Gibsen. She was sure she had heard that name before. His tunic was much finer than the tunics worn by the men outside. It was a soft red and the bear over the chest was embroidered in silver. *He must be someone important*, she thought. She raised her eyes to meet his again and realized he was looking at her expectantly.

"Oh! Yes, Ayra," she eked out and silently cursed herself for such a brilliant response.

Just then Kelton burst into the room with another guard on his heels, consequently adding to her embarrassment.

"What's this all about?" he demanded. "I've been doing my work. And I didn't take anything!" He scanned the room and realized Ayra was there, too. The tension drained from his face, and he looked at her with a puzzled expression. "And what do you need with my sister?"

"You must be Kelton," said Gibsen with a slight bow. "If you will have a seat I will explain what *this is all about*."

As Gibsen spoke, Kelton's demeanor shifted from youthful cockiness to subdued subject. He quickly took a seat next to

Ayra, shooting her a wide-eyed look.

"Now, as I was telling Ayra, my name is Gibsen, Son of Leofric of the House of Yofreid, long may he live."

It dawned on Ayra why his name was so familiar. He was a prince of Mihtengard. A prince of Mihtengard was standing in front of her, addressing her by name. A snort escaped her throat. Kelton glanced at her with a barely suppressed smirk, but Prince Gibsen either hadn't heard her or gallantly pretended not to and continued.

"You are the only two remaining members of your family present in this location, correct?"

Ayra and Kelton nodded in unison.

"Good. Well, it has come to our attention that records of your family are unclear. It appears we…lost track of your line."

"Lost track?"

Gibsen cleared his throat. "Yes. One of our historians has been piecing together years of records—a painstaking process, I assure you—and we think we have found the first of your ancestors to arrive in camp. Do you have any family papers?"

Ayra shook her head.

"I assure you there would be no trouble if you knew anything about a false history."

"We know nothing, I promise."

"Well, that is a disappointment. You see, some time ago, my father received correspondence from a man now in the northern country of Tiseden who has been searching for a lost line of relatives. From the House of Regnan. He had some information that indicated that line may have a history in one of our camps and promised to pay the debt if we could discover the where-abouts—or fate—of any members of his family."

Ayra glanced at Kelton, seeing a far-off look in his eyes.

"If you have no papers, there is one other way we might verify you are of the line we are searching for. Do either of you have any sort of mark? One that you were born with?"

Ayra shook her head and reached for Kelton's hand, but her brother didn't remain silent.

"She does! Two lines on the left, close to her shoulder. Show them, Ayra."

Gibsen stepped closer. "May we see it?"

Ayra considered denying it, keeping her promise to Tanna. But Kelton's words were too sure. And something in Rooney's eyes made her certain they would see it, willing or not. She pulled on the sleeve of her frock, revealing the two dark lines.

Prince Gibsen exchanged a look with Rooney.

He smiled at Ayra. "Exactly as he said. The debt is to be paid upon your reunion with your family in Tiseden. It is for this reason my father has sent me to fetch you." Prince Gibsen glanced at Rooney again before he continued. "Obviously, we will take precautions in your exchange, ensuring that his claims are valid and that you will be safe."

Ayra could do nothing more than stare. She was unsure if the ground was beneath her feet or not. For a moment she even for-got anyone else was in the room. Gibsen's words flitted through her mind like a covey of confused birds. *Tiseden. Family. Safe.*

Kelton let out a whoop. "What are we sitting here for? Let's go!"

His outburst pulled her from the flapping thoughts. She grabbed his thin arm protectively. "No! I mean no, thank you. We can't go. We will stay here. Thank you for your offer, but we will stay here."

Kelton looked at her in disbelief. "What are you talking about? Stay here? We have the chance to *leave*, Ayra."

"I heard what he said. But...we can't go."

"Maybe *you* can't, but I can," he said shrugging off her hand.

Ayra took a deep breath and let the air escape slowly. "Can I have a minute with my *younger* brother, please?"

With one nod from Gibsen the room cleared. Kelton put his head down in his hands, and the mess house was still for a few minutes.

Ayra used the silence to carefully gather her words. Kelton was not easily swayed, and she needed to make her reasoning clear. With all the authority she could summon, she said, "It is my responsibility to keep you safe. The quarry is where we are safe. Nana said. We don't know what's out there, who this man in Tiseden is. We don't even know for sure who this Gibsen is or that he'll do what he says."

"Ayra! Did you see how he was dressed? The horses out there? I think he's who he says he is. He said he would make sure we were safe."

It wasn't difficult for Ayra to believe Gibsen was the prince he claimed to be and that his intentions were true. There was an air about him that felt trustworthy. But she did not want to admit that to Kelton. Tanna had said numerous times the world was very dangerous for them. She had called the quarry a sanctuary. And Ayra trusted her grandmother's words more than anyone else's.

"Kelton. Remember the story Nana told us about the wolf who tricked a boy into going with him into the woods? He promised the boy all sorts of treats. That he would be happy. But his promises were false. And the boy was gobbled up. I don't want you to be the boy who follows the wolf into the woods."

"That was just a story Ayra. It didn't mean anything. Have you ever thought of my future here? Do you really want me to die with lungs full of dust or be buried by rocks? And what about you? I know you aren't happy here."

"I'm happy here," she said weakly. He raised his eyebrows at her lie. "At least we are protected."

"But for how long? Accidents happen, you know that. And food is short. Think about it." Kelton put his hands on her shoulders and gave her a shake. "We could see trees, Ayra."

She hesitated. He knew this was a weakness of hers. The colorless image of trees in a book she no longer possessed passed through her mind. With a shake of her head, she axed the pictures. "I am not leaving."

Kelton shot up with a growl and stormed out the door. She almost chased after him but instead let him go. If she gave him time to think about what she had said, maybe he would not be so difficult. He had threatened to go without her, but she knew he would never leave her behind. If she refused to leave, he would stay, too.

Prince Gibsen reentered the hall flanked by two of his men. "I assume you did not reach a consensus?"

"No."

He nodded. "I realize this information has taken you by surprise, and you might need to think it over. My men and I will stay one night to allow you some time." He glanced around at the mess house and settled on her face again. "I hope you will reconsider, Ayra. A girl like you should not have to live in a place such as this."

She thanked him and hurried out of the hall and past the group of scoffing men. She was afraid if Prince Gibsen continued to speak to her, she would weaken and change her mind. What did he mean by 'a girl like you?' The phrase scratched at her brain. She should have returned to work, but the stinging behind her eyes turned her toward the hut. It took all the control she had to not break into a run.

4

WHEN she reached the little shack, she clumsily closed the door behind herself and stared blankly into the dim room. The darkness was only broken by the little rays of sunlight that found their way through the wooden shutters and the cracks of the door. The sound of pounding mallets outside matched the sudden pounding in her chest. She folded her arms over her stomach to still her shaking hands and calm her insides.

When her heart slowed, she walked over to the wash tub and splashed her face with the cool, brown water. Finding comfort in the barely noticeable tingle in her fingers, she dipped her hands in for a second splash and watched the water trickle over her dusty skin in murky trails. She released the cupped water and inspected her hands more closely. The rough calluses on her palms made them look coarse, and her short fingernails were caked all around with dirt. She straightened to analyze the rest of herself.

A film of dust made her thick, wavy hair a shade lighter than it truly was. She should have worn it in a braid like the village girls but having it loose gave her a feeling of freedom. She touched her face to try to get a sense of her features. She had never seen her own face, aside from the distorted, dingy reflection in the metal pots at the mess house. Her nose felt straight and her cheeks thin. She imagined she looked something like Kelton, but no one had ever said so.

Her hands trailed off her face, down her neck, and to the dress that hung on her body. She looked down at her wool frock, riddled with clumsily sewn patches. She never took the time to wash it properly, only occasionally shaking out the fine dust.

Attracting any boy's attention had always been far from her thoughts, not that any even looked her direction anyway. Her father had been a laborer from the village. He had moved to Doren from Midivard and fell in love with her mother. He had no known family anywhere and chose to stay and work in the camp to marry her. Ayra had always loved to hear their story and had shaped it into a sort of fairytale in her mind. But it seemed ridiculous to think her life could replicate her mother's.

Having now had the attention of a finely dressed prince from Midivard, even if only for a few minutes, she felt more awareness of her body and appearance than she had ever felt before. *What does he think of me?* she wondered. Surely at the head city he was surrounded by pretty, rosy-cheeked girls with long, glossy braids and soft, clean hands. She snorted at the idea he could think *anything* of her—much less something spectacular—and shook her head at the absurdity of wondering.

Ayra stayed hidden behind the stone walls of the hut, immersed in troubled thoughts, the remainder of the day. None of the guards came searching for her, and she felt grateful the prince's arrival had at least brought her that much peace.

As the sun fell, she heard the sounds of supper—banging pots and clamoring voices—coming from the mess house. When she peered out the sleeping room window, faint firelight flickered in the distance near the north bend in the hills. That could only be the prince's camp. She willingly pulled his handsome face and curly brown hair from her memory and smiled.

The door banged shut, making her jump away from the window. Kelton marched into the room and without a word readied for bed.

"Aren't you going to supper?" she asked.

"No," he grouched.

Ayra felt a flicker of heated frustration and knew talking to him now would not go well, so she quietly readied for sleep, too. A couple hours after she slipped into bed, the sounds of camp became hushed. She wished for her fingers to tickle, for the comforting sound of rainfall on the roof. But neither sensation came. There was only the uncomfortable silence of an anger-filled room.

Even in sleep she could not escape the agitated thoughts. She tossed for hours, finally drifting to sound sleep late in the night.

When she awoke again, gray light could be seen behind the cracks of the shutters. She rolled over and glanced at the cot across the room. It was empty. She shot up. The little hut was silent. In her bare feet and underclothes, she rushed out of the sleeping room toward the door but skidded to a halt when she found Kelton sitting at the table, his arms crossed and his face set in a scowl.

A night's sleep—or at least the night's hours—had evidently not changed his feelings.

Ayra swallowed, unsure what to say to ease his temper. She did not want him to be angry anymore. "You're up early."

His eyes narrowed, but he didn't look at her. "Couldn't sleep."

"Me neither. Not really anyway." She looked down at her feet against the dark, earthen floor. She could feel frustration kindling in her chest and took a deep breath to clear it. Trying to mimic the way Tanna always responded to her own defiance, with an even tone she said, "I have to keep us both safe. Try to see as I do. I'm doing what is best."

"Best? No, you are doing what is easiest." He uncrossed his thin arms and leaned toward her. "You're a coward, Ayra."

"A coward!" she hissed. The kindling flickered into a burning in an instant. "Is that what you think I am? I'd rather be a coward than a fool. You are only just fourteen, and you've lived your entire life surrounded by rocks and guards. You can barely defend yourself against a deer fly. Taking you beyond these hills would be like putting a one-legged goat in a bear's den and hoping it lives!"

He jumped to his feet and jabbed a shaky finger at her. "You think you're the boss of me. You think you can make me stay here. But you're not and you can't. I'm going without you, Ayra. I have made up my mind and you can't change it." Utter defiance glinted in his eyes, and he recrossed his arms.

Ayra felt all the air rush out of her lungs. She thought he would not leave her, but here she found herself mistaken. He would leave. And if he went without her, she would have no control over what happened to him. She would probably never hear what became of him. And she would be completely alone.

They stood staring at each other. Neither one moved for a moment.

Then Kelton relaxed his shoulders and let his arms drop to his sides. "Ayra. I don't want to leave you. But I can't be here anymore. It was fine when I was a small boy and Nana was here, but with just me and you, it's not worth it. This might be our only chance. Please come. Please don't stay here alone."

Deep down inside, she wanted to go. Her heart yearned to go. She closed her eyes and before her logic took over again, she relented aloud. "All right. I'll go."

Kelton threw his scrawny arms around her and gave her a squeeze. "Whew! That's good to hear. I wasn't sure who would make sure I ate my meals."

Ayra laughed despite the unsettled feeling that still lingered in her gut. "Should we really do this? Can we really leave?"

"Yeah, we really can. C'mon, let's pack our things."

They dressed, and after looking herself over, Ayra took the time to plait her hair. The braid was messy since she couldn't get all the knots out with her fingers, but she felt more presentable. Neither of them had a bag, so they placed what belongings they needed in the middle of a blanket and tied the corners.

Minutes from the time they started, they sat down at the table one last time.

Ayra looked around the humble little room. This was the house she was born in. The house her closest family members had died in. And she was leaving it. She was surprised how little remorse she felt in leaving it. Neither her parents nor her grand-parents were still in this home. They were elsewhere, and she could feel that. This was just a simple hut, built of wood and stone. Her memories were within her, not within these walls.

5

WHEN the rising sun changed the sky from gray to pink hues, Kelton picked up the makeshift pack, and the two siblings stepped out into the morning. They had decided to eat and then wait in the mess house for Prince Gibsen.

With pots clanging and boiling, the hall gradually filled with laborers hungry for their morning meal. A few times Ayra over-heard whisperings about Prince Gibsen being in the camp and smiled at being the secret reason why. While she stood in line for her food, she watched the people form clusters around the tables, conversing and laughing with each other.

She had the sudden feeling she should say goodbye to some-one but did not know whom. They had no firm attachment to any of the guards and all the laborers were strangers. A few of the villagers she only knew by face might appreciate a farewell, but she did not know where or how to find any of them.

She sat down next to her brother and stirred the lumps of overcooked barley in her bowl. A quick glance at Kelton revealed his bowl was untouched. She found a bit of comfort knowing she was not the only one whose stomach felt full of stones.

As Ayra watched the laborers file out of the hall heading to the lineup, a strange sense of satisfaction settled over her. She was no longer one of them. The kitchen crew quickly scrubbed and dried the pots before hurrying off to their other tasks. A few shot them questioning looks but said nothing and scurried out the door. Kelton drummed his fingers on the table, and the hollow sound echoed softly into the rafters.

"Do you think he changed his mind and has taken back the offer?" Ayra asked.

Kelton shrugged and opened his mouth just as the door opened and Prince Gibsen entered followed by the man named Rooney and another man she had not seen before. The prince looked at her, then down at the pack, and smiled.

"Have you made your decision?" he asked, though it didn't really sound like a question.

Ayra fiddled with her braid. "We have and we will go…with you."

Gibsen's smile widened. "Wonderful. You have my word no harm will come to you. Rooney, make arrangements with the guards for their parting." Looking back at them, he pointed to their pack. "Is that all you have to take with you?"

"Yes. This is all," Kelton said scooping up the pack.

"All right then. Tress, please take their belongings." He held out his arm for Ayra. "Come, I will show you your horses."

Horses? She would have to ride a horse. She had not thought out the journey this far. As they approached the beasts, she concluded they must have eaten well last night because they were much bigger than they were yesterday.

Gibsen grabbed the reigns of a black horse and handed them to Kelton. "This one is yours. And this," he said grabbing the reigns of the beautiful white and deep brown patched horse, "is yours, Ayra. Both are mild, and I think you will find them obedient."

Ayra hesitated before reaching out to grab the reigns from Gibsen. The horse reared its head but mellowed quickly. She reached her hand up and stroked its muzzle. It blinked its round, dark eyes and puffed hot air out its huge nostrils. She smiled and looked at Gibsen. He beamed back at her, and she quickly turned toward the horse when she felt her cheeks warm. The braid that tied her hair back from her face didn't seem like such a great idea anymore.

"My other men are packing up camp. We will meet them and begin our journey."

Ayra nodded and watched him mount his horse, then watched the other two men mount theirs. Kelton imitated their actions, placing his foot in the stirrup and pulling himself easily to a sitting position in the saddle. He gave her a look that asked *Did you see that?!* If he could do it, surely she could. She put her foot in the stirrup, bounced on her grounded foot, and pulled herself up. It wasn't as graceful as Kelton had done it, but she blamed that on her skirt. She shot back the same look he had given her.

The road leading around the quarry was rocky and rough. Ayra's horse stumbled a few times, and she struggled to keep herself in the saddle, wool slipping against smooth leather. Her skirt had tucked up awkwardly underneath her, and already she felt it rubbing uncomfortably against her thighs.

The road smoothed and cut through the center of Doren. Children stood in front of homes in clusters to wave and watch the small procession pass. It occurred to Ayra that seeing a prince of Mihtengard was probably as exciting to them as it was to her.

By the time they reached the camp, the soldiers had a large wagon packed and were mounted on horses waiting for the missing members. The prince guided them into the company line up just before the wagon and its team of four horses, placing Ayra next to him and Kelton behind them with Rooney. Four mounted soldiers, two on each side, moved into position next to them, and the company began to move.

Ayra glanced back at the quarry. The familiar sounds of pounding and cracking and workers' shouts were softened by the distance. But the work continued. It stung a little to see how easily the quarry carried on without them. Not even a pause to lament its loss.

The company rounded the bend in the hills, and the village and pit disappeared from view, the road and the faint echoes of pounding bouncing off the hillsides the only evidence of their existence. Ayra straightened her shoulders and shook off the sting. She had no idea how far they had to go before hills disappeared and whatever was beyond them could be seen. But the stones in her stomach morphed into butterflies as her anticipation to see the unknown grew. The corners of her mouth tugged into a smile.

Gibsen looked at her and smiled, too. "I am glad to see you are excited for your journey."

"Yes, I guess I am excited," she replied, surprised it was the truth. "I have never been outside the quarry. I think I'm most excited to see trees. I have always wanted to climb one."

Gibsen laughed. "That is an odd thing for a young lady to want to do. But there is no reason why you should not, I guess."

He meant the last part to be encouraging, but Ayra felt her excitement flutter away. It suddenly occurred to her how little she knew of customs and manners. What was right for her to do and what was not. Kara had laughed at a lot of things Ayra had said that she hadn't meant to be funny. She shifted in the saddle feeling anew the irritation caused by her skirt.

The slope of the hills gradually decreased and with each bend Ayra expected the world to open before her. Turn after turn ended in disappointment as the company slowly descended out of the hills. Finally, the hollow widened further, and the slopes tapered into flat, open lands. Her shoulders slumped as her eyes took in more gray brush and brown grass in the land surrounding them. Landscape she had looked at her whole life stretched out before her, only horizontally instead of vertically.

"Where are the trees?" she asked.

"That depends on what kind you would like to see," Gibsen replied. "The bush pines are on the mountains behind you. Along this road heading north, as we are currently doing, there are no trees for some distance until we reach the Life River. Much of southern Mihtengard is desert, you know."

Ayra nodded and only admitted inwardly that she did not know that. Her knowledge of Mihtengard was not only lacking in its customs, but evidently in its geography as well. She wished at some point someone would have lent them a book that contained information that was useful. But maybe those types of books did not exist. She wanted to ask Gibsen but decided to keep the question to herself.

The company traveled the dusty road through the morning. When the sun was high, they stopped for a brief rest and a small meal of dried mutton and hard biscuits. Ayra decided to stay on her horse to avoid having to get back on. She noticed a few men, including Gibsen, look at her up on the horse. She was glad Kelton asked if she was going to get down, so she could loudly claim she wanted to observe the area from a higher perspective.

They rode on through the afternoon, and Ayra continued to wait for the horizon to reveal something different from the brown, rolling hills. As they topped a small bump in the earth, she thought she caught sight of a green line and leaned from side to side trying to see around the soldiers. Unable to see much, she watched the land to her right pass by.

When she looked ahead again, she could clearly see a line of green. A smile twitched onto her face, and her grip on the reigns tightened. She imagined herself breaking away from the group with her horse in a dead run toward the green and her hair whipping free of its loose, sloppy braid. Since she did not want to draw attention to herself more than she already had and because she didn't know exactly how to get her horse to run, she sat back in her saddle, tapping her foot in the stirrup.

The ground became a patchwork of old brown and new green long grass, and the green line ahead gradually stretched upward as they neared the woods. The trees were taller than she ever imagined them. Soon they were near enough for her to hear the gentle whispering sound of the leaves as a breeze pushed its way through. The tree trunks were white, scratched with rough, black scabs. Each leaf was a vibrant, early green and seemed to shimmer as it moved in the sunlight. Ayra felt as if a smile had been permanently etched on her face.

Once into the trees, they crossed a bridge that spanned a river. She stifled a laugh when she saw the pristine water flowing lazily below them. She and Kelton exchanged a look, and the laugh bubbled out. To think she had almost convinced herself to be satisfied with colorless pictures in a book made her laugh louder. A small distance beyond the bridge, a narrow meadow opened before them, and Gibsen asked the soldier beside him to halt the company. The man gave a sharp whistle, and the horses stopped.

"We will rest here until tomorrow," Gibsen called out.

The prince gracefully dismounted his horse and approached

Ayra's with his hand held out to her. She worried her legs would not hold her up once on solid ground, but she slowly placed her hand in his anyway and allowed him to help her slide off. She hoped no one noticed her wobble when she stood.

Gibsen pointed across the road. "The river is over that hill. I thought maybe you two would like to take turns washing up. Rooney, will you please fetch them their things. I am going to inquire what Arty is planning for supper tonight."

Rooney nodded, but instead of going to Kelton's horse for their bundle, he trotted off toward the wagon. When he returned, he held out two leather satchels and a bundle of folded clothes.

"Prince Gibsen anticipated you would come with us, and he prepared for such. In each satchel you will find a bar of soap and a large cloth with which to dry yourselves. You do know how to bathe?" The two dirty quarry rats nodded and with a return nod the man continued. "You may keep all items as your own." He gave them more specific directions to the river and described the section that had a natural hot spring flowing into it.

As the pair walked toward the referenced hill—finding walking normally to be much harder than merely standing—Ayra heard a soldier utter, "Woo-eee! I hope they're heading to clean up!"

"Yeah, I think my horse smells better even after a good run!" remarked another.

Ayra whipped her head in the direction of the voices. She saw four young soldiers standing together laughing. She noticed the dark-haired one with the bow. Something about him—the cocky grin or the stupid way he laughed all the time—made her fists ball up. She tried to think of something nasty to shout back but noticed Rooney still watching them go and held her tongue. Kelton kept his head facing forward, though Ayra was sure he had heard.

When they reached the river and inspected the flowing water, she decided it was a little wider and much deeper than she had thought when crossing the bridge. They walked upriver a bit until they found the hot spring Rooney had described—a small section where the trees and willows grew thick. Kelton bathed first while Ayra waited on a boulder amongst the trees. She could not stop admiring the canopy overhead and inhaled deeply the warm, mingled smell of bark and brush. It was almost as good as the quarry after a good rainfall.

Kelton emerged from the willows dressed, with damp hair and a radiant face. She had never seen her brother so clean before. The orange tunic he had been given was a couple sizes too big and looked more like a blanket draped over his shoulders.

"Your turn. I'll keep a look out for you," he said, switching her places on the rock. "And the water only came to my waist, so don't be afraid," he added, as neither could swim.

"Thanks," she replied, hesitating for just a moment before pushing through the willows.

"And don't take forever like you do, all right?"

Ayra stopped just before walking into the water. She slipped off her boots and looked at the slow-moving river. Streaks of sunlight dipped into the water, reflecting off the green, mossy rocks in the bed. She had never been fully immersed in water before. In the hut, she only had the small wash tub to wash her hair and face in and an old cloth to wash the rest of herself. It had taken so much effort she didn't care to do it more than she had to. She lowered one foot into the water and felt a tickling sensation prick at her fingers. It was warm enough that she immediately felt her foot relax.

Taking a deep breath and a thorough look around for any unwanted spectators, she stripped down to her underclothes and waded into the water with soap in hand. She felt the gentle pull of the current around her calves, then her thighs, and finally her waist. The tingling in her fingers grew stronger. She laughed at the sensation, and the water seemed to laugh with her as it babbled around boulders and brushed against the banks. She bent her knees and let the water rise over her shoulders. As she washed her hair, she made an effort to really work out the tangles. She also took care to scrub out her fingernails and wash around her ears.

"Are you almost done?" Kelton yelled from an unseen location. "They're going to eat without us if you don't finish up. Or worse, come looking for us!"

The last part put some hurry into Ayra's scrubbing. She dunked herself several times to rinse out the lather, scrambled onto the bank, and dried off with the large cloth. She picked up the bundle of fabric Kelton had left and was relieved to find the dress had underclothes folded into it. She had not thought about her current set being too wet to wear when she waded in.

She removed her old soggy underclothes without dropping the cloth and wiggled into the clean, ivory-colored set. As she slipped the deep blue dress on, she wondered what it was made of. It was lighter than wool but still heavy enough to feel durable. And though it was more snug around the chest and waist than she would have liked, it wasn't itchy and she felt comfortable in it. The neckline was cut to rest just under her collarbones and gently scooped the same in the back as it did in the front. A thin embroidered pattern that looked like intertwined leafy, yellow vines decorated the hems.

She wrapped the cloth around her hair and squeezed to draw out as much water as she could. As she combed her fingers through the brown waves, she debated whether to leave it down or braid it. Prince Gibsen's face popped into her mind's eye. Braid it, she decided.

She divided her hair into three sections and crossed one over another. As she bent her head forward to make the hand movements easier, the foreign blue color of her skirt distracted her from the braid. Her hands slowed to a stop before her fingers released the sections and raked them back into one. The new dress and lack of dirt made her feel strange enough. It would be more comfortable to feel the familiar swish on her back.

She found Kelton stretched out on the boulder, his hands behind his head. The evening sun shone through the trees, creating shadows that danced across his face. She had not seen him look this peaceful in a long time.

"I thought you were keeping an eye out for me."

He sat up and let out a slow whistle. "Well, look at you. Not a rat's nest in your mane or a speck of dirt to be seen. What did you think?"

"It was…" She tried to think of a word to describe it but only came up with a feeling. "Happy."

"That's what I thought, too."

They roughly retraced the way they had come and made it back to camp. Brown, rectangular tents of all sizes were up, and the men were gathered around the wagon, thin metal bowls in hand. Ayra did a quick head count and came up with eighteen. She was used to being surrounded by men and boys, but this felt different. Maybe it was because she no longer had familiar guards keeping watch. Or maybe it had to do with a new blue dress and smooth hair.

Gibsen spotted them returning to camp and crossed to meet them. "Kelton, that tunic looks natural on you," he said. Ayra stifled a snort, looking at the drape her brother wore. "And I am glad to see the dress fits, Ayra. I actually brought three different sized dresses just in case. What luck my first pick fits. Forgive me if I am too forward, but that blue compliments your green eyes well."

An inward silliness overcame her. The prince had just complimented her eyes. Or had he complimented the dress? Either way she liked the sensation she felt. If he hadn't been making all the orders and wearing the different tunic, she might have forgotten he was royalty. His manners were so friendly and not at all aloof like she expected a prince's to be.

The evening passed pleasantly, with happy chatter and full bellies for all. Ayra and Kelton sat with Gibsen and Rooney a little apart from the other men. Though she felt a little foolish and her hands never quit feeling damp, her face was never without a smile as she listened to the prince describe his castle home and his talents with the sword and horse riding.

Night overtook day, and the siblings were escorted to their small tent. Two cots with several blankets on each had been prepared, and the sleeping hours passed just as easily as the evening. In the morning, camp smoke hung heavy in the air, and they ate a filling morning meal of cured pork belly and seasoned potatoes.

When the camp was packed, the men began to mount their horses. Kelton again seemed to have no trouble getting onto his horse's back. Ayra put her foot in the stirrup like before, but as she pushed off her other foot, her boot slipped out of the loop. Her face bounced off the horse's side igniting a burning in her nose, and she stumbled back a step or two. With watery eyes she glanced around to see if anyone had seen her clumsiness.

She locked eyes with the dark-haired boy, his lips curved into an amused smirk. He raised his eyebrows at her. She narrowed her eyes and huffed out a deep breath. As she gripped the saddle again, a horse trotted up behind her. Determined not to make a fool of herself again, she placed her foot further into the stirrup.

"Need a hand?"

Without turning around, she knew whose voice came from behind her.

"No," she snapped over her shoulder. "I can manage it."

She bounced her right foot and mounted the horse with only a little struggle. Thank the stars for strong digging arms that made it possible to pull herself up. She put her chin in the air, but the dark-haired soldier's smile remained as he moved to his position in the front. Kelton's horse moved in behind hers, and when Gibsen's was in position, the company began to move.

To soothe her wounded pride, Ayra breathed deeply the smell of the trees—a fresh, green scent unlike anything she had ever inhaled. As they put more distance between them and the quarry, she could not keep the giddiness she felt from penetrating every piece of her body. The dust, the pounding hammers, the brown water, the bland soup, the pitiful looks. They were all staying behind her.

6

DAYS passed quickly for Ayra. Travel was moderate, and while the prince seemed to continually urge the company to move at a faster pace, Ayra wished the horses would not trot down the road so efficiently.

Like a little child from his mother, the happy river wandered away from the road at times but always found its way back before long. Ayra loved the challenge of separating the sounds of rustling leaves and flowing water and detecting when the river was going to return. She relished basking in the green light that flooded through the canopy and enjoyed chatter both from the birds flitting about and the companion riding beside her. Five days into their journey, she felt no regret leaving the quarry.

Most of the soldiers paid her no attention, other than a friendly nod here and there. Prince Gibsen was by far the most attentive member of the group, taking special notice of her and Kelton. He personally ensured they were comfortable each night and took all his meals with them. She liked the way he prattled on about his own doings. She could watch the goings on of the woods without needing to think too much about what he was saying.

Tress was one of the friendlier soldiers, in Ayra's opinion. The streaks of gray in his hair gave him a fatherly appearance, though he appeared more fit than several of his younger comrades. He was not boisterous like some of the other men, but he often initiated conversation with her and Kelton, asking about their family and the quarry, telling them things about his wife and children.

The camp cook, Arty, was another new friend. He was the oldest man in the group with a round belly and ruddy, bearded face. He always dished Ayra's bowl for her and said things like, 'Here you go, young lady. Hope it sits well with your gut.' And his food always did. She had tasted more flavors in one week than she had in all her seventeen years. The second day of travel he had cooked spiced apples in a large pot. At the mess house, they cooked apples when they were starting to spoil and mashed them into sauce, so she assumed Arty's would be similar. One whiff and she knew she was mistaken. She had never tasted anything more delicious.

She had learned the dark-haired soldier's name was Edvin. She guessed him to be near Prince Gibsen's age. Gibsen didn't say much about him other than he was a reckless brawler and unmatched in archery. The way the prince stuck out his jaw and hardened his tone when he spoke about Edvin gave Ayra the impression he liked him about as much as she did. On her own she gathered the other men seemed to like him despite his obnoxious behavior, and often laughter erupted from whichever group he was in. Edvin had tried striking up a conversation with her several times in camp, but she flatly ignored his attempts. Since his riding position in the company was in the front, she never had to ride near him. To her relief he mostly left her alone.

The company rolled into a large clearing. A sharp whistle came from the front. They would be staying here for the night. Ayra slid out of the saddle and felt only a little ache. Her legs and hips were getting used to being astride a horse for hours on end. She was proud of herself for mastering basic horse riding rather quickly.

"It is fortunate this road follows the river much of the way, or we might have run out of water—a group this size and my demand for *real* food at least once a day," said Gibsen, gesturing to the soldiers heading into the trees with pails. He looked at his hands and wiped his sleeve across his forehead. "Though it would be nice to be able clean up in the river. This time of year many sections, including this one here, are too high and rough. Only a fool would dare to get in. Have to settle for a bucket."

Ayra listened for the distant rumble of the river. "I'm surprised there is so much water. I thought the country was in drought."

"True. We are. But renewal season brings the melt of the

snow in the mountains, the streams and trickles from the Aster and Western Wolfjaw Ranges join the Life, as well as water flowing from the southern countries. But this water is not enough to supply the farms with all the water necessary. We need rain, and the mountain heads have decided to stop most of the clouds from entering the valley these last few years." He looked toward the western Wolfjaw Range. "My father always says the mountains that surround us are some of the best soldiers we have, but even good soldiers can cause trouble."

"What will happen if the rain doesn't come?"

He bent over and picked up a sharp rock, turning it over in his hands. "Our bordering countries do not have the same problem we do, and we are on peaceful terms with all of them at the moment, especially Tiseden. We will trade with them— quarried stone, gold from the mines." He glanced up from his rock to look her in the eye. "We are secure," he said with a rigid smile.

Ayra wanted to continue asking questions, but he ended the conversation by excusing himself to direct the setting up of his tent. She looked at the trees and wondered if the rest of Mihtengard looked more like the desert they had come from. When she was reunited with her cousin in Tiseden, she would not have the worrisome trouble of not having enough water. That country borders the Azure Sea, with many rivers and lakes.

"I know that face," Kelton said, walking up beside her. "You are thinking about what Arty is cooking up for dinner, aren't you?"

"I'm sure I'm the only one who isn't. No, I was just thinking about Mihtengard. It's not going to be our country anymore—when we get to Tiseden. I'm just getting to know it and soon I'll leave."

"Yeah, I had no idea it was more than rock and rubble. Maybe Tiseden is even better."

"Maybe." She looked at the trees that lined the clearing. "I'm going to go find the river. Want to come?"

"Nah, I think I'll go snag an apple and wait around to see what the others are doing."

"Are you ever not hungry?"

He put his hand up to his chin and rubbed it thoughtfully. "Nope, don't think so. Not when there's good stuff to eat."

She gave him a swift kick in the rear as he trotted off, then headed in the direction the soldiers with buckets had gone and followed the sound of the river through the trees. The water seemed to call to her like a honey hive to a bear, though she was careful not to get too close to the edge. The thought of falling in frightened her enough to keep her distance.

She found a tall boulder a safe measure from the water and climbed to its top. With her knees tucked up under her chin, she watched the river crash down its course. The rush of the water made her blood pump faster and her fingers tingle, yet at the same time calmed her mind. Absently, she rubbed the mark on her shoulder.

Thwack! The unexpected sound made her jump. She glanced around. About thirty paces downriver she spotted a rusty orange tunic through the trees. She ducked her head lower to try to glimpse a face. She saw the drawn bow before she saw the face and realized it was Edvin.

Another *thwack*.

He was a quarter turned away from her. Maybe he had not seen her on her tower. She slipped over the opposite edge and made her way down, her foot slipping and scraping against the rock only once. The trees all looked the same, and it took her a minute to remember exactly which direction she had come from.

She had only taken three steps from the boulder when Edvin jumped to her side and shouted, "HA!"

She let out a startled cry reminiscent of a goat bleat and stumbled away from him, stepping on her dress and nearly going down.

"Sorry," he laughed. "I didn't think you'd scare so easily."

"I don't!" she shot back. "I just wasn't expecting anyone to jump out at me."

He lifted both his hands. "Take it easy, Pit Girl. I didn't know I had an audience when I came here for some target practice. You following me?"

"No," she said quickly. Of course he would assume she had followed him. "I was here first. But I was just on my way—"

"Now, wait a minute." He grabbed her arm as she tried to scamper away and let go before she could think to pull it free. "I don't mind having some company if you want to stay."

"I really think I should get back," she said, resuming her steps.

"Well, I'm on my way back, too. I'll come with you," he said striding up next to her.

"Please don't."

"But it's my pleasure, Pit Girl," he said with a lopsided grin. He knew he was annoying her, which annoyed her even more.

"Stop calling me that. That's not my name."

"I know. But Pit Girl just suits you. So what did your family do to end up in the debtor camp so long?"

Ayra balled her fists. Of all the things he could ask. She looked the other way and pretended not to hear him.

"Kind of touchy on that one, huh?" he quietly mused. He was silent only a few seconds before he tried to resume conversation. "I'd never been to a debtor camp before. Looks like a good time. I was surprised when Prince Gibsen directed us further south past Bowgen instead of north, but I think we all were."

"You were surprised? Didn't you know what the company was setting out for?"

"Sure I did. Well, I thought I did. We were only told we were going on a trade mission, to set up trade with the surrounding countries, Tiseden to start. We went to Bowgen to pick up some supplies and instead of taking the north road from there, we went south. But now I think I understand." He looked her up and down. "Your cousin must be an important man for Prince Gibsen to go to such effort."

Ayra felt her throat warm, and she picked up her pace.

His long legs kept up effortlessly. He looked at her face and hurriedly added, "Wait, I didn't mean that how it sounded. I was just thinking out loud and—"

"Maybe you should try thinking in your head instead of letting it all fall out. Then you wouldn't sound so stupid."

He stopped walking. "Now hold on, I just meant your family must be of some value to the crown. I didn't mean you—"

She spun around to face him. He was well over a head taller. She lifted her finger to him. "You can just stop talking to me. I don't need you to try to gather any more information to embarrass me with. And I don't need you to be my friend either."

"I'm not out to be your friend. I just have some questions about your...never mind. Anyway, where I come from, people are civilized. They make small talk. They have *manners*. I guess I shouldn't have expected the same from a girl who was raised by thieves."

Ayra's mouth dropped open. If he had known Tanna or her parents, he never would have said a thing like that. "Well, maybe *you* should have paid more attention to your people."

She wished she could come up with something harsher—cleverer—but he had her irritated beyond being able to think. After a pause she spat, "I don't like you," and marched the rest of the way to camp alone.

Kelton found her right away to tell her some of the men were going to practice sparring and had invited him to learn a few things. He raised his eyebrows when she told him to go right ahead.

"Really? I thought you'd say something like 'You're not old enough,' or 'You'll be killed,' or 'That's like you being a chicken trying to fight a bear with a pebble.' You're really all right with it?"

She really wasn't sure what she thought but felt too flustered to really think about it, so she sent him on his way. Sitting alone in their tent she ran through her conversation with Edvin again. Why was he interested in her family? She couldn't think of a reason why he should care a scrap about them. Rooney said the journey would be weeks. Ayra hoped she could avoid Edvin for all that time.

She shook her head and laid back on the cot to think of pleasanter things—the rustle of the trees, the little purple flowers she had noticed growing all along the road, Gibsen's curly hair bouncing as he rode his horse. This last thought almost made her outright laugh. She did like his hair, but he was a prince. And she was nothing. But just the same, she let herself think of him until supper.

7

AYRA'S eyes opened and stared into the dark space above her. A noise like the snap of a twig had pulled her from a light sleep. She looked in the direction where Kelton was still sleeping.

It was just one of the horses, she told herself.

A southern wind tickled the trees and made them shiver, their rustle drowning out other sounds of the night. She closed her eyes again and told herself to sleep.

Out of the darkness, a hand clamped over her mouth, warm and heavy. Her eyes shot open to see a dark figure crouched at the head of her cot.

"Don't make a sound," said a low voice. "It's me, Edvin. I can't explain, but you and your brother need to come with me."

She shook her head, too afraid to even eke out a noise. Kelton's soft breathing continued undisturbed.

"I didn't want to do it this way," he said. Cold metal pressed against her neck. "Now get your dress and boots on. We need to hurry."

The blade moved from her neck, but he stayed crouched as if ready to strike any second. If she screamed, surely the men in the camp would come running. But what might happen to her or to Kelton before they could get to the tent kept her silent. She obediently slipped her dress over her underclothes and put on her boots.

Edvin stood. He seemed so much taller in the dark. His hand wrapped around her arm and pulled her to her feet facing away from him. Then he brought his other arm around her and pressed the knife to her neck again. With his left boot, he gave Kelton a nudge. He rolled over and stretched, reluctantly opening his eyes.

"Kelton," she whispered.

"What's going on?" he whispered back.

"Get your boots on," Edvin ordered. "Make any moves or sounds and your sister will get it."

Kelton shot up like a rabbit from danger, threw on his tunic, and set to putting on his boots.

Edvin motioned his head toward the tent opening. "Quickly." With Ayra still at knifepoint, Kelton moved out the flap first. "This way," Edvin whispered, directing them toward the woods.

Little light from the partially masked moon reached the ground, and Ayra stumbled and tripped over the cloaked rocks and dips, each time expecting the blade to slice into her skin.

When they reached the edge of the clearing, Edvin paused and moved the knife from Ayra's neck. "Keeping going," he whispered with a wave of his knife.

He moved to follow them into the trees when Kelton suddenly whipped around and threw his fist through the air with all his might, connecting with Edvin's jaw. Edvin stumbled back, and Ayra heard the knife hit the dirt. She dropped to her knees to find it. Edvin lurched forward and threw his shoulder into Kelton's gut, effortlessly knocking the boy to the ground.

"Kelton!" Ayra cried as her fingers searched over the cool dirt for the blade.

Edvin pinned Kelton to the ground with one hand over his mouth. "Kelton, listen to me. You—" Edvin's head snapped up, looking toward the camp. A few seconds later shouts erupted through the clearing.

Edvin tried lifting Kelton to his feet but as he came up, Kelton twisted out of his grip and broke into a run.

"Over here!" he shouted.

When she saw her brother was no longer captive, Ayra pushed off her feet and sprinted after him. She only made it a few steps when a yank on her hair pulled her back. Edvin grabbed her firmly under the arm and scooped his blade off the ground. Kelton was already halfway back to camp, shouting the entire way.

"Move!" His tone sent a chill down her back and for a moment her feet wouldn't obey.

Impatiently, he twisted her arm up behind her back and pushed her into the woods. As they moved through the trees, Ayra struggled to place her feet as quickly as Edvin did his. She slipped once on a rock and yelped as pain shot through her contorted shoulder.

Shouts from the men left behind echoed around them and whistles carried through the trees. The rushing sound of the river grew louder. They did not stop moving as Edvin smoothly grabbed a pack tucked behind a boulder. He slung it over his shoulder in one quick motion.

And then the river was at her toes. The bank dropped sharply, shadowing the churning water. She could no longer hear any noises from behind over the roar of the river.

"We'll have to jump," Edvin said in her ear.

"What? But I…I can't swim." She dug her heels into the dirt and leaned backward into him.

"Then don't let go of me." He spun her around, wrapped his arms around her, and jumped.

The river swallowed them whole in one gulp. The shock of the icy water constricted Ayra's lungs, seizing the air inside. She felt the current press against her back, and instinctively threaded her arms around Edvin's neck. They surfaced, and her lungs relaxed to allow a sharp breath of air, gulping water with it. She sputtered and opened her eyes to see silvery, moonlit trees rushing past.

Edvin kicked his legs forward and leaned back, directing them past rocks and other debris.

The realization that she was rushing downriver in water that was over her head with a boy who had threatened her with a knife ousted Ayra's ability to be rational. She began thrashing her legs thrusting herself further above Edvin's head, pushing him down. His arms flailed as he went under, but she didn't care. With one kick of his legs his head shot out of the water again.

"Stop!" he shouted.

She continued to thrash and push, unable to gain control of herself. He reached up his hands and gave her shoulders a solid push. In an instant they were separated. Sheer terror pulsed through her body as she flailed her arms to find something to grasp. Water continued to swirl around her. Pushing her up and down. She glimpsed Edvin swimming toward the bank just as her head went underwater. She pushed against the water with her exhausted limbs and resurfaced.

The current shoved her into a rock and dull pain pounded through her leg. As her body rounded the partially submerged rock she felt a quick pull, and the current changed from flowing to churning. Darkness surrounded her, and she could no longer tell up from down as she rolled with the frustrated water. Seconds dragged on, and her lungs began to burn, begging to suck in a breath. *This is it,* she thought. *Buried by water instead of rocks.*

In one final effort, she put her hands above her head and thrust them down. The water around her pushed away with surprising force. She felt the pocket's suction break and the normal current push against her body. She surfaced into the night air, gasping and hurling downriver once again.

"Ayra!" A hand grabbed her wrist, and she felt Edvin pull her toward him. He had found a short log. "Grab on."

He guided her hand to the smooth wood. Ayra draped both arms over the float and pulled it to her chest.

"We need to go a little further," Edvin shouted. "Can you hold on?"

When she gave no answer, he leaned back into the water and stretched his legs in front of them again to maneuver around obstructions.

The torrent water continued only minutes more. The white waters smoothed, and the din became hushed behind them. The current continued to push the log, and Edvin changed position and began to kick.

Ayra was certain her legs were paralyzed, and if it weren't for the sharp point left by a broken branch digging into her arm, she would have been concerned about her arms, too.

"I can't hold on much longer," she whispered through chattering teeth.

"We need to go on just a little further."

He moved closer to her and placed his arm over her back to hold her to the log. Questions swirled in her head, as chaotic as the water she had just passed through. Where was he taking her? Was he working alone? Or was there a band of men waiting for them? What would they want with her?

How long would she have to wait to find out?

The log moved toward the bank on her left. They ran aground on a low spot covered with smooth pebbles. Ayra crawled out of the water as much as she could and dropped to her stomach. Every part of her body felt numb except her tingling fingers. She looked at Edvin, who was lying awkwardly on the pack on his back, panting heavily.

"Well," he breathed. "That did not go as planned."

A few quiet minutes passed. Then, as if he suddenly remembered something pressing, he sat up and swiftly got to his feet. "C'mon. We need to move away from the river."

"I can't. I'm too tired." The stones pushed into her face and chest, but the feeling of something solid beneath her was too reassuring to pull away from. "What do you want with me?"

He nervously glanced around. "I'll explain when we get to a safe place. They're still searching." He crouched over her, put his arms under hers, and pulled her up.

Ayra's legs felt wobbly beneath the weight of her body. She didn't think she could make them move, but Edvin grabbed her arm and forced her to move them. She was relieved he didn't twist it like before. She couldn't see his knife anymore but decided it would be useless to try to break away. The only way she was moving anywhere was if he was pulling her. After an hour of brisk walking in silence, Edvin stopped and slightly tilted his head to the side.

"I think we should be safe here for a couple hours. You can rest if you need to." He dropped his waterlogged pack into the dirt.

Ayra glanced around. A large pile of rocks created somewhat of a sheltered area. She dropped next to them and leaned her back against one. The faint blue light of the moon seeped through the branches of the trees, casting cold shadows around them. She shivered as the heat from walking drained from her body.

"Are you cold?" he asked.

She blinked at him. Was she cold? It had to be one of the most ridiculous questions he could ask.

"Of course you are," he said with a light laugh and a shake of his head.

He crouched down and untied the bow and capped quiver that were strapped to the pack. He muttered to himself as he examined them with his hands more than with his eyes. Then he jerked back the flap to open his pack. He pulled out a dark bundle and held it up.

"Swiped this from the wagon in case you got yours wet. Not much use now."

The folded dress hit the ground with a slap. He reached into his pack again and pulled out a thick stick, bent it until there was a cracking sound, and held it out to her.

"We can't have a fire, but this will be enough."

She looked at him, unsure she wanted to take anything he offered. He impatiently held the stick out closer to her.

"It's a heat stick. Army uses them. Just take it."

Ayra grabbed the stick and felt its warmth flow into her hand. A little surprised laugh escaped her throat. She examined the plain stick and wondered how such a thing could work.

Edvin's voice cut in on her inspection. "You're going to have to take off your dress."

"No, I will not!" she hissed and crossed her arms over her chest. One of the guards had warned her to be careful of boys like him.

"Take it easy, Pit Girl—last thing on my mind. That dress is made of cotton. It'll suck the heat right out of you." He untied a rolled blanket attached to the bottom of his pack and gave it a few squeezes to get out most of the water. "Here, take this. It's wet, but it's wool. It will be better than nothing. Now do as I say before you freeze to death. I'll even turn around."

He swiveled on the balls of his feet so his back was to her. She stared at him for a minute and felt her body grow colder. Reluctantly, she leaned forward and got to her knees. The wet dress clung to her body, making it difficult to get off. But she yanked and wiggled until it pulled over her head. She kept her underclothes on even though they were probably cotton, too. She wrapped the damp blanket around herself and clutched the heat stick to her stomach.

"All right. You can turn around."

He turned back to his pack without even glancing up at her and pulled out a few items Ayra couldn't make out. Everything he had was laid out between them. He didn't say anything to her, but Ayra could tell by his rigid form and quiet cursing he was not pleased. He pulled off his boots and shirt, cracked his own stick, and wrapped his tunic around his shoulders.

Neither one spoke as they sat in their little camp of rocks. Ayra's thoughts flowed through the events of the night— Edvin's hand over her mouth, Kelton pinned to the ground, the terror of churning waters, a knife pressed to her neck. Her blood began to pulse quicker as her temperature and temper rose. His silence was making her angrier by the minute.

Finally, she said, "Are you going to explain to me what under the stars you are doing or not?"

He drew in a breath and exhaled slowly. He rubbed his hand over the back of his neck. "Not real sure where to start. Wouldn't you rather sleep?"

"No," she said shortly. "How about you start by explaining the part where your put a knife up to my throat, dragged me through the woods, and threw me into a river."

"I told you I didn't want to use my knife, but you weren't moving. And I didn't think you'd stay quiet unless you had incentive. And since you seem to have forgotten, I didn't *throw* you into the river. I jumped in *with* you."

"Pretty much the same thing."

He stared at her a moment. "I don't think it is. And jumping into the river wasn't even part of the original plan. If your brother hadn't woke the whole camp, we could have left on foot and crossed the river in a sane place instead of plunging into rapids."

"If my brother hadn't woke the whole camp," she scoffed. Now he was trying to put the blame on Kelton. "If you hadn't put a knife to my throat he wouldn't have."

"Circles. You are taking this conversation in circles. Are you always ornery? I don't know how I'm going to convince you the truth of anything else I'm going to say if you won't even accept I never wanted or tried to kill you."

"It's kind of hard to see it any other way."

He stiffened a little and calmly said, "Ayra, I need you to be honest with me. Does your family have any special…skills? Anything that would be of value?"

Ayra wasn't sure how to answer his question. She thought of Tanna's words. 'We have an important purpose.' She wished she knew what Tanna had meant. But she didn't trust Edvin anyway. At all. "We're really good at picking dirt."

He studied her for minute, swallowed, and said, "When this mission started, we were told we were going to Tiseden to arrange a trade agreement. After leaving Midivard, we went south to Bowgen, supposedly to pick up some needed supplies we couldn't get in the head city. Instead of going north from there, we went south."

"You told me that already."

"Right. When we picked up you and your brother, we were told we were taking you to your relative in Tiseden. What we weren't told is who the supposed *relative* is." He paused until she looked up at his face. "Prince Gibsen is planning to trade you and Kelton to…Covalt." He looked at her meaningfully.

"So my cousin's name is Covalt?"

"You can't be serious. Have you never heard the name Covalt?"

She shrugged.

He ran both hands through his hair. "Why am I surprised?"

She glared at him, but he didn't flinch.

"Covalt is a Tisedenian. A dangerous one. A maniac. He formed a secret army of disgruntled soldiers and citizens and raged war against his own brother, the king of Tiseden. I guess he's technically a prince, but no one gives him the title. After decades of peace and losing many men to Covalt, King Tobian's military structure was weak. My father's army was sent to provide relief to King Tobian, and Covalt's army suffered heavy losses. But he survived. And, unfortunately, the Tisedenians don't believe in punishment by death—for royalty anyway—and King Tobian spared his brother. So Covalt was banished to an old fortress on an island somewhere out on the Azure Sea. You've heard of the sea at least, haven't you? Right. Well, word was he died a while ago, but evidently those were just rumors."

Ayra shivered. She wished she knew more of what happened in Mihtengard. Most of the time her family had pretended the outside world didn't exist. It would be nice to have some way to validate what Edvin was saying. She could not remember Gibsen telling her that Edvin's father was the commander of one of Mihtengard's armies, which seemed like an important thing to mention.

"So what does this Covalt want with Kelton and me?"

Edvin put one hand up to his forehead and rubbed it with his fingertips. "I don't know. For some purpose. I was hoping you could tell me. Ayra, think hard. Think of your parents—did they ever say anything? Or your grandmother. You were with her a lot. Did she ever say anything to you, or did you notice anything special she could do? Obviously he is looking for a specific family."

How did Edvin know about Tanna? She had hardly spoken to him before tonight, much less told him about her grandmother. "I told you. We're really good at picking dirt. That's about as special as we get. No, I really can't tell you any reason why we would be important."

He studied her face again and was quiet for a bit. "It's obvious you aren't fond of me," he said finally, "but I feel like I can at least trust your word. Whatever the reason is, we are trying to prevent him from succeeding."

Ayra took a few minutes to process the information Edvin had just given to her. She began to think that maybe she should have just gone to sleep because not much of it was making sense.

"You said 'we.' Who is we?"

"Tress and me."

"Tress? I don't understand. If Tress made the plan, why didn't he come to get us instead of you?"

"To be clear, I made the plan, not Tress. And that's a good question. I told Tress he should take you. You were more friendly with him than me. But he thought with his experience it would be better if he stayed with Prince Gibsen. Also, he wasn't sure he could find where we are going, and I have been there before. And mostly, he thought it was a rocky plan. But now I'm positive he should be the one sitting across from you.

This isn't going to work. I don't know what I was thinking." He put his head down and buried his face in his hands.

"Why didn't Tress mention any of this to me?"

"He tried but couldn't get you alone," he said through his fingers. He popped his head up. "Prince Gibsen kind of kept you to himself as much as he could."

The mention of Gibsen's name again made something else connect in Ayra's mind. "Wait, so are you suggesting Gibsen is a traitor?"

"First name basis with a prince of Mihtengard, huh?" Ayra felt her cheeks warm, and he smiled with satisfaction at her silence. "I didn't say that exactly. But yes, I guess a traitor is what he would be. I've never liked him much—pompous little pup, al-ways chasing his elder brother's glory—but I never thought he'd betray his father and country."

"How do you know all this?"

"I…" He shifted his weight and rubbed the back of his neck. "I can't say. Just try to trust me, all right?"

Ayra had nothing else to say. She let the rest of the information sink in. She did not like Edvin, but what he offered seemed honest. She surprised herself by believing him. And she did trust Tress. What could Covalt want with Kelton and her? They were quarry rats. Nobodies.

She looked at Edvin again. He was staring at the supplies laid out on the ground between them. Moonlight touched only half his face and his dark eyes appeared almost black. He had a cowlick in his hairline on the right that forced his hair to swoop up on its own. She hadn't noticed it before now. She felt her eyelids become heavy and soon released herself to sleep.

8

AYRA woke when the first promise of light shone behind the eastern mountains. She was surprised how well the heat stick had worked, though its warmth was fading and the early morning air felt cool on her face. Edvin was asleep across from her, still in the sitting position. She wondered if Gibsen and his men were looking for her or if they had given up.

She moved to sit up and flinched. Every muscle in her limbs and back ached. She managed to push herself all the way up and wrapped the wool blanket tighter around her body. She looked over the items Edvin had laid out that she couldn't identify a few hours earlier. Now she could see a circular device with a needle in the center, flint stones tied together, a hatchet, a leather water pouch, and a box similar to the boxes she had seen other soldiers tuck noon meals in. Her stomach growled.

Edvin stirred and stretched. When he opened his eyes, he gave her a faint smile. "You're still here. I was afraid you'd try to run off."

"I considered it, but I didn't know what I would eat for my morning meal."

He chuckled. "Was that a joke?"

"No." She felt a tug to smile but tightened her mouth to stop it. "Maybe. But I am hungry."

He tilted his head for a moment. "I think we're safe, but we better get moving. Hopefully, we will find something soon."

"Hopefully? Did you not think we would need to eat when you made your heroic plan?"

He lifted the metal box. "Again, wasn't planning on going for a swim. And I know I *can* find us food, just not sure when I will find it. We can't have a fire yet, so I need to find things we can eat raw." He dropped his tunic and pulled his shirt on. "Your dress is probably still damp, but it should dry quickly when the sun gets higher."

Edvin stood as he replaced his tunic and turned his back to her. Ayra pulled her dress over her head and tugged it into place. She sat back and pulled off her wool stockings to look at her feet. They were both red and blistered. They must have been too numb for her to realize they were rubbing in her wet boots. When she slid her sore feet back into her boots, she could still feel some moisture inside.

Edvin loaded all his items except the bow and quiver back into his pack.

"It's a good thing I brought my watertight quiver," he muttered to himself.

Ayra slowly rose to her feet and tried to stretch out her soreness. "You still haven't told me where you are taking me."

"Oh, right. We're going to find a hermit."

"What?"

"A hermit. A person who lives alone. In the mountains."

"I know what a hermit is," she snapped.

He smiled. "I think there we can learn why Covalt wants the Regnan siblings. We'll curve west—away from the company—as we head north to Gowen."

They moved through the woods quietly. Every once in a while, Edvin stopped and tilted his head. As his confidence grew, she felt her hope diminish. It wasn't long before she gave up her last flake of hope that anyone in the company was still looking for her. Or at least that they were looking anywhere near the right area. Perhaps they thought she and Edvin had both drowned in the river. She wondered what Kelton was doing, what he was feeling. She knew he was safe, for now at least, but he didn't know she was.

Now that he was her only traveling companion, she studied Edvin more closely as she walked. She welcomed any thoughts, even about *him*, to distract her from the pain of each step. He was lean, but not scrawny and his shoulders were broad. He moved fluidly, as if it took little effort to maneuver his long body around. Wrapped multiple times around his left wrist was a strap of brown leather. Gibsen had told her he liked to pick fights. She wondered if the scar by his right eye was from one of his brawls.

After an hour of walking, Edvin pointed to a patch of green stems. "Wild raspberries. Too bad they aren't ripe yet."

"Really? Raspberries? I've never had any type of berry before," she said, examining the little white blossoms and fuzzy-looking nubs on the cane.

"You've never had a berry? I really am beginning to question everything about your upbringing."

She rolled her eyes. He spoke as if her family had chosen to raise her in a debtor's quarry and to never leave. He obviously didn't understand what life had been like for her. "In the quarry, we eat what we are given. Potatoes, cabbage, onions, barley for porridge, sometimes squash and beans. Stuff like that. Every so often we get meat. And pears or apples. But I've never had any other kind of fruit."

"Hm. When you come to Midivard, I'll buy you a raspberry tart. There's a little bakery in the Crawford District near my home that makes the best in the city."

A day ago she thought she would leave Mihtengard before seeing the head city. She smiled at the prospect of seeing it after all. Edvin found a small spring near the berry patch and filled the water pouch. He pulled some little shoots from the wet earth around the spring and rinsed them in the clear little pool.

"These will have to do for a meal."

They continued beating their own path through the trees as they ate. Ayra grew tired of turning through anxious thoughts about Edvin, Gibsen, and Kelton in her mind, so she focused on the new world around her. The lower brush and grass were still in early growth, embellishing the ground with varying shades of green, but predominantly the ground cover was still a lifeless brown. The trees grew thick in some areas and in others thinned into lonely groups.

She smiled to herself as brown, long-legged insects jumped away from her grass-crushing feet like sparks fleeing a fire and even found herself pouncing a few times to scare up as many as she could in one spot. All around she could hear the mild clicking and humming sounds of insects and the tittering of birds in the trees. For some time, these and the sound of the gravelly dirt and dry, snapping sticks under their feet were the only sounds she heard.

In the silence of their mouths, she unearthed questions in her mind about the world she had not bothered with in recent years. She had asked Gibsen a few questions, but most of their conversations had been about him and life in the castle. She had not learned much about anything else.

She had been told what trees grew in the region but couldn't remember the names. She wondered what the little gold-bellied bird hopping around a rock was called. And what bird made the rasping call, or which one made the high-pitched trilling sound.

The only birds she heard around the quarry were ugly cawing crows and occasional screaming falcons flying overhead searching for mice in the rocks. And some mindless clucks from wandering village chickens.

She also wondered about general life in Mihtengard. What types of tasks do girls her age do and what do they do for fun, among dozens of other questions, meandered in her head. She couldn't ask Edvin any of them, though. He already thought she was ignorant, and she did not want to feed his notions any more.

"I forget you haven't been around trees much," he said suddenly. He must have noticed her constantly looking up into the branches. "Have you had a chance to climb any yet?"

Ayra shifted her gaze from the untouchable treetops to his face. "How do you know I want to climb trees?"

He looked away, but she could still see the flush of color in his ear. He shrugged. "You just seem like the kind of girl who would like to do that."

She wasn't sure what he meant by that but decided she didn't care to know. The sun was high in the blue, cloudless sky. Edvin stopped and listened like he often had that morning. Then he dropped his pack into the dirt and adjusted his bow and quiver on his shoulder.

"I think we can have a fire now. And the trees are thick enough here to give us some cover. Stay here while I go look for something to eat." He watched her sit down on a rock as if that would ensure she would not run off when he left her alone.

She watched his easy jog through the trees until his rusty orange tunic disappeared. For a minute she entertained the idea of an escape plan. She could run in the opposite direction to the river, find a shallow place to cross, and find the road that would lead to Gibsen's company.

Her plan seemed easy enough until she thought of complications such as how she would find food, which direction the river actually was, and the possibility of there being more than one road. It was no use trying to get back to Kelton if she was putting herself more at risk than she was now. As much as she hated to admit, she needed Edvin to survive.

And what if the story he had given her was true? In that case, she really was better off where she sat.

She slumped her shoulders and rested her chin on her hand. Her eyes fell on a large tree a little off to the right. It was the same type of white barked tree, but it was noticeably larger than the others around it. She left her rock and strolled over to the tree. She looked up at its thick branches clustered with leaves and glanced around for any sign of Edvin returning. No rusty orange tunic was in sight.

A wide smile spread across her face as she traced a path up the branches with her eyes. She reached up to the first branch and hoisted herself up, placing one knee on the branch, her skirt hindering her movements a little. Then she lifted her hand to the next branch and pulled up her other foot. She laughed quietly to herself at how easily she moved higher into the tree.

When she was three quarters of the way up, the branches above looked too thin to support her weight, so she sat on the highest thick branch and rested her back against the trunk, using a smaller branch as an armrest. She basked in the green sunlight that felt so much warmer away from the ground. She grinned as birds moved around her, not bothered by the giant who had entered their realm. A squirrel with a short bushy tail was not quite as comfortable and scurried back the way it had come upon seeing her.

She had almost forgotten she wasn't alone in the woods when she heard jogging footsteps nearing. Edvin's figure came into view through an opening in the leaves. When he got to his pack, he turned, looking in all directions. He tilted his head for a minute before shaking it and running both hands through his dark hair.

She smiled wickedly to herself to see him frustrated. Then she noticed the two birds dangling over his shoulder, and her stomach protested its hollowness.

"Caw-caw," she called out.

His head snapped up directly to her secret hideout in the trees, and she couldn't hold in her laughter any longer. Relief washed over his face accompanied by a sheepish smile as it dawned on him she had been watching him.

"That was pretty good," he called up. "You really got me. I didn't think there was any way you'd be able to get away without me hearing you, but for a minute…" He trailed off.

"You're not the only one who can sneak around, you know."

"I've got your grouse, but I'll only let you have it if you apologize."

"I am *not* sorry," she called back.

He laughed and shook his head as he gathered pieces of wood for a fire. She watched him from her loft as he carefully placed each piece of wood and tucked kindling pieces in between. He cracked the two flint stones together, sending sparks into his creation. With a few blows, the fire took.

He picked up one of the plump, feathery birds and set to work. Everything he did looked easy, like he didn't even have to think about what he was doing. Ayra wondered if she could learn to be like that. Self-sufficient.

In the quarry, all their food and housing were provided for them. Getting clothing and necessities like soap and blankets was a little harder. Those kinds of things usually came from what families in the camp left behind when they returned to their homes or from the villagers who took pity on her family. She had worked hard in the quarry, but it really hadn't been necessary to do anything for survival.

When the smell of roasted meat wafted into the trees, Ayra reluctantly climbed down.

"How was your first tree climbing experience?" Edvin asked as she sat down next to the fire.

"Even better than I dreamed."

His mouth twitched as he fought back a smile. "You know, most girls your age in Midivard would never even think of climbing trees."

Her curiosity got the better of her pride, and she let herself ask one of her questions. "What do they like to do then?"

He checked the roasting meat and shrugged his shoulders. "You know, girl stuff. Like fist-fighting and rolling around in pigsties."

Ayra sat back and folded her arms. He was making fun of her.

"Never mind. It was a stupid question."

"What? No," he said looking up at her. "Sorry. My mother's always telling me I don't know when to keep my jokes in. No, the girls I know like to go to dances. They like to go to the First Day Market at the beginning of the month to eat and look at the fabrics and jewelry. Watch plays. Paint. A number of them like to ride horses. But I've never known any of them to play in the dirt all day or climb trees." He didn't say the last part with disgust. Just matter of fact.

She still felt slightly irritated, but his frank response made her relax. "I didn't play in the dirt...at least not much since I turned twelve. I worked in it."

"Right, well, pretty much the same thing," he said with a wink.

They finished the rest of their afternoon meal in near silence. Edvin buried their small fire in dirt before they set off again. He told her Gowen was a village at the base of the north mountains where they'd be able to get some better supplies. It was about ten days off by his estimate. Ayra felt more at ease about the situation as he seemed to freely offer information about his plan.

But she decided to keep the rest of her questions to herself. She did not like that there was so much she didn't know, but she would rather Edvin not know the depth of her ignorance. Instead, she let the birds fill the silence for her.

9

THE landscape gradually changed as days of walking passed—large rocks dotted their path and long-needled pine trees now mingled with the aspens as they skirted around low hills and cliffs. The northern section of the Wolfjaw Mountain range was close and extended along all of the horizon. It had been seven days since Ayra was separated from Kelton and the company.

She tried not to think about how much easier travel had been on horseback as she rolled her ankles in unseen holes and tripped over brush and stones. But at the end of each day, she could feel her legs were getting stronger and her body not so weary. When they stopped to rest, she usually tried to find a tree to climb to observe her new world and her new escort.

Her feelings toward Edvin had changed with the face of the land. She refused to speak more than necessary, but she let him talk as often as he wished. He did not offer a lot about himself, talking more about his family, mainly his four brothers—Ronan, Tavin, Peter, and Lee—or Mihtengard's proud military history when he attempted to stir up conversation. It was not hard for her to see that he was deeply loyal to his country.

She was surprised the conceit she had perceived upon first meeting him was not so evident. He was self-assured, that was certain. But he was not boastful. She even occasionally failed to hold in her laughter when he told his stories.

The air was cooling around her as the sun drifted lower in the sky. She heard the wild cry of a bird and looked up into the trees to try to spot it. She was startled when her face bumped into the back of Edvin's shoulder.

She stood still and waited while he listened in his usual way, his head tilted. He didn't move.

"What? What is it?" she whispered.

"Shh," he glanced around, then ducked his head with his eyes closed. When he opened them again, he whispered, "We're being followed."

"Gibsen? Er…Prince Gibsen?" she asked, trying to determine whether she felt relief or fear. A confusing mixture of both, she decided.

"No. Not men. Wolves. I first heard them a while ago, but they are definitely coming closer."

"What do we do?"

"Keep moving and hope they change course. I can't tell exactly how many yet, but there are at least four." He shifted his bow and uncapped his quiver as they entered a large meadow.

Ayra narrowed her eyes. She looked around and strained her ears to pick up any unusual sound, but she saw and heard nothing. How did he know how many there were? Before she could form the question, he grabbed her by the arm and pulled her along at a faster pace. Her heart picked up with her steps.

In the quarry, coyotes and wolves occasionally came near the camp or the village. Usually only one or two at a time, when on the brink of starvation. It was not difficult for the guards or village men to take them out before doing any harm. But wolves were big, and if there really were four or more, they were out-numbered and under armed. Edvin was good with his bow. She, however, was utterly defenseless.

Halfway to the trees Edvin stopped again and looked south. Ayra followed his gaze, her heart thumping. A cold howl broke through the air, sending a chill down her spine.

Edvin dropped his pack. "Run!"

Ayra took off, heading toward the far end of the meadow. She was so focused on making it to the trees, she barely noticed Edvin's hand pushing against her back, increasing her speed.

Movement to the left caught her eye. Two massive, silver figures glided through the trees along the edge of the meadow. These were not like the wolves she had seen at the quarry.

Suddenly the trees seemed very far away.

"On the right, too. Three of them," Edvin breathed.

Ahead, Ayra realized the trees were small and thin. "We can't climb those!"

"The rock—I'll give you time."

Across a stream, just behind the trees, Ayra saw it. A jolt of energy shot through her legs. She splashed through the wide, shallow creek, slipping once on the mossy rocks. At the base of the boulder, she dug her fingers into the thin ledges that traced over the rock and swiftly moved up its face to the top.

She scrambled around just in time to see Edvin release an arrow. It did not miss its mark and sank into the chest of the nearest wolf. The creature yelped once and collapsed. Another wolf already stuck through with an arrow lay on its side nearby. The remaining three wolves were closing in from the other side.

Edvin still stood with his back to Ayra, the creek rushing between them. Her blood ran cold and heavy as she realized he did not have time to get to the boulder. He nocked another arrow and drew back. The arrow sliced through the air and dropped another wolf. The remaining two separated, slowing into attack positions, heads low and teeth bared. Their menacing snarls rumbled through the air.

Ayra scanned her surroundings for something to use as a weapon, but there was nothing. She watched helplessly as the wolves crept closer to Edvin from both sides. He slowly stepped backward making his way to the creek, bow drawn and ready. He released his arrow and dropped the fourth wolf just as his boots entered the water.

Wasting not a second, Edvin reached back to pull the last arrow from his quiver. The lone wolf snarled and leaned back ready to strike.

As Edvin brought the arrow forward and took another step back, his boot slipped across a wet rock. His arms flailed, and he fell backward into the water, his shoulders hitting the bank. The arrow dropped from his hand into the water and was instantly swept out of reach. The wolf seized its chance and lunged forward with a guttural snarl.

"Edvin!" Ayra screamed. Instinctively, she reached her right hand out toward the arrow floating downstream as if she could will it to stop. She felt a pull on her fingers, and the arrow stopped, water rippling around it. She whisked her hand back toward Edvin and watched the arrow glide upstream in unison with her hand. "Your arrow, Edvin!"

Edvin turned to find his arrow within reach. He snatched it out of the water, nocked it, drew back, and released just as the wolf leaped. The gray beast came down on Edvin with a splash.

All was still. The creek water flowed its natural course, sweeping over smooth stones and whispering to itself. Ayra held her breath waiting for either Edvin or the wolf to move.

The wolf's shoulders lifted, then slumped to the side as Edvin pushed his way out from under the animal. Ayra exhaled and clambered down from the rock, ran to the creek, and dropped to her knees.

"Are you all right?" she said, searching him over with her eyes. His tunic was deep red across his chest.

He propped himself up on his elbows in the water, breathing heavily and scanning the meadow edges. "I think so. Are you?" He turned his head to look at her.

She nodded. Relief rushed through her body, cleansing it of awful dread.

"What just happened?" Edvin asked, still looking at her face.

Confused, she replied, "We were attacked by *five* wolves. And you killed them all with your bow. That was incredible!"

"No, I clearly understand that part," he said sitting all the way up. He looked up the creek and then down it. "What just happened with the water?"

In her anxiety for him, she had forgotten about the water. She stood. Her fingers were pulsing. "I...I don't know what you mean," she stammered.

He turned away from her. His shoulders lifted and dropped with a deep breath. He stood and slung his bow over his shoulder. With his hands on his hips, he turned back to face her, his jaw flexed. Gesturing to the creek, he said, "The water, Ayra. I know that arrow was swept downstream. How was it next to me, then, when I turned back?"

The anger in his voice rattled her. She didn't know how to answer him. She had seen the water move in an unnatural way, had felt the pull of the current on her hand, but her mind struggled to make sense of it. She looked down at her hands. When she didn't answer, he turned away from her muttering under his breath words she didn't try to hear. He walked to each wolf and yanked out the arrow.

"I'm going to get my pack," he called back to her. Then looking up and down the creek, he lifted his finger and bitterly added, "Don't do anything tricky."

As she watched him jog away, the events of the last five minutes replayed in her mind. The image of Edvin surrounded by three snarling, gray wolves lingered, making her feel nauseous. She moved several paces away from the dead wolf. As the adrenaline in her veins thinned, she realized how exhausted she felt and dropped to her knees again. Her right arm throbbed as if she had been digging for hours without a break. She wiped her clammy hands across her skirt and looked down at the creek. The pulsing in her fingers had relented into the familiar tingle she felt off and on around water.

When she first noticed the sensation, she had told Tanna about the tingling. Her grandmother had just smiled and told her she felt it, too. But when she later asked Kelton, he didn't understand what she meant.

Edvin was still across the meadow. Hesitantly, she reached out a hand over the water, concentrating on its movement. A swift tug pulled on her fingers, and the water rippled where a small section halted from its regular flow. A laugh bubbled up in her throat, and she dropped her hand. She held her opposite hand up and tried again with the same result.

A branch snapped.

She tucked her hands in her lap and looked up to watch Edvin coming through the trees.

"We need to move away from here," he said, eyeing her suspiciously. "Those weren't wild wolves. We're still being tracked. Might even need to keep moving into the night." He walked past without waiting for her to get up.

With a pang of guilt, Ayra got to her feet and trailed behind him. She really did not know how to explain what had happened with the water but recognized it must be part of the purpose her grandmother had spoken of. Perhaps she should have told him what Tanna had said. But she had not trusted him then.

She stared at his back as they briskly walked through the trees. It irritated her to feel guilty when she had done nothing wrong. To ease her own discomfort, she shifted her irritation from herself to Edvin.

How had he heard the wolves before she had? Or seem to know things about her she hadn't told him? And he still had not told her why they were going to the hermit or where he learned all his information about Gibsen working with Covalt.

He was keeping things from her, too.

Long after the moon won its position in the sky, Edvin stopped and without a word, set to building a small fire. When the flames licked into the space between them, he sat down opposite her with his ankles crossed and his folded arms propped on his knees. Ayra stared into the fire, avoiding his gaze. Frustration, guilt, and confusion churned inside of her like the rapids on the river.

"Ayra, why didn't you tell me you can move water?" he asked abruptly. His words were tight, as if his tongue tried to suppress what he really felt.

She kept her eyes on the flames. "I didn't know I could."

"What do you mean you didn't know? How could you not know?"

His tongue was losing control, and she felt the heat burning beneath his words.

"I mean I didn't know, Edvin. That was the first time anything like that has ever happened."

"Well, that's a fine thing," he snapped. "Pretty interesting you would have a rare and very useful skill and not know a thing about it."

She looked up and matched his fiery gaze. "Why are you mad at me? I did *not* know. I can't do anything about that. And what about *you*?"

"What about me?"

"I don't think I have any good reasons to trust you."

"Reasons to trust *me*?" He covered his face with his hands and pressed his fingers to his eyes.

"Yes, you have to admit taking a girl at knifepoint is a little shifty. You never mentioned how you came by your knowledge of supposed treacherous acts. And why are you always tilting your head to the side when we walk? How do you know things about me that I never told you?"

He took a deep breath and slowly exhaled. The fire crackled and snapped as it slowly consumed the wood. Even without the fire Ayra's face would have burned. But her back felt the chill of the night, so she wrapped herself in the wool blanket.

She wanted to go to sleep and forget today but knew it would be pointless to even try. Her mind felt too alert to sleep. So she stared at the fire some more, chewing her lip and cursing Edvin in her mind. She startled when he spoke again.

"I have very acute hearing." His words came out relaxed and easy, his tone steady. He was looking at the fire instead of at her, and his jaw still flexed when he paused. "A gift from the Creator. It tracks in my family, on my father's side, but not all of us have it. I'm the only one out of my brothers. And near as we can tell, only a person with the gift can pass it on. It's not something that's supposed to be general knowledge. My father has told me before that I need to be more discreet when I use it, and evidently he's right."

"Very acute hearing? And it came from your father."

He leaned back on his hands. "Yeah. The kings of Miht-engard have long tried to surround themselves—in the military and in their staff—with gifted families. Some can see farther than average eyesight, some can loosely communicate with animals. Tress comes from a family with a strong sense of smell, which is what makes him a good tracker." He paused. "I don't know all the gifts—they're supposed to be secret. To protect the families. But," he pointed to his ear. "Anyway, I'm not sure many people even believe they really exist. The gifts have kind of worked their way into folklore." He raised his eyes to hers. "I've never heard of anyone having the ability to manipulate an element, though."

Ayra felt the weight of those words. Manipulate an element. That was what she could do. She also felt the weight of his trust. He had told her something that could jeopardize the safety of his family. She bit her lip.

"Just before my grandmother died, she told me I had a

purpose. But she passed before telling me anything. I really didn't know, Edvin."

He was quiet for a minute, then said, "It's all right. I believe you. You just…really surprised me. Shouldn't have since we know Covalt wants you for some reason. But you did." He looked up at the stars. Ayra studied his face and watched the muscles in his face relax. Still staring at the sky, he asked, "Do you think Kelton also has the gift?"

"I don't know. He doesn't feel the same thing I do around water. My grandmother did, though." She followed Edvin's gaze and looked up at the dark sky. The stars stared down at them, unblinking at the dim world below.

She hated that there were so many things she didn't know. In the days she had been out of the quarry, she hadn't learned much about anything. She didn't know the names of the birds, the trees, or the flowers. She didn't know how to defend herself or provide anything for herself. She didn't know the customs of her own people. She hadn't even known about the rare skill she possessed. She felt tears stinging her eyes, but she held them back and blinked until the sensation faded.

"The hermit we are going to has a unique gift, too. The gift of sight but not the ability to see far distances like the family in Midivard. Wil can see the past. It's hard to explain, so I think it will be best if you just wait until we get there to try to understand." He sat up straighter and his tone lightened. "But actually, I guess we really don't need to go there anymore now that we know what Covalt wants with you."

Ayra thought for a moment. A gift that allowed one to look into the past. "No, I still want to go."

"But we don't need to. We can—"

"I want to go," she said firmly. "I know so little of my family's past. Maybe I can get some answers. Will you still take me? Please?"

He sighed and closed his eyes. "Yeah. All right. I'll take you."

"And then we can get Kelton."

"Right. And then we can get Kelton."

He stretched out on his side, propped up on his elbow, fiddling with a stick in his hand. As he stared at the fire, his brown eyes flickered with the flames. She hated to admit being ignorant, but he was not wrong in his perception. Maybe she had been wrong to not ask him her questions. He seemed to know something about everything. And he had just killed five wolves, all on his own, to save them. Well, almost on his own. She had helped with the last one.

She wrapped the blanket tighter around herself and took a deep breath.

"Edvin." He looked up at her when she hesitated. "Will you teach me...some stuff?"

His eyes glinted with interest and a slow grin formed on his face. "Some stuff? Like what?"

She grabbed a thick section of her hair and absently began braiding it. "Like things about the forest. How to use a knife or a bow. And the right way I should act. You know, around people. Everything you know...that I don't."

He tossed the stick at her and with an air of self-importance said, "So you want lessons from Tutor Edvin, huh?"

She threw the stick back. "Well, I thought I did—for just a minute—but now I take it back."

He chuckled and laid all the way on his back resting his head on his hands. "Too late. Yes, I'll pass on my vast knowledge about everything to you. But starting tomorrow, all right?"

"Thank you," was all she could think to say. She tucked into a ball on her side. Her right arm still ached a little. But she smiled despite the ache. Tomorrow she would begin building her knowledge of the real world.

10

THE sun peeked over the eastern mountains, reaching its golden fingers through the trees to stroke Ayra's face. She sat up and glanced around. The fire had been built back up, but Edvin was nowhere in sight.

Just how sharp is his hearing? she wondered.

"Edvin," she said quietly, putting him to the test. "You are a stinky badger of a boy. I hope you are somewhere washing off your awful smell." Some minutes later she heard his confident footsteps approaching from behind and smiled in anticipation.

"First of all, I am not a boy," he said rounding her right side. "I am a man. Secondly, I have a fine, masculine musk that does not wash off. It's natural. Most girls appreciate it."

A chirpy laugh slipped out of her throat as a tickle of delight rolled in her stomach. He *had* heard her.

"I've been listening for you to wake up. And just your luck, I've brought you a morning meal, pupil."

She rolled her eyes at the word 'pupil.' What had she done? But the smile didn't leave her face.

"I've decided you may call me Master Edvin instead of Tutor. Pretty sure I know enough to be on the master level."

He knelt and emptied pale green shoots and a few brown mushrooms from the flap of his tunic onto a rock. Then he set to cleaning the rabbit that had been hanging over his shoulder. He instructed her as he worked, showing her how to squeeze to expel the innards and where to cut the hide on the back leg to pull the skin from the flesh in nearly one piece. Ayra listened intently, trying to remember each step.

While the rabbit roasted, he told her about the different kinds of mushrooms in the woods, where to find them, and how to recognize the poisonous varieties.

During the course of her first lessons, Ayra learned more than just mushrooms and rabbits. She felt more comfortable than she had in days. There was an easiness between them, as if a wall that divided them had crumbled into rubble. The more he spoke in his smooth, animated way, the more she realized she had been the one who hastily built that wall, stone by stone. She thought she would feel humiliated if she had to take it down but was surprised to feel relief in being open. And she began to use the wall stones to build a bridge. A friendship even.

The morning was full of questions from Ayra and answers from Edvin. Each bird or bug she pointed out, he knew its name. He told her which wildflowers were edible or medicinal, and they chewed sweet leaves or spicy stems as they walked.

When they weren't talking about things of the woods, Edvin described some of the holiday festivities of Mihtengard, injecting his own amusing stories as he went on. He told her about traditional pear cakes, carrot puddings, and seasoned, braided bread. He briefly explained games with spears and targets and with numbered pins and wooden balls. And every celebration ended with dancing and music.

Ayra tried to squelch the pang of resentment she felt as she quietly listened. She recalled hearing celebrations from the village every few months, celebrations that were not allowed in debtor camps. The things he described were commonplace to every other citizen, but her ancestors had deprived her of all of it. Like the roots in the soil beneath her feet, her bitterness silently spread deeper into her bones.

When the early afternoon sun beat down on the two travelers, Ayra felt the tingling in her fingers. She looked up at the cloudless sky.

"There must be water nearby. I can feel it in my fingers."

"Yeah, I can hear the river just a little bit east of us, and not far ahead should be Lake Iridan. The village we are looking for will be just on the other side of the lake." He looked sideways at her. "Have you never noticed the feeling in your fingers before?"

She wiggled and clenched her fingers.

"I have. It started when I was eight or nine. Only felt it sometimes, the strongest with heavy rain. There isn't a lot of water in the quarry otherwise, you know. Only from the well. But I feel it near the river and creeks, too. It feels like it's getting more sensitive."

"Really? And before rain, huh?" Edvin looked up at the sky thoughtfully.

She nodded and tried to listen for the river. "What does it feel like to hear so well? Is everything just really loud all the time?" Realizing she might be yelling in his ear, she lowered her voice to a whisper. "Should I talk to you like this?"

"Yes! Thank you! Your regular voice is deafening." He smiled at her playfully. "No, I can control it. Make things louder if I want. I hope one day I can make it reach as far as my father can. I guess it's kind of like stretching a muscle. I can stretch my hearing." He shook his head. "I've never tried to explain it to anyone. Does that make sense?"

"I think so." Ayra tried to imagine what it would be like to stretch her hearing. She squinted her eyes and flexed her neck in an attempt to get any kind of ear stretch and laughed at herself when she looked at Edvin's amused face. "I don't have that gift, I guess. But how far can you reach?"

"A mile or two, I think. I'm not proficient in estimating distance yet—you saw that with the wolves. I can figure out direction and what it is, but distance is hard. Harder when it's something on the move."

She thought of the way he often tilted his head. He had to consciously extend his hearing. So he knew things about her because he had listened to her conversations with Gibsen from his position at the front of the company. She wondered if Edvin had listened out of duty or because he was bored. Or because he was interested. She quickly threw out the last thought before her mind sprouted any ideas.

"So is that how you found out Prince Gibsen's plan? By eavesdropping?"

He made a pained expression. "Eavesdropping is such a dirty word. I prefer the word 'investigating' for what I do. But, yeah, that's how I found out. The night before I came to get you, I was awakened by movement in the camp. I know fellows get up for various things, so I tried to ignore it and go back to sleep. Couldn't so I just laid there. Sometimes when I can't sleep, I stretch my ears. Try to see how far I can hear when it's mostly quiet. So that's what I did. I heard all the usual sounds—owls, raccoons, leaves rustling. And then I heard voices. Two men talking. One I recognized as Rooney and the other I had never heard before. Rooney told the other man we had you and your brother, and we would be to the meeting place in about three weeks. And then Covalt would have what he needed. As a high-ranking adviser to the king, Rooney knows about my hearing, so he must have thought they were out of my range." He sounded pleased he had been underestimated.

Ayra was surprised Rooney would have dealings with such a villain. He seemed like a wise and quiet man—she had only seen him speak to Gibsen. "If you heard only Rooney and the other man, how do you know Gibsen is involved? Maybe he doesn't know about Rooney working with Covalt."

"That's what I hoped. The next morning when I was trying to decide what to do, I listened to everything I could, and I overheard Prince Gibsen ask Rooney if he was certain you and Kelton could be exchanged for the Azure Sea Stone—whatever that is—and that it would work. Rooney assured him that he had found evidence of the stone's existence. Anyway, I just couldn't trust him. Or anyone else in the company. Rim and the other fellows would never have been able to keep it shut. Except Tress. He and my father are close friends. I've known him all my life. That's why I went to him. He thought if I took you and Kelton, he could stay behind to throw them off our trail. Prince Gibsen and Rooney would trust him and his nose."

Ayra thought of Gibsen's promise that she and Kelton would be well taken care of. He had seemed so sincere. It was alarming to realize how easily a person could lie. It gave her the awful feeling she was being stalked by an invisible predator. In the quarry, no one ever had secret motives or sly words. She had never had to distinguish between truth and a falsehood.

She stole a few glances at Edvin as they continued making their own path through the trees. It was an odd feeling to realize the person she trusted the least a few days ago was now the person she trusted most.

Up ahead, the green and white of the trees thinned, and the open patches filled with gray blue. Ayra felt the tingling in her fingers grow stronger. She quickened her steps, and Edvin matched her pace. The trees opened and revealed the deep blue waters of Lake Iridan.

Ayra gasped. She had never seen so much water.

The sun's rays bounced off the lake and sparkled like an early night sky crowded with stars. There was a break in the pine and deciduous trees that surrounded the lake almost directly across from where they stood. Tiny structures filled in the gap where trees had once stood, and the northern section of the Wolfjaw Mountain range, half dressed in white, towered protectively over the village.

"It's the most amazing thing I have ever seen," she whispered.

Edvin looked as pleased as if he had created the body of water himself. "I thought you would like it. Lake Iridan is the largest lake in Mihtengard. The Life River empties here, along with other streams down out of the Wolfjaw Range. Then on the far side over there, the United River begins and flows to the sea. But see the exposed lakebed around the edge here? The water level is not as high as it used to be since the rains stopped. Our groundwater is low—the number of springs decreasing—and we used to have much heavier snowpack in the western range there, but this year's won't last long. And all this water here doesn't do the eastern side of the country any good. Because of rock flats and hills, we can only irrigate so far. There are two small lakes near Midivard, but they are being depleted quickly to supply the farms, livestock, and the city."

Gibsen had mentioned some of this to her but not as in depth. She scanned the edge of the lake, noting the whitewashed rocks all along the shore. "Prince Gibsen said the lack of water isn't a great concern. That we can trade with other countries."

Edvin raised his eyebrows. "Well, I guess that is what a king's son would say, isn't it? Admitting to anything else would diminish power. Admit weakness. Our people and our livestock need water. And we can only trade so long as we have something to trade. Our mines do not produce as they once did. Once the wealth is gone, there is nothing to exchange, and the country becomes weak and susceptible to collapse. Or invasion."

Ayra gazed out over the shining water. She had felt comforted by Gibsen's words. This new idea that Mihtengard was amidst a real struggle left her feeling like the sky was not as blue as it had been minutes ago.

Edvin watched her for a minute before dropping his pack and sitting down on a big rock. "We can stay here for the rest of the day and head for Gowen tomorrow morning."

Ayra welcomed the idea and sat down on a rock near his. She breathed in the scent of the sweet woods mingling with the peculiar smell of the lake. They had never stopped traveling this early in the day before, and she felt happy to become acquainted with an area during daylight.

Dragonflies zipped around them and waves lapped against the rocks as Edvin amused Ayra with stories of his childhood—unwittingly filling his pants pockets with worms the day before laundry day, hiding in sugar barrels at the bakery, loading his eldest brother's boots with mud during the night for an early morning surprise.

He showed her how to skip smooth, flat stones across the water and challenged her to a competition to see whose stone could skip the most. Edvin won by five skips and whooped over his victory. She pretended to pout and plopped down on a rock.

"Why don't you practice using your newfound skill," he said with a smirk. "Maybe it will make you feel better to do something I can't."

She accepted the new challenge and extended her hand toward the water. The pull on her tingling fingers felt like an invisible rope tied her to the water. She flicked her hand toward Edvin, and water splashed onto his boots.

He glanced down at his feet and cocked his head to the side. "Not bad. Try again—bigger."

She reached her hand out again, and the water under her gaze stilled. Instead of flicking her hand, she swooped it. Water shot up and drenched him from the waist down. He yelped and jumped back, stumbling over the rocks until he fell on his backside. Ayra thought her gut was going to burst from laughing so hard.

"I was not expecting you to make it that big," he said from the ground, laughing with her.

"I wasn't either." She lifted a bent arm to the side and rolled her shoulder. "But it makes my arm sore. It's almost like I'm actually lifting or holding the water. I don't know if I can do it bigger than that. I don't think it's as useful as your hearing."

With soggy pants, Edvin moved to sit next to her and tossed pebbles at the water, watching the ripples spread. "Maybe it's more like my hearing than you think. Maybe the more you use it, the stronger it will become. Like a muscle."

It *was* possible. She hoped she could learn to manage it well and be of use. She looked out over the water and wondered about her family. Who had wielded the gift before her? Did it occur randomly in her family like it did in the other gifted families? Was anyone able to make it useful?

An ache for her grandmother to be sitting with them surfaced. Tanna would have loved this little spot at the edge of this vast lake. And she had felt the tingling, too.

Edvin abruptly stood. "I think I'm ready for something to eat." He unwrapped a long piece of twine from the strap of his pack and picked up his quiver. "If you're lucky, you'll have a belly full of trout before the evening is over."

Ayra had never tasted fish before and was anxious to try it. She watched Edvin tie one end of the twine to an arrow just above the fletching. He wrapped the other end a few times around his left hand, leaving a long stretch of twine between the two. He flashed her a smile, while bouncing his dark eyebrows up and down, and nocked the arrow on the bowstring.

With one wide step from the water's edge, he was perfectly perched on a partially submerged rock. He looked over the water for a minute and stepped over a few more rocks. After another quick scan of the water, he raised his bow and drew back. When he released, the arrow broke through the water's surface with a slight splash.

Edvin whooped and pulled the string, bringing up the arrow shot through a writhing, silvery fish. He bounded back with his trophy to where Ayra sat and gave the fish a solid tap on the head with a rock to make it still.

"For you, my lady," he said, holding out the slimy creature. "Your first fish. An important event in every Mihtengardian girl's life."

By the way his brown eyes twinkled, she knew he was joking and was secretly pleased with herself to now be able to pick up on his jokes. She grabbed the fish with both hands near the tail and instantly felt it slip out of her grip onto the rocks. She picked it up from the middle and held on a little firmer. Edvin instructed her where to cut down the fish's belly and then how to pull the jaw to draw out the colorful innards in one piece.

As she watched the fish rotate on a willow over the fire, she felt a sense of pride for doing something new and helpful. When it was finished roasting, they picked at the orange, flaky meat together. Though Edvin laughed when she gagged on the pin bones, Ayra could tell he was pleased she liked the fish.

Before the sunlight completely faded, Ayra asked Edvin if he could begin her self-defense lessons, so she would be prepared for whatever she might encounter when rescuing Kelton. She wanted to learn about archery, but Edvin told her blades—knives or swords—would be better.

"Honestly, I'm afraid you would break or lose my arrows. I only have five," he said.

She accepted his reasoning and agreed to start with knives. Using shards of wood, he showed her several different grips and described situations each would be used. He then explained the basics of knife defense. He showed her how to make herself smaller by tucking in her head and shoulders and how to get the most out of her arm movements without exposing herself too much to her opponent's attacks.

Then with the pieces of wood, they practiced. Each time Ayra parried or jabbed, she could see his mouth twitch, fighting a smile. A few times he let a laugh escape.

"What am I doing that you find so amusing?" she finally asked. "Am I doing it wrong?"

"No. No, actually your form is quite good, and you're quicker than I expected." He rubbed his free hand over the back of his neck. "It's just weird to be fighting…a girl. I've never had a girl ask me to teach her to knife fight."

"Really?" she said, straightening. "Do you think it's wrong for me to learn?"

"Not wrong. Just unusual."

"Unusual." The word tripped into her ears. "What else do I do that's unusual?"

He laughed. "I don't think I should answer that question."

Ayra pressed him relentlessly for an answer, poking at him threateningly with her practice knife. When he couldn't hold her off any longer, he gave in.

"Well, aside from being tricky with water…you wear your hair loose. Most girls in Mihtengard—all of the girls I've ever seen—braid their hair."

Ayra knew that from the Doren village girls and the few who came to the camp. She reached her hand up and pinched a lock in her fingers.

"But I think it suits you," he added quickly. "Don't change that."

"What else?"

"Ayra, why do you worry so much about being different? It doesn't really matter if you braid your hair or don't. Or if you are the only girl in two hundred who can gut a fish. You have more to offer the world than a pretty braid and daintily kept hands." He put his left arm in front of his chest and put his knife-wielding hand forward again. "Come on, put your knife up and let's keep going."

She fell asleep that night with Edvin's words repeating in her mind. When she was in the quarry, she had not cared what anyone thought about her looks and manners. She had even prided herself in not caring. But the last two weeks had drawn out feelings she didn't understand, as if she were made of hundreds of pieces she couldn't fit together.

The thought of walking into the head city with her hair down and people staring made her feel panicky. She was more different than she had ever thought—her abilities with water proved that.

But Edvin seemed confident that her differences were acceptable, and she clung to his reassurance she had something to offer.

11

LATE the next morning, after another meal of roasted fish and more knife practice, the two friends began the trek around the lake. They happened upon a well-worn trail that hugged tightly to the lakeshore and kept to it.

With encouragement from Edvin, Ayra practiced manipulating the water as they walked. Her arm ached, but she continued her attempts, stopping rows of waves, making splashes of various sizes, and creating little whirlpools. She found the water did not simply obey her hand motions. Concentration was needed to get a reaction.

Edvin found her tricks immensely amusing. He pointed to a cluster of ducks paddling through the water and dared her to pester them. She whipped her hand in a circle causing a sudden whirlpool to swirl one of the ducks around. They laughed as the poor bird quacked and shot out of the water, along with his startled friends.

"Just think what you could do with more power. I really am curious what else you are capable of doing."

"I'm not," she said quickly and instantly wished to take the words back.

She was relieved Edvin only gave her a questioning look instead of asking her why.

Being responsible for Kelton the last four years had created a constant dark cloud that loomed over her head, always threatening to shroud her in darkness. If she developed "more power," more might be expected of her. Her want of purpose and desire to be unfettered battled inside her in a way she couldn't explain to anyone, even to herself.

The day was bordering hot with the warm season months drawing nearer. When the prematurely warm sun began to feel unwelcome, Edvin suggested they stop for a small break on some shaded boulders near the water.

As Ayra plopped herself down and breathed in the clear air, she felt grateful Gibsen had given her a light dress that allowed the breeze to flow through its threads. She would have been near melting in her wool dress.

Edvin removed his tunic and sat down near her. She watched as he carelessly rolled the sleeves of his shirt to his elbows and began digging through his pack for the water pouch. Ayra felt her cheeks burn when she caught herself staring at the lines of muscle in his forearms.

She quickly turned her head away from him and concentrated on making ripples in the water.

"What would Pupil Ayra like to learn from Master Edvin today?" he asked, handing her the pouch.

She thought for a minute about all the questions stockpiled in her head and picked one of her newer curiosities. "What's it like going to the market in Midivard?"

"That's all, huh?" he said with a grin. He tossed a pebble at her shoulder. "I thought you might want to learn how to dance."

"With you? Not on your life," she quipped, turning to the water hoping he didn't notice the embarrassment all over her face. She could only imagine the horror of stumbling over her own feet, trying to keep up with his agile movements.

"That's a relief. I don't want to dazzle you too much and ruin you for any other potential dancing partner."

"Not what I was worried about, but at least we agree it's not a good idea."

He threw a smooth stone at the water, skipping it six times. "The market takes up a whole district of Midivard. Carts and stands line the streets—food, jewelry, dyed fabrics, knives, you name it, it's there. In the center of it all is a round stage for performers. Skits and music from locals. Sometimes acrobats and animal trainers from southern countries. Some new things and a lot of the same things each month. You'd like the market."

She smiled as she tried to envision the market, imagining herself weaving through the displays. Her smile ebbed a little when she added crowds of people to the vision.

"What's your favorite thing to do?"

"Eat," he said simply.

Food. Even though she had eaten Arty's food for less than a week, she missed his cooking each time she ate unseasoned shoots, rabbit, and fish. To have a wide array of foods to taste and fill her belly with would be bliss. For the remainder of their break, Edvin told her more of the market and some of his experiences there.

For days, aside from the wolves, they had been undisturbed. Edvin had used his hearing to guide them clear of any other hunters, herders, or travelers. As they neared Gowen and the smell of woodsmoke and fish weaved through the wind to her nose, Ayra's stomach fluttered and her palms dampened.

What if she was being searched for or if questions were raised regarding the purpose of their travel? Edvin talked as if he was unaware of any pending conflicts, but she noticed him stretching his hearing more frequently and swiping his hands on his pants a couple times.

The village of Gowen was larger than it looked from afar. At least three times the size of Doren. It was a prosperous settlement that gained its support from mines and fisheries. The buildings were made of stones pulled from the lake and from lumber harvested from the surrounding forest.

The street they entered was bustling with villagers hard at work. Fish fillets were lined out on racks to dry in the sun. A group of women were repairing a damaged net spread between them. Carts of firewood or stones wheeled past them. Men were loading and unloading small rowboats of fish or nets. Ayra noticed several paths winding up the side of the mountain, likely leading to mines. The rotten, fishy smell that hung in the air during one stretch assaulted Ayra's nose and almost made her stomach turn.

Edvin strode along with his usual self-assured gait. He had put his tunic back on, and although it was brighter than any of the others she could see, somehow he seemed to fit right in.

She, on the other hand, felt like she stuck out like a fish head in spiced applesauce. Every woman and girl either had her hair in a long braid or up in a cap. Hers was down and blowing wildly in the breeze. And her finely made, deep blue dress was filthy and slightly tattered at the hem, while all the village women were clean and tidy in dress. This struck her as miraculous since she could see many of the women were hard at work on one job or another.

They must also work hard at washing their clothes, she thought.

She noticed many sets of eyes turn to watch them pass, but she could not bring herself to look directly at their faces to see if they smiled or scowled. Instinctively, she moved closer to Edvin.

The trading post Edvin was seeking sat on the other side of the village where the main road led out. Ayra could not think what either of them had to trade, but Edvin was confident they could get what they needed.

They found the building, mostly stone with a door made of carved pine. Ayra could not help running her fingers over the wildflower design. She had no idea anyone could transform a door into a work of beauty. Inside, a long counter divided the room in two with waist-high shelves on either side of the customer half and two sets of tall carved shelves, heavy with merchandise, lining the far wall on the proprietor's side.

Edvin breathed a sigh of relief. "We're in luck!" he whispered.

Behind the counter, an old, whiskery man sat in a chair leaning against the doorframe between the shelves. He was so still, the possibility of him being dead flitted through Ayra's mind. Edvin rapped on the counter.

The man snorted and sat up in his chair. "Weevil in my boots!" he snapped.

"Hello, Marn, old fellow! It's me, Vansar's son Edvin."

The old man hoisted himself up and leaned over the counter, placing his face only a couple handbreadths from Edvin's. A gappy grin spread across his face. "Yes, young Edvin. Well, what brings you to these parts?"

"Just passing through with...my new wife." Edvin wrapped his arm around Ayra's shoulders and hugged her to his side. She felt her face flush and a stinging irritation he had decided to surprise her with this plan. What was more, she hadn't even seen it coming.

"Married are you? Well now, you can't be more than twelve years."

"No, sir. I've just turned nineteen. And, well," he looked down adoringly at Ayra, "when two hearts beat as one..." His brown eyes twinkled.

The old man chuckled, "You young 'uns these days have no

patience." He leaned over into Ayra's face. "Can't say I blame you. Can't say I blame you. Well, you here looking for something or just come to say hullo?"

"We're in need of some supplies, but I'm afraid we're low on coin and trade goods. We need a wool blanket, some heat sticks if you have them, and two wool caps." He pulled a couple items out of his pack. "What can you give us for this supply box and compass?"

"It's 'bout warm season. What you need cold season supplies for? Not going up the mountain, are you?"

"Yes, sir. We are."

Marn shook his head and clucked his tongue. "Can't give you much for the supply box." He looked up at the two of them and squinted one eye. "How are you on food?"

"Just taking what the forest will give."

"Hm," Marn grunted. He turned with the box and limped through the doorway between the shelves. Ayra could hear him muttering to himself and caught the words 'don't give much' and 'foolish lovebirds.' A few minutes later he came back through and pushed the box toward Edvin. "Got some hard biscuits and fish jerky here for you. To fill in the gaps of what you can't find."

"Thank you, sir. That will help us a lot."

Marn turned his attention to the other item on the table. "This compass is purdy shiny," he said as he picked it up to examine it.

"It was used in the Tiseden battle."

"Was it now?" Marn said with interest.

Edvin looked down at Ayra still tucked to his side and raised his eyebrows. She bit her lip fighting back a laugh.

"I can give you six heat sticks and two caps for the compass." Marn turned around to the shelves and began to gather the items. Then he pulled out a bundle and placed it on top. "And I'll throw in the blanket for a weddin' present."

Edvin and Marn chatted for a half an hour about Midivard, mutual acquaintances, and Edvin's family. During their conversation, Ayra wiggled herself out of Edvin's grip and moved about the room admiring the expertly carved animals and toys that were carefully placed on the shelves.

When Edvin and Ayra turned to leave, Edvin said, "Thank you, Marn. You have saved us. We'll think of you every time we snuggle under this blanket."

The old man laughed, "That's not necessary. Now git out of here and take care of yourselves. And tell your father hullo for me."

"I will. Thank you again!"

They left Marn standing behind the counter with a wide smile. Ayra's embarrassment over the whole display had faded into relief, but she still went along with being irritated. When they were a good distance away from the post, she punched him hard in the shoulder.

"You rat-brained, beast of a boy! You planned that and didn't tell me."

He laughed, "I did not, on my honor. Didn't even think of it until we were standing there in front of Old Marn. I was going to call you my cousin, but that wasn't very clever. Brilliant ideas just come to me, you know, and I have no choice but to put them into motion. And I'm not sorry. The look on your face…it was worth it. It was worth it."

Ayra pretended not to hear that last part. "I don't know if brilliant is the word I would use, but it worked, I'll give you that. How do you know Marn?"

"He was a woodworker in Midivard. One of the best. Was always kind of an odd man, never really fit in. But he and my father became good friends. Marn has a fascination with the military, so he enjoyed my father's stories. A number of years ago he couldn't stand the city anymore and moved himself out here. I was hoping he was still running the trading post. Feel a little bad about taking the wool blanket as a wedding present. I'll have to send him something nice when I get…" His words trailed off and some of the amusement slipped from his face.

Ayra watched him tuck the new items into his pack and tightly roll the thick blanket. She shook her head. She could not understand how Edvin's schemes always seemed to work out. He was just one of those lucky people, she guessed. Without a glance back at the village, they set off for the mountains, heading back to the west.

"You say you have been to this seer before?"

"Yeah," he said looking away from her. "When I was younger, I came out here with my mother." He paused for a moment. "Have I told you about the time Tavin and I said some unpleasant things to a fellow, and I ended up getting my face smushed into horse manure? No?"

Ayra looked up at him as he told her his story of black eyes and unpleasant mouthfuls, though she really wasn't listening. She wondered why he had changed the subject so abruptly. As much as she wanted to ask, she held her tongue and forced a laugh when he laughed.

A little bit up the mountain slope and a good distance from Gowen, they happened upon a spring with a nearby flat spot.

Edvin dropped his pack and sat down. "We can stop here for the night, it's as good a spot as any."

The evening was quieter than usual. Even the birds seemed to be tired and withdrawn. Ayra's thoughts about Kelton, about what the coming days would bring, and about Edvin's visit to the seer kept her occupied.

The latter unsettled her more than she thought it should, and she didn't feel much like talking. As her mind wandered through the forest of speculation, she practiced stopping and releasing the water flowing from the spring.

Edvin seemed out of sorts, too. He fed the fire when it did not look hungry, peeled green bark off of twigs, and tossed pebbles down the mountain to watch them bounce. Watching him fidget and move around like a rabbit searching for a place to hide left Ayra feeling even more unsettled. She tried not to even look at him.

Before the sun had completely retired from its day's work, Ayra wrapped the new wool blanket tightly around her body and laid down on her side. Edvin still sat on the other side of the fire watching the flames. She hoped sleep would squelch her agitated thoughts, but hope was not enough, and she drifted into a restless sleep.

12

AYRA raced through the woods, rocks tripping her, branches scratching her face.

In any direction she could see only trees and darkness. She stopped. The gray-leafed trees on her right shifted, and the earth heaved upward, like a giant wave over her head. Trees hurled downward and washed over her.

When she opened her eyes, everything was gone. Bubbles floated from her mouth. Ahead, a dark form moved toward her. Her heart began to pound as it grew before her eyes.

"Ayra."

She recognized her name being called from above, but it was murky and distant. The dark form reached for her. A hand gripped her shoulder.

"Ayra!"

Her eyes flew open, and she shot up, nearly colliding with Edvin's face.

"You all right?" he asked.

She rubbed the mark on her shoulder and nodded, feeling the pounding of her heart.

He nodded back. "I can't remember the exact way to Wil's, so we should get moving. We might need the whole day to find it." He rolled the other blanket and tied it in its place on the pack. He paused. "Are you sure you want to do this?"

Ayra's heart continued to pound. She couldn't decide if she felt anxious or excited but was ready for the unknown that gnawed her conscience to be gone. It had crossed her mind several times that knowing might be worse than not knowing, but she dismissed it once again. "Yes. I need to go."

He nodded and rose to his feet. "Well, let's go then."

She was disappointed to hear the melancholy still lingering in his tone. As they walked along the windy mountainside, she found herself continually looking up at his face. His jaw flexed often, and his eyes seemed darker. It looked unnatural for his mouth not to hold even the promise of a smile. She watched her feet and searched her memory for anything he might find entertaining.

"When I was small, my grandmother used to call me Bare-ah," she blurted out. "Because I preferred to…be bare." It was the first worthy thing that came into her head, but as she heard the words out loud, she wished she had kept thinking. Then she looked at his amused face and decided it had been worth saying.

"Bare-ah, huh? What else did you do as a child?"

They had talked about the quarry and what general life was like, but she had guarded her own life tightly. Spurred by his interest she told him of her old love of creating mountains and castles out of the pebbles and mud, of letting tiny Kelton chase her around their hut. Of catching lizards in the rocks and falling asleep to the rain pelting the stone outside, among other happy memories. Edvin's expression relaxed with each story, and her words came easier and easier as she carried on.

Without meaning to, her thoughts drifted to harder memories. She told him her vague memories of her parents' deaths from the fevers, about her grandmother's accident, and about her responsibility for Kelton—how she had struggled under the pressure of caring for him and how she hurt not knowing where he was.

She looked at Edvin walking beside her. The cloud seemed to have evaporated, but he looked more thoughtful than light-hearted like she had set out to make him. "I shouldn't have told you all of that. I didn't mean to burden you with my thoughts."

"No," he said quickly. "Don't be sorry. I like hearing you talk—your stories I mean." He stopped to listen for direction and shook his head. When he began walking again, he added, "I'm sorry I failed to bring Kelton out with us."

Us. She liked that word. "It was his fault, anyway. Who reacts like that to a crazy man with a knife?"

He laughed like she hoped he would, and she smiled to herself, pleased she could stir a reaction from him. They continued to hike up the mountain, slowly pushing west. The uphill walking seemed easier without the heavy feeling from earlier in the morning. When they were halfway up, Edvin looked around and listened again.

"Even with this wind, I should be able to hear something by now. This isn't the right mountainside." He changed course and directed their path down, moving toward the next hillside over.

The trees came in thick bundles, then the terrain opened again to rock, small shrubs, and grasses. Where the second peak connected with the third, the gravelly ground turned to a rocky slide. Ayra struggled to keep on her feet, constantly sliding and stumbling, putting her hands on the rocks to her side to steady herself. Edvin moved below her and a few times saved her from tumbling down the hillside with a steadying hand on her arm or shoulder. He kept her laughing with jabs at her clumsiness.

"Keep this up, and I might have to throw you over my shoulder and carry you. For a girl who grew up on a rock pile, you sure don't navigate one well."

"Shows how much you know. I lived where it was *flat*."

"Well, I seem to remember you tripping over the rocks there, too."

She blushed at the memory and laughed at herself, imagining what he had seen. "Yes, well rocks are tricky. They don't like my feet. And if you were any sort of hero, you would have come to my rescue instead of laughing at me."

He looked at her frankly. "That's true. I should have." His hand flew up to her hip as she teetered toward him. He granted her one of his crooked grins. "I think I'm making up for it now, though."

On the other side of the rockslide, they stopped for a rest. Edvin handed her a small piece of dried fish and took the same ration for himself. As she chewed on the jerky, Ayra looked out over the valley. Most of the land immediately before her was forest. Lake Iridan, long and blue, stretched out on her left. She squinted at the land beyond the lake hoping to see Midivard from where she sat but no structures rose out from the ground. Way off in the distance she could, however, see cleared land that she thought might be farmland.

She closed her eyes and lifted her face toward the clear, blue sky. The mountain wind was cool, but the beams from the bright late afternoon sun warmed her skin. She listened for the whisper of the trees. Pine trees spoke softer than the leafy trees in the lower land. *I could live in these trees*, she thought.

"There!" Edvin said suddenly. "I hear it. We'll find it before dark, I'm sure."

Ayra felt the anxiousness in her stomach return. She tried to imagine how the seer would reveal the lives of her ancestors. Surely it would take a long time for him to tell her everything. Days even. She wondered if they had that much time to waste. Prince Gibsen's company might already be in Tiseden, and before long, Kelton would be in the hands of Covalt. The thought made the nervous butterflies turn to stone.

They continued across the mountain, slowly making their way up. This mountain was wider and taller than the first two they had tried. The higher they climbed the rockier it became and trees grew fewer. Edvin listened constantly, adjusting their path as he thought necessary. The sun was behind the western range now, but Edvin grew more confident the lower it got.

Ahead, Ayra could see a section of rock that jutted out of the mountainside. Above it she noticed a thin wisp of smoke that faded in the wind.

"Yes. There!" Edvin pointed to where she was already looking. "I remember that formation now," he said triumphantly.

They pressed on, aiming for the formation, and rounded the bottom of it, before climbing the steep side next to the crag where a cluster of trees stood like sentinels. Ayra thought she could hear a faint tinkling sound. The trees granted passage, and the two of them walked into the tiny establishment.

Carved out of a mound that blended into the mountain was a little home with a round, painted door and a single glass window. Neatly plowed rows and shaped mounds showed the beginning work of a large garden. A nanny goat tied in front bellowed once at the intruders and carelessly returned to chewing its pine branch. The crag rose sharply like a hand cupping something precious, sheltering the homestead from the valley and the wind, making it feel instantly quieter. The little chimes she had heard swayed on the end of a staked crook just on the inside of the crag. The whole place reminded Ayra of homes in the tales her grandmother spun.

The door creaked open and a short, stocky young man with black, curly hair stepped out. Ayra guessed him to be somewhere between her and Edvin's age. He folded his arms and looked each of them up and down.

"What is it you come for?" he asked sharply. His words had a distinct sound she had never heard anyone speak with before. His stance and tone struck Ayra as unnatural, like a mouse trying to prowl like a wolf.

"We're looking for Wil," Edvin replied with a friendly tone that countered the other young man's. "Is she home and able to see us?"

Ayra looked from the young man to Edvin. She was surprised to hear him say 'she.' She had assumed the hermit was a man.

"She is home. She is *always* home. But I don't think she wants to see anyone, so you'll just need to be on your way."

A frail voice called from inside, but Ayra could not make out the words. She looked at Edvin for an indication of what had been said, but he did not look at her. The sternness in the young man's face disappeared as he held up one finger and ducked back inside. Minutes later he returned and penitently said, "She will have visitors today. Go in." He picked up an ax leaning against the house and walked past them to a woodpile near the natural rock wall.

Edvin turned to Ayra and held his hand out toward the door in a way she knew meant she was to go in alone. She hesitated and said, "Please don't listen, all right?" He nodded, and she slowly entered the little home and stopped just beyond the door.

The room was dim with only a small fire burning in the fireplace and an oil lamp set on a table at the opposite end of the room. The walls were mud and straw, but the floor was hardwood. Dried flowers in bottles decorated the table, windowsill, and hearth.

In front of the fire sat a woman in an ornate, splintered rocking chair. Ayra wasn't sure which was more ancient, the chair or the woman. Her long, snow-white hair rested in a tidy braid on her shoulder, and the lines on her face numbered her years of life.

"Come closer, child." Wil's voice was shaky and stern, a voice that had no patience for dawdling.

Ayra glanced around the room again before she obeyed. The wood floor softly moaned under her feet. Wil motioned for her to kneel beside her. She examined Ayra's face and squinted one eye for just a moment.

"What is it you seek, girl?"

"My name is Ayra. And I want to know…my family's past. My mother's line."

The woman's mouth curved into a thin smile. "Then you have come to the right place." She began to rock again and looked into the fire. "I have lived here all my life. My mother had the same gift, you see. People didn't try to understand her abilities, only desired of her to do what they wanted. Most people want to know only the future. They do not think much of the past. She was so plagued with people knocking on her door that years and years ago, my father moved her here. Only people who really want to know make the effort to seek it."

She looked down at Ayra again, her gray eyes intent on being understood. "But the past keeps secrets just as the future does. We all carry within us the memories of our ancestors. Locked deep inside when we are born. My gift allows me to both see these memories and waken them in your mind. Sometimes they are worth remembering. And many times they are painful. You must be sure you want to see." She looked back to her fire as if to leave Ayra alone in the room.

Minutes passed and the old woman's words penetrated Ayra's mind. She thought of her own memories that caused her heart to ache. Bringing the memories of others into her conscience could pour more pain into her heart. But she would rather have a heart filled with sorrow than a mind filled with questions. She needed to know why her family was banished to the quarry.

She squared her shoulders and sucked in a deep breath. "I am sure."

The old woman nodded and drew her face close to Ayra's. "The memories that are the strongest are what I can most readily access. If you do not obtain what you seek tonight, we will try again tomorrow. We will begin with your own history." She reached out her crippled hands and slid her cold fingers over Ayra's ears, pressing her thumbs to her temples. Ayra closed her eyes and instantly saw silent images of her and Edvin walking along the mountainside. She smiled the moment Edvin caught her from sliding down the mountain. Suddenly, the image vanished, and Wil's hands withdrew.

"The boy. I have seen him before."

"Yes, he came here to see you when he was little." Ayra bit

her lip and let her curiosity loose. "What did he learn?"

Wil narrowed her eyes. "I tell history only to the one who owns it," she said. She paused a moment before adding, "But understand a darkness can follow those we least expect."

Ayra leaned away from Wil's hands. What could she mean by that? Before she could raise the question, Wil's hands were holding her head again, and she closed her eyes. Visions from the wolf attack came next, and Ayra held her breath as she witnessed for the second time the snarling beasts surround Edvin. She smiled at an image of Kelton sleeping safely in the hut and winced as the rockslide that buried Tanna flashed before her. Images of her childhood flitted quickly past. Presently, memories that were not her own flowed into view. A baby being born. Her father digging in a small pit. Hands she recognized as her grandmother's, with hills surrounding the camp before them, the clouds in the sky growing thicker.

Another memory showed the same hands playing a game with a little girl she instinctively knew as her mother. A man walking away, a bag over his shoulder. A different man with a little girl and a little boy pulling rocks from a pile, someone eating alone in a mess house, a parchment laid out with a pen writing a name across the bottom, a man kneeling at the bedside of an ill child. Memory after memory flooded her closed eyes. They flowed quickly yet she could grasp and understand each one. Some were brief, others seemed to stretch on. All of them in a quarry.

One memory, a possession of a young beholder, showed a couple older women she didn't recognize, standing on a hillside motioning their hands discreetly, clouds gathering above. Wil's voice broke through Ayra's concentration, reminding her of the present. "Your family is gifted. See the clouds? The women in your family only, it seems. Gifts tie us tighter together. We are now five generations back. Continue?"

Ayra kept her eyes shut trying to absorb every person, every detail. Her head was beginning to ache, and she felt like lying down. But she had not received the answer she sought. She swiped her hands on her skirt and nodded.

A few more memories in a quarry revealed themselves, and then the rocks and brush disappeared. She saw a small company of soldiers surrounding a small girl with bound hands on a green, forested road. A memory of a group of people in a large stone room stirred. Ayra gripped her hands to her knees and tried to pay attention. A tall man held out a large, blue stone that was perfectly round. *Safner.* The precious gem found only in southern Mihtengard. Through a metal door, he handed it to a boy who dropped it into a satchel and disappeared.

Next, she saw a crowned man draped in furs enter the same room. His fingers pointed and mouth moved, shouting orders. The tall man spoke, his face pleading. Ayra strained to hear his words, but all memories were mute. Soldiers seized him and all the people in the room.

A framed structure with a raised floor and two posts supporting a beam appeared. The king and a handful of soldiers surrounded a woman and the memory holder—the view from a child's eyes. The woman clutched the child to her chest, but the girl fought to see the event unfolding, Ayra struggling with her. Her heart pounded and her hands began to shake. Nine adults and four children lined up with nooses before each face. One by one, a rope was looped around a neck. The king signaled with a casual wave of his hand, and the trapdoors dropped, taking her people down with them.

Ayra jerked her head out of Wil's grasp. "It isn't true." Her chest felt tight and refused to draw in enough air.

"Memories do not lie, Ayra," Wil said gently.

Ayra shook her head trying to expel the memory from her mind. Over and over she saw ropes tightening under the weight of her family. She shot to her feet and bolted out the door. It was dark, but the moon was large and shed its blue light across the mountain. Edvin was leaning against the rock and straightened when she burst out the door.

"What did you learn?"

"Leave me alone," she hissed as she blew past him.

"Ayra," he said falling in step with her. He grabbed her arm, pulling her to a stop.

She yanked out of his grip. "Don't touch me, Edvin!"

They stared at each other for a moment. She could see the hurt in his eyes, but she felt nothing for his feelings. When he opened his mouth to speak, she turned away and darted into the trees. She stumbled through the little grove and out onto a stretch of brush and rock. She felt the burning in her chest spread to her throat and into her eyes.

The dam that had held strong for years threatened a breech.

She scrambled to build it higher, but heavy breaths slipped into sobs. She fell hard on her knees, and for the first time since Tanna's death, the dam gave way and tears began to fall. Her sobs came unchecked and harsh. For just a few seconds she remembered Edvin's listening ears, making her feel like he was beside her, watching her lose control.

"Please just leave me alone, Edvin," she choked out.

All her life she had blamed a long forgotten ancestor for her problems. She had harbored and nursed a deep bitterness toward him that followed her like a shadow. She had never dreamed for a moment that someone else was to blame, much less a king of Mihtengard. Her family must have worked for him like Edvin said. And he had slaughtered them. She could not understand it.

She wanted to forget their faces. She wanted to forget the terror in the children's eyes. The images stayed and haunted her as she continued to weep. She tucked her legs under her chest and rested her head on her folded arms. The cold rock beneath her was a surprising source of comfort.

Slowly, the sobs faded and her breathing steadied. The rocks dug into her knees and arms, but she did not move them. She remained tucked in a ball on the rocks for some time thinking of what Wil had told her. Only the women in her family wielded the gift. One by one she recalled each of the women and hands she had seen until arriving at her grandmother's. Each had evidently used the gift to call rains to the wide valley despite being trapped in the quarry.

How did they do it? she wondered. *What did the safner have to do with anything?*

She tired of working through the maze of motives and heartache and closed her weary eyes, trying to invite sleep to overcome her. The crunch of gravel behind her startled her wide awake.

"Ayra," Edvin said softly. "Wil said we may stay in her home tonight. I know you want to be alone, but it will be a cold night and this is bear country. I can't leave you out here."

She pushed herself up out of her balled position. Her back and limbs were stiff as she got to her feet. He handed her a blanket with eyes full of pity. She turned away from his face and wrapped herself in the warmth of the blanket. She had not realized how cold she was. Edvin didn't speak as they walked back over the rocks and through the trees. The little house glowed warmly like a little ray left behind by the sun.

It had been days since Ayra had slept with shelter overhead. As she stepped through the door into the comfortable room, she felt a sweep of gratitude for the old woman's offer. Behind her, Edvin ducked his tall frame through the low doorway and stepped in. Only the two of them stood in the room. A narrow bed was made up on the floor near the fire. Ayra looked back at Edvin.

"I'm going to sleep outside," he whispered. He stood in front of her for just a minute, as if he wasn't sure that was really what he wanted. When Ayra didn't say anything, he ducked back out the door and left her alone.

She dropped onto her side on the little bed of blankets and stared into the fire. Her eyes felt heavy and swollen from the scalding tears and begged for more rest. She closed them, feeling comfort in the darkness, and embraced the sleep that came to her.

13

AYRA woke feeling heavy and swimmy, as if her head and limbs were full of water. She glanced around the unfamiliar surroundings. When her eyes fell on the rocking chair, the memory of the evening before flooded back to her.

The room was still dark, but the gray light from the window told her it was early morning. She hugged the blanket tighter around her body hoping she could sleep until the sun was a little higher, but her eyes, still slightly swollen, were tired of being shut and her legs felt restless.

She sat up and poked the embers in the fireplace with a rod she found near the hearth. The orange light flickered brighter before dying down again. She put another log on, hoping Wil would not mind, and watched the flames wrap around the wood.

As she watched, she remembered Edvin's face the night before and a twinge of guilt trickled into her gut. She did not regret needing to be alone. Only that she had treated him so coldly.

An hour passed before stirring in one of the rooms reminded her she was not alone in the house. A door slowly opened, and Wil hobbled out, her hair already groomed with not a hair out of place in her white braid.

"Ah, my child. You are awake," she said with a small smile. "I hope your dreams were peaceful."

Ayra hesitated to speak but did not want to hurt the woman as she had her friend. She tried to return a pleasant face. "I don't remember any if I had them."

"Well, better empty sleep than troubled dreams." She set to work making a pot of porridge without another word. The floor moaned as if it were not ready to wake as she effortlessly went about her morning ritual.

Ayra sat on the little floor bed, fidgeting with her hair as she watched the woman's gnarled but deft hands work. She did not know if she should offer to help, say something to break the silence, or move herself off the floor onto one of the chairs. She frequently glanced at the door hoping Edvin would come to get her, but the door remained quiet.

The goat bellowed from outside.

"Oh," breathed Wil with a tsk. "I nearly forgot about Nanny. She usually comes in at night, but I gave you her spot. Do you know how to milk a goat?"

Ayra shook her head.

The old woman bobbed her head just as the other door scraped open.

"I'll do it," said the curly-haired boy as he strode past Ayra and grabbed a bucket by the door.

The little woman smiled fondly at him. "Thank you, Arman. She will be happy to see you."

Just before the front door pulled closed, Ayra jumped to her feet. "I'll come with you."

Arman smiled as if the idea was a welcome one and held the door for her. The morning was brisk, cool enough to see their breath. The mousy brown goat looked at Arman with unforgiving eyes and bellowed again.

"Quiet you. One would think a badger was gnawing on your knee with the way you're carrying on." He looked at Ayra and winked.

She had been so anxious and the lighting so dim the night before, she had not paid much attention to his features. He did not stand much taller than she did and was built much thicker than Edvin. The messy curls in his black hair made Ayra think of a mouse nest. If it weren't for his strong, square jaw, his hair would have left him looking very boyish.

Ayra briefly smiled back before glancing over the settlement for signs of Edvin. Remnants of a fire lay near the rock face. But he was not there. Nor his pack. Ayra swallowed hard to push down a feeling of panic. If he had left her, how would she find Kelton? She didn't want to acknowledge the other reason she had for hoping he had not left. He was her only friend.

While Arman milked the goat, Ayra walked over to the edge of the trees. The sun was high enough now that golden light shone through the timbers. She bit her lip and looked for orange in the little grove. She listened for snapping twigs and Edvin's assertive footsteps.

The birds were wide awake now, darting from branch to branch. Trills and cheeps filled the quiet of the trees, not the familiar sound she was straining to hear.

"Edvin?" she asked simply. She waited, but the woods remained just trees and birds.

"I'm turning back inside," called Arman from behind. "Porridge is probably near ready."

Ayra waited ten minutes more before she stepped away from the trees and headed toward the door. Her eyes began to sting, and she quickly wiped them.

Inside, the small table was set with four wooden bowls. A bottle of fresh goat milk proudly stood in the middle. Wil gestured for Ayra to have a seat, and the three began to eat without a word.

Ayra tried not to stare at Arman as he used his spoon like a shovel, filling his mouth to capacity with each scoop. She would have laughed if her stomach hadn't felt so heavy. She looked back at her own bowl and forced a bite up to her mouth, wishing she could enjoy the rare treat of having creamy, sweet milk.

"Your friend," said Wil. "Is he not going to join us?"

Ayra fought to keep control of her tone. "No. I don't think so." She was proud of how calm she sounded.

"I looked out the window in the night to check on Nanny," Arman said with a mouthful. "Saw him heading into the woods."

Wil looked quizzically at Ayra. She set down her spoon. "I see. You are welcome to stay here as long as you need to, child."

"I..." Ayra did not know what to say. She needed to find Kelton before he was taken to Covalt, but she knew she would not make it if she tried to go alone. She could not believe Edvin would leave her without at least saying goodbye, but that was what he had done. She cleared her throat and bravely put her spoon up to her mouth.

A knock sounded at the door. Without thinking Ayra jumped to her feet and ran to it, bumping the table with her legs and causing the milk bottle to tip onto its side. Thick white liquid flooded the table as Arman called out and jumped away from the spillage over the table's edge.

She yanked the door open and faced Edvin standing on the other side. Relief flooded her entire body. She wanted to wrap her arms around him but gripped the door instead.

"You didn't leave me," she said, feeling foolish as soon as the words were out.

"Leave you?" He gestured toward the woods. "I went to try to scout out a pass over the mountain." He cocked his head and raised his eyebrows. "You really thought I left you here?"

"No," she lied. She tried to laugh, but it came out more like a grunt.

He grinned. He saw right through her bluff.

They stood there awkwardly for a moment before Wil gruffly said, "There is enough porridge for you if you are hungry."

Ayra turned and remembered the tipped bottle of milk. "Oh! I am so sorry. Let me clean that up."

Arman insisted on wiping it up himself, and Edvin tucked into a milk-less porridge. Ayra tried to give him hers, but he wouldn't take it.

After finishing their morning meal, Edvin told Ayra what he had learned. He had ventured up to the ridge of their current mountain and spotted a low notch where two of the greater mountains met. As near as he could tell the snow was not too deep at that point, but he admitted he didn't know what the other side of the mountain looked like. Ayra could hear the apprehension in his voice.

Wil listened quietly as Edvin laid out the course. When he finished, she asked, "What supplies do you have?" Edvin listed what they had, and the old woman shook her head. "The mountains behind mine are much higher and rougher than they appear. The thaw is nearly through down below, but it has hardly begun in the mountains that lie ahead of you, certainly not on the Tiseden side. Your supplies won't last you through the snow and cold. You are ill prepared, and I would advise you not to try it."

"We have to," said Ayra. "We don't have time to go around the mountains. Do we, Edvin?"

"No. We'll be far too late for Kelton, but I agree. Going over the mountains will be risky."

The room was quiet a minute before Arman piped up. "They could take the Wolf's Eye." He looked at Ayra. "I'd be willing to take you."

Wil looked at the boy and squinted. She clucked her tongue. "That could work. If it is still clear."

"It was seven years ago."

Edvin looked back and forth between them. "What's the Wolf's Eye?"

"It is an old, old mining and trade tunnel that passes through one of the mountains," replied Wil. She shook her head. "No guarantee it has not caved, but if it is still passable, it will make your hasty journey possible."

"I took it when I came from Tiseden. I know I could get you through." Arman nodded his head reassuringly.

Edvin sat back and rubbed his fingers over his closed eyes. "We're probably already behind the company. If it will save us some time—"

"And frostbite," interjected Wil.

"And frostbite, it's worth a shot." He turned his face to Ayra's. "What do you think?"

Ayra was stunned. He had never asked her opinion about their travel plan before. "I think we should try it."

He leaned back again with his hands behind his head. "All right then. Through the Wolf's Eye we go."

When the sun was overhead, the three travelers were ready to set off. Arman had insisted on finishing a few of his chores to ensure Wil would be all right in his absence, and Edvin worked with him to speed things along. While they labored, the old woman fashioned a burlap bag into a pack with one strap that Arman slung over his chest. She also packed him a box with dried fish, goat cheese, and some flat, dry bread cakes and gave the same to Edvin to fill his box the rest of the way. Arman estimated it would take the entire rest of the day to reach the tunnel opening.

"Are you sure you'll be all right without me?" he asked Wil just before parting.

"The question is will *you* be all right without me," she replied placing her hand on his face. "Be careful and come home as soon as you can." With a fleeting glance at Edvin, she turned to Ayra and said, "Should you need a place to go, remember you are welcome here."

Ayra was surprised by her generous offer and thanked her sincerely for everything. As they entered the little woods, Ayra turned back to look at the little home once more. It was such an unassuming place. One would never guess from looking at the outside that a little, old woman with the ability to unlock the past lived inside.

The Wolf's Eye was located on one of the great mountains over the ridge, back to the east. Edvin walked behind Ayra while Arman led the way, weaving a course back and forth up the steep, rocky mountainside.

Ayra found it easier to keep her footing at Arman's pace, and she was grateful for all the days of walking that prepared her legs for this trek. They burned despite their regular exercise, and she imagined without that exercise she would have needed frequent rests.

Soon smears of snow awaiting a sunny demise became a part of the terrain. Ayra could feel the air cooling around her, and for the first time wished she had worn her old woolen clothes. A chilled wind whipped around her and snaked its way through the fibers of her cotton dress.

Neither of her companions seemed inclined to talk, so to distract herself from her discomfort, Ayra let her mind wander where it would. She found herself staring at the back of Arman's head. He had said he had come from Tiseden years ago. She wondered what brought him to this side of the mountain. He seemed like a grandson to Wil, but she felt certain they had no blood relation. And he had been so quick to offer his help to Edvin and her. What made a person so willing to help strangers?

A loose rock under her foot made her wobble. Edvin's hand flew up to her side and steadied her. "I was starting to worry you didn't need me around anymore."

"That's my plan," she quipped. He laughed but not his usual lighthearted laugh.

Edvin's demeanor had changed since they left the village below. He joked and laughed but not in the effortless way he had before. It seemed forced. She wanted to know what had caused the change.

Wil's words returned to her mind. 'Darkness can follow those we least expect.' She glanced back at him, and he quickly turned his unsmiling face away from her.

Near the top of the ridge, Ayra asked for rest. Arman wandered a small distance away and sat down, leaving Ayra and Edvin almost alone. She climbed up a boulder, and Edvin followed. She shivered when a cold bolt of wind blew over them.

Edvin rummaged through his pack. "Here." He handed her the extra dress he had snatched from the company wagon. "Let me know if the extra layer doesn't help. You can have my tunic if you need it."

Ayra took the dress. "Thanks. This should help." She stood and gratefully slipped it over her head. It was green and a size or two bigger than her blue dress, but the length was about the same. After twisting and adjusting, she sat back down.

"You hungry?" he asked.

"No, I think I can save it for later."

Edvin nodded and placed his folded arms across his knees. The tightness in the air felt foreign to Ayra, even though a couple weeks ago she did not want him to even look at her.

She took a deep breath. "I learned some interesting things from Wil." She hesitated and looked at his face to see if he was interested.

He sat up straighter. "Yeah? Go on."

She told him everything, beginning with the happy things she saw. Her parents working together, her young grandmother playing with her mother. Family members she did not know reading together, telling stories. She told him the gift seemed to only be bestowed on the women of her family. It was easy to talk to him about those things, and she liked to watch the gloominess about him lighten as she spoke. But she had to pause before telling him the rest.

The dark memories dug up from the depths of her mind were still raw and uncomfortable. She told him that her family was forced into the camp by a king and with tears blurring the valley below, she told him about the dungeon, the safner, and the execution.

"It must have been King Ivar. He was a tyrant. A controlling warmonger, unlike his father or any of his successors. He probably tried to use your family to stretch the borders of his rule. He took some land in the east countries, but his empire failed even before he was killed. I wonder if the safner you saw is the Azure Stone Gibsen wants."

"Maybe. I don't know what it would be for, though."

He placed his hand on her shoulder. "I'm sorry, Ayra. Something like that should never have happened. King Ivar is a blight in our history," he added with disgust.

Ayra nodded not knowing what else to say. Blight did not seem ugly enough of a word for the man. She could still see his wicked face when she closed her eyes. She didn't want to talk about him anymore, so she changed the subject.

"I never imagined the rain I loved so much was a gift from my grandmother. I have been trying to imagine how strong she must have been to pull rain clouds into the valley—into the whole country—while she stood on a hill near the quarry. I saw her pull clouds over the western Wolfjaws, but surely most of the rain comes from the North. Such a long way."

"Yeah, that is very far," Edvin said thoughtfully as he threw a pebble. "You could do it, though."

Ayra looked at him wide eyed and snorted. "You're joking. I can hardly make a splash."

He looked back at her with a smile and shrugged. "No. I'm not. You could do it."

"Swishing water out of a lake or stopping up a spring is one thing. To pull rain from the sky…it's impossible. For me. My arms get sore with just little tricks. I'm afraid it would take every bit of me to do something like that."

"Maybe you just need more time to understand it. To build up strength. I bet your grandmother's arms weren't bursting with muscle."

Ayra laughed at the thought of her petite grandmother with biceps the size of her waist. "No, they weren't." She tossed a small shard of the boulder at him. "You're so ridiculous."

"I'm ridiculous?" he chuckled, tossing the shard back. "I'm not the one who thinks I can't do anything."

He was smiling, and seeing the spark in his eyes, she remembered the hurt she had put in its place the night before. She thought about telling him something nice or doing something for him but at the same time knew he wouldn't recognize her veiled apology like Tanna always had. She cleared her throat and shifted on her seat.

"Edvin. I'm sorry I was…mean to you yesterday. I should not have talked to you the way I did. Thank you for listening."

He tossed another flake of rock at her. "Apology accepted.

And don't hold anything in anymore. I'm always ready to listen."

She wanted to say something witty about his ears but felt too content to joke. His face seemed lighter than it had when they sat down, and her heart felt lighter with it. "Me, too," she replied.

Edvin threw another rock downhill. Minutes passed before he asked, "Did she tell you anything about me?"

Ayra immediately recalled Wil's words about him. They were not exactly pleasant. "No," she lied. She forced her face and voice to sound uninterested. "She didn't."

He studied her for a minute, and she fought the urge to look away. If she did, he would surely catch her fib. She felt guilty for lying to him but didn't want Wil's words to irritate him. She wanted to casually ask why he thought she would say something about him, but Arman called out from below. They needed to get moving.

Ayra noted the sun's place in the sky. She hadn't been thinking about time as they talked, but the break had probably been much longer than it should have been. Arman rounded the side of the boulder and began making his way toward the ridge again. Ayra and Edvin followed.

The trees were all behind them now. Only rock lay ahead.

The rock on this mountain was different than the rock that littered the quarry. Instead of shades of gray and blue, the rocks were white and brown with streaks of red, orange, and silver. Some even sparkled in the afternoon sunlight.

Ayra began picking up any piece that especially caught her eye. When her hand was full, she wished for a pocket or little pouch to put them in. Unable to find a place to save them, she decided it was silly to keep rocks anyway and slowly released them from her hand one by one.

14

THE ridge neared sooner than Ayra thought it would and soon they stood atop it. She drew in a sharp breath at what lay ahead. The mountain sloped down a good distance before it rose again to the next peak. Snowcapped mountains in either direction filled her eyes. Dense clouds hung in the northern sky refusing to step over the peaks.

"The Wolf's Eye is over there, where the mountain is at its narrowest," Arman said, pointing northeast. "We should reach the opening soon after the sun disappears, I think."

The north side of the lesser mountain was steeper than its south-facing slope. And the crusty snow was denser on this side but patchy enough they could still maneuver around it. They switchbacked their way down until the earth turned to small, loose rock.

Only a few steps in, Ayra slipped and fell hard on her backside. Suppressing a smirk, Edvin helped her up and showed her how to turn her feet and shuffle. She laughed with glee as she found herself almost gliding down the unstable ground.

As they neared the deepest part of the ravine, Ayra could see a creek running along the bottom. It looked wide enough to be difficult to cross without getting wet. And she was certain getting wet in these temperatures was not a good idea. Her hands and feet already stung.

"Looks like we'll need someone to help us out down there," Edvin called over his shoulder, raising his eyebrows at her.

Ayra's fears were confirmed when they reached the bottom of the ravine. The stream was deep enough the rocks were covered, and wide enough they couldn't jump across.

Arman let out a low whistle and sat down to unlace his boots. "I don't think it'll be any better further down. We'll just have to wade across."

"No," Edvin said calmly. "Keep your boots on. Ayra will get us across."

Arman looked up at her with his thick brows knit together. Ayra looked at him and back at Edvin. She shook her head.

"Go on. Give it a go," Edvin prodded.

"I don't think she should have to carry—" Edvin silenced Arman a wave of his hand.

Ayra felt her gift was not something she should go around showing off. The less anyone knew the better. Edvin evidently trusted Arman, but she was not sure she did. And aside from that, she had never sought control over this much water.

She stood with her arms pressed to her sides. Both of her companions stared at her waiting for her to do something, one confident and the other confused. She closed her eyes and pictured Tanna's face. She would have been able to do this. She would want her to develop the gift.

Ayra opened her eyes and watched the flow of the water for a minute. She looked for a section where the rocks looked near the surface. That way she would not have to hold back as much water to allow passage.

"Fine," she said begrudgingly. "Be ready to move."

Arman got to his feet without taking his eyes off her. Ayra took a cold, deep breath. She put out her hand and focused on halting the water's movement. A ripple set across the stream and a small wall of water began to build. The rocks appeared to rise out of the water as the flow from above thinned.

Edvin gave baffled Arman a push, and they both dashed across the rocks. Ayra felt the strength in her arm give out and released the short wall of water. It fell with a swoosh, and the stream returned to its regular flow.

Edvin turned around and found her still standing on the other side. "You were supposed to come across, Ayra," he chided with his hands on his hips.

"I couldn't. I couldn't hold the water and move my legs at the same time!"

Arman still had a stunned expression on his face but said nothing.

Ayra stood alone, holding her arm, looking at the two boys across the frigid barrier.

"Hold it again using your other arm," Edvin suggested.

Ayra shook her head. Already she felt worn down. It was too hard, too much water. Edvin pushed her again, and she tried once more, this time only managing to hold back half as much before her invisible dam broke. Edvin blew out a loud breath and sat down. He jerked at his laces and yanked off his boots and stockings, muttering under his breath.

Ayra chewed on her lip as she watched him begin rolling up his pant legs. "What are you doing?" she timidly called over.

He stopped midroll and looked at her with an expression somewhere between irritation and surprise. "Coming to get you!" he called back.

She heard his breath catch as he stepped into the freezing, knee-deep stream.

"Sorry," she eked out when he reached where she stood.

Without a word he stooped down and threw her over his shoulder like a sack of potatoes, then turned and waded effortlessly back across the creek.

By the time they were all on the same side of the stream and Edvin's feet were dressed, the sun was well on its way to hiding. With the shadows of the mountain, they would lose light soon. Arman was still confident he could find the tunnel and within an hour the trio stood before a black hole in the mountain's side.

The opening appeared to be smaller than it once had been, with large rocks strewn around the bottom and up the sides. If

Arman had not guided them to it, Ayra was sure they would never have found it, especially in the dark.

"There's a cavern about a hundred paces in that we can bunk in," Arman said, lighting a small oil lamp. "There's enough room for smoke ventilation." He handed the little light to Edvin and maneuvered his stout body through the opening.

"How will we build a fire without wood?" Edvin asked. "I have heat sticks if we need them."

"I made a stockpile last year. Should still be here as long as no one has taken it," Arman called back from inside the tunnel. His voice echoed into the darkness.

The opening looked more like the mouth of a vicious beast with jagged teeth than the keen eye of wolf. Ayra remembered what one of those looked like. She shivered at the memory.

Edvin waited for her to slip in and followed after her. When they were both inside, he grabbed her arm, holding her back a minute. He tilted his head and listened. Ayra could hear Arman's feet stumbling over the rocks somewhere ahead of them but nothing else.

Edvin shook his head. "I don't like it. The echoes throw me off. As near as I can tell it's safe. But I can't hear clearly very far. Just stay close to me, all right?"

Ayra nodded and stepped closer to him, putting little space between them. In the faint light of the lamp, she saw him grin at her and realized he didn't mean *that* close to him. But she stayed right up next to him anyway as they navigated their way deeper into the tunnel.

The little lamp's glow seemed to be swallowed up in darkness, and Ayra blundered over rocks as if she had no light at all. A few times she put her hand out to the side, just to make sure they were surrounded by protective rock and not an ambush hiding in a pocket.

They reached the cavern and found Arman waiting for them.

"About time you got here. Thought you'd be right behind me with the light. It's darker than the inside of a goat in here. We could probably continue and make it through tonight, but I feel better about sleeping here than on the other side."

Edvin handed him the lamp, and Ayra watched the small ball of light with an arm move to the far side of the cavern.

"I come here every once in a while," Arman was saying, "usually in mid-warm season after the snow melt is over. Wil doesn't like me to leave her too long, so I just stay a night here and there. Just in this part. Only been all the way through the tunnel one time. Ah! Here's my pile."

Without the lantern, darkness seemed to bear down on Ayra, cold and lonely. The only way she knew Edvin was still near was just a feeling, an instinct. Afraid he might move away from her, she wanted to grab his arm or hand to have tangible reassurance. But she pressed her arms to her sides instead.

A few sparks jumped out of the darkness. Arman gave the little kindling fire a few blows, and the flames bloomed into life. He added logs one at a time until the fire was a comfortable size.

The cavern did not light up as much as Ayra had hoped it would. The ceiling and all sides but the one directly to the side of the fire remained hidden. But the darkness did seem less formidable with a broader radius of light.

As she ate her late supper, Ayra looked at the other two faces around the fire and couldn't miss seeing the contrast between them. All the lines in Arman's face were relaxed. He wolfed down his fish and cracker bread as if he were on a sunny picnic. Edvin kept rubbing his eyes and furrowing his brow. He picked at his food as if it were rotten, and several times Ayra noticed him try to listen, then shake his head. She wondered if his feet were still cold from walking through the creek.

"I'm sorry I couldn't stop the water again," she said quietly.

He glanced at her and turned back to the fire. "It's fine, Ayra. I shouldn't have gotten mad. I just think you could have done it if you really had tried."

His tone pricked at her temper. "I *did* really try. You have no idea what it feels like."

Arman's hand stopped halfway up to his mouth and slowly lowered back down. He looked from Ayra to Edvin, suddenly aware of the tension between them. He ducked his head and trained his eyes on the fire.

"Not exactly, but I know my ears get stronger as I use them. I'm gaining more control all the time. You hardly even try to do anything."

"Well, maybe what I can do doesn't work the same way. And I haven't exactly had years to practice like you have. Why are you pushing me so hard?"

He raked a hand through his hair driving the cowlick further upward and leaned back on his hands. "I don't know. I didn't really think things out this far—I didn't think past visiting the seer. And I was supposed to have you *and* Kelton. I'm not sure taking you to get him is a good idea, especially when you are so weak."

The word weak felt like a slap. But the part about Kelton angered her more. "Not sure taking me to get my brother is a good idea? They'll probably kill Kelton when they find out he can't do anything. I can't just let them take Kelton to Covalt."

At the mention of Covalt's name, Arman's head snapped up. Ayra had forgotten he was there.

Arman swallowed. "Wait, you have dealings with Covalt?"

Edvin sucked in a deep breath and laid all the way back, covering his face with one arm. The cavern was silent except for the crackle of the fire. A log collapsed sending tiny, red sparks flying like a frightened flock of birds. Ayra glanced at Edvin, but he did not seem intent on answering Arman.

"Not exactly," she began. "My brother and I came from Darkwater Quarry in the Aster Range." She hesitated, unsure whether she should mention Prince Gibsen. She decided against it. "Edvin's company came to get us, claiming they were taking us to a relative. But it turns out they were taking us in exchange for something from Covalt. Edvin…helped me escape, but my brother did not make it out with us. So now we are going to Tiseden to get him."

"What does Covalt want with you?"

Ayra bit her lip unsure if she should tell him. Then she

remembered he had already seen her use her gift. "It must have something to do with my little tricks with water. I doubt he realizes I'm not worth much."

Edvin uncovered his face. "Ayra," he began. But Arman spoke, too.

"I lived in Tiseden once. I guess you might already know that. But my family moved from Prashura to a small fishing village in Tiseden near the sea. My Papa hoped he could do better for us there. I had one elder brother and two sisters." He spoke thoughtfully, as if his memories were being pulled from somewhere deep inside. "Prince Covalt was head commander of the army then. Everyone thought he was a hero. Rumors that he was working against King Tobian were slow to spread. No one wanted to believe it. I remember my Papa arguing with a neighbor about it one day. He was worried."

He paused and drew in a deep breath. "I haven't thought about these things for a long time. Hard things you want to forget. Anyway, Covalt's own army had been building but quietly. From within. Convincing soldiers King Tobian was not allowing Tiseden to obtain its rightful place in the world, and that he—as the new king—would bring riches and pride to the country.

"When the army divided, he needed more men, so he tried more aggressive tactics. I was only four or five, but I remember the day Covalt's Army came through. Instead of the green feathered, brass helmet of Tiseden, they all wore black helmets. Coarsely crafted—ugly as rage. Our village was so small there was nothing anyone could do. He stood in the center and shouted that if we wanted to live, we had to join him. I was too small to understand but could feel the fear. I could *feel* it."

His voice broke. "But my Papa was the first to speak out. He said no. And right there, Covalt slit his throat. One swipe of a blade, and my Papa was gone. It's hard to remember much after that. But I can still hear my mother's screams. Everyone was rushing around. Mina—my sister—grabbed me and ran to the cooper's. Tucked me in a barrel and said to stay put. Made me promise not to get out. I was too scared to move—to even cry. I heard screams and banging and pounding. All sorts of ruckus. I could smell smoke seeping into my barrel. And then it all stopped. I fell asleep waiting for Mina to come get me. But she never did." He swiped the tears in his eyes with the back of his hand.

Ayra's mouth felt dry, but her cheeks were wet. She let the tears go unashamed this time. It felt natural to cry for someone else rather than herself. She tried to process what little Arman had seen but could not. She had seen death a number of times, but nothing like that. And she knew how the new, secondhand memories haunted her.

Ayra never would have thought Arman to have such a history. He seemed so genial and happy. She realized as she listened she was not the only one with a history that hurt.

"Arman, I'm so sorry," she said. It seemed a pitiful response, but there was nothing else to say.

His mouth pulled into a half smile, accepting her sympathy.

"Me, too. Covalt terrorized a great number of other small villages like mine. After word spread, some joined as soon as his scout rode in. People from distant areas went into the demolished villages and took in any of the children they could find. Some of those people were good, some were not. The man who took me in...was not. He was a merchant and moved all around. I worked for him for six years, beaten if I did right and beaten if I did wrong. Finally, I worked up the courage to run. We were in a village at the base of a mountain. Overheard two men talk about the Wolf's Eye one day. I just felt like I had to get there. I had to find it. So I left in the night.

"Lucky for me it was late warm season, and there wasn't any snow. By no small miracle my foolish self found the tunnel. Came through with a makeshift torch that I don't know how stayed lit. Up and over and stumbled upon Wil's. And she took in the little mutt I was." He let out a light laugh. "She saved me. And has given me a real home as if she were my own grandmother." He looked down at his hands. "I don't know if you understand the man you are running from. I have not heard anything about him since I left Tiseden, but I know him to be ruthless. He doesn't care one scrap about anyone or anything. Why they let a man like that live, I don't know. I'd kill him with my own hands if I could. Would that the Mihtengard army had got to him before Tiseden leaders did."

The mention of the Mihtengard army turned Ayra's attention to Edvin. His dark eyes were locked on the fire. His jaw muscles flexed, but he said nothing. Arman obviously didn't know that

Edvin's father had led that army, but since Edvin didn't offer the information, she kept quiet.

The air hung heavy with the melancholy mood of the cavern occupants. Ayra had many thoughts in her mind but did not feel like speaking any of them. She had to get Kelton, but she felt more afraid than ever. And Edvin's moodiness scratched at her nerves. She didn't know how to help him if he wouldn't talk to her. Everything had seemed so light and hopeful just a week ago. But it all felt spoiled now.

Edvin was the first to stretch out and close his eyes. Arman followed shortly after and was snoring almost as soon as his eyelids met. Every part of Ayra felt exhausted, except her mind. It would not quiet when she begged it to, so she sat with her legs tucked up under her chin and watched a log turn to glowing red coals.

"Hey." She jumped when Edvin's whisper broke through her thoughts. She turned her eyes to meet his. "It's going to be all right. We'll figure it out." He reached his hand out and placed it on her foot. "We'll figure it all out. I promise."

She nodded and wiped her sleeve across her wet cheeks. He rolled over and grabbed the extra blanket from his pack and handed it to her. She wrapped it around herself and laid the top of her head near his. Even though they were only words, his promise carried enough peace for her to close her eyes and let go for a time.

15

AYRA sat up and blinked several times to make sure her eyes were open. The fire had gone out completely. They must have slept far longer than planned. She squinted but couldn't make out any lines or shapes. She felt around the ground and found what she was looking for.

"What!" a startled Edvin practically shouted when her fingers touched his head.

"I think we've slept too long." A snort came from a few feet away. "Arman. Wake up."

"Hm? Where's the fire? Oh, it's out. How long have we slept?"

"I don't know," Edvin answered, his voice gravelly and dry. "Can you light the lamp?"

Ayra listened to Arman fumble through his pack. A few

sparks burst into the darkness and the lamp lit. The meager light dispersed the chill in the cavern and cleared their sleepy fog. They rolled their blankets and readied for their journey through the tunnel. Ayra wondered if there would be sunlight when they reached the other side or if they had slept an entire day away.

The passage was not wide enough for the three of them to walk shoulder to shoulder, so Arman led the way with Ayra and Edvin walking side by side behind him. The little light did not have to work as hard in the narrow tunnel as it had in large cavern and proved itself more useful in helping them place their feet. The deep, earthy smell intensified as they made their way further into the mountain. Ayra brushed her hand over the rock to her side and wondered how many diggers it had taken to etch out the tunnel.

"Why don't they use this anymore?"

Arman shrugged. "Not sure. Wil said it was dug out before she was born. When the tunnel was complete, the Tisedenians mined one side and the Mihtengardians the other. Maybe it wasn't productive or maybe working conditions became unsafe."

"Oh," she replied and squinted at the ceiling hoping it wouldn't decide to give out over their heads.

Edvin bumped his arm into her shoulder and flashed her a smile. "Don't worry. I'll be able to hear any shifts in the rock if it starts to give way. But I think we'll get through just fine. The echoes still carry a good distance ahead, so it's still clear as far as I can tell."

They walked in near silence, the scraping of their boots over rock the only constant sound. Ayra tried to imagine what it had been like for little Arman to pass through this maze alone. He must have been a brave child. Or just desperate, she decided.

Time seemed to have stopped for Ayra without the heavenly lights as guides. The chill of darkness seemed thicker than before and pressed at her from every direction. She glanced back a few times hoping she would somehow see a way out behind her, as there certainly was not one anywhere near ahead. The thought struck her that if she died in this dark place, no one would ever know. Her breaths quickened, and she wiped her clammy hands on her green dress.

Edvin glanced sideways at her. "One time when I was just a little Edvin, I found my way to the bakery down the street from my home. Some idiot had set up a display of cakes on a table low enough anyone could reach. Just little cakes, about this big." He held up his hands making a circle to represent the size. "They were iced pink with sliced strawberries on top. The little devils practically begged me to eat them. I made off with as many as I could fit in my arms and hid myself behind the water barrel at home. Ate every crumb and berry right then.

"After I finished, I was so tuckered out from my labors, I nestled in and fell asleep. When Mother found me, she shook me awake and asked what I had been doing. 'Napping,' I said. She didn't take that like I had hoped and asked again. 'Nuffin. Just napping.' She stood there with her hands on her hips and her eyes shriveling my courage with every passing second and asked, 'And how do you explain the pink crust all over your face and shirt?' I looked myself over and knew I had to think quickly or I'd be done for. 'I dunno. But it sure isn't frosting.' Brilliant, really. Mother's hands stayed on her hips, but I knew I had won her. I could see it in her eyes. She took me up and scrubbed my face with cold water from the barrel before letting me run off."

Arman chuckled a little from the front. Ayra imagined a little wild-haired, brown-eyed Edvin with an armful of cakes. The more she pictured it, the funnier it became.

"I can't believe you got away with that," she said through a laugh.

"Oh, I didn't say I got away with it. Mother didn't have the spirits to whittle me herself but had no trouble telling my father when he returned home that day. He didn't think any of it was very cute or clever. I got a licking not to be forgotten, then dragged down to the bakery to apologize and pay for the cakes. My father was surprised to hear from the baker I had made off with six of them."

"I'm not at all surprised to hear you were a greedy, little thief."

"What?" He put his hand to his heart. "As charming, honorable, and charitable as I am? I'll have you know there may have been a time when every shop owner followed me around their shop like a hawk after a mouse, but I have since amended my ways and have become an exceptional, upstanding citizen. Now when they see me enter, they beam with joy. Pure joy."

Edvin continued to tell stories of Little Edvin. Ayra watched

Arman's posture relax in front of her and felt her own muscles slowly release their tightness. If it weren't for the dank scent in her nose and the blackness ahead, she might have forgotten they were walking through a mountain that could collapse and crush their bodies at any moment.

Sporadically they passed through small caverns. A few times they came to forks in the tunnel that Arman wasn't sure which branch to take. Each time, Edvin picked up a pebble and threw it down the tunnel. Usually by the echoes he could decipher which one was deeper. Only once did he pick the wrong tunnel and force them to retrace their steps.

After a time, the tunnel noticeably sloped down and a white light appeared ahead. Each of them quickened his or her steps, anxious to escape the mountain. The light grew wider and brighter until they found themselves out in the open once again.

Ayra squinted in the light of day and inhaled the fresh air. The sky was thick with white, puffy clouds. The sun was high in the sky above them, but the north-facing mountainside felt shadowed and cool. The peak overhead was heavy with snow, and the slope immediately around them was thinly skiffed. Not far below where they stood, a thick forest spread far and wide.

"Going the other way isn't nearly as confusing," Arman said turning to Edvin. "If it weren't for you, we might not have made it out so quickly."

Edvin gave one nod of his head.

"Made it out so quickly?" questioned Ayra, still drawing deep breaths of fresh air. "That felt like hours and hours and hours."

Arman chuckled. "Felt like it but it wasn't. But I know what you mean—it's hard to keep track of time without the sun."

Before taking a rest for their first meal of the day, they decided it would be best to get to the protection of the trees and trekked down the mountainside. Tall, deep green pine trees surrounded them. A different sort of pine than the variety in Mihtengard, with short needles and massive trunks. The scent of the trees was as thick as their boughs. Bright green, leafy-branched plants and mossy rocks covered the ground. Ayra felt a tiny tingle in her fingers. The moist air felt even cooler than it had up on the rocks.

Arman set to work gathering wood for a fire while Edvin, bow in hand, went deeper into the trees to see what he could find to eat. Unsure what to do, Ayra sat down on a fallen log. She looked around wishing there was something she could contribute. Water droplets clung to the leaves of the groundcover.

She picked up the water pouch Edvin had left for her and removed the cap. With the lip of the pouch touching the branch, she gathered the little droplets using the pull of her finger and guided the trickle into the pouch. She repeated this task several times before deciding it would take days to fill the pouch this way.

"I'm going to see if I can find a spring," she announced, getting to her feet. "Want me to take your pouch, too?"

Arman nodded and continued to throw sparks and blow on his rebellious, damp firewood.

Ayra followed the tingling in her fingers through the trees.

She knew she was moving in the right direction when the sensation grew. She felt pleased she had a skill that could help them on their journey, even though Edvin could find water, too.

The babbling sound of a stream grew louder as she weaved her way through the trees. She had thought the pine trees of Mihtengard were tall, but they were dwarfs compared to these trees. Some of the trunks were too thick for her to even wrap her arms around. She walked directly to the mouth of the spring and filled each pouch. A few times she practiced stopping up the flow.

She heard a quiet whistle and glanced around. Edvin was about twenty paces away from her on the other side of the spring. He pointed downstream. A massive animal, with fuzzy prongs on top of its head grazed at the edge of the water. Its brown coat was dark with patches of light, scruffy hair. It was either unaware or unconcerned it was being watched.

Edvin stepped across the narrow stream and silently made his way to her side. He grinned as he stared at the animal.

"That's not a deer, is it?" she asked.

"No, it's an elk," he whispered back. "They only live on this side of the mountain range. I've actually never seen one in person. Only drawings. I think he's a good size. I wish I could see those stumpy antlers in a few months."

They watched the animal for some time before Ayra remembered they had left Arman. She was not used to having a third companion. Reluctantly, Edvin followed her away from the spring.

They found Arman sitting by a blazing fire with a scowl on his face. It disappeared when Edvin dropped two hares in front of him.

The three of them discussed the plan for the coming days as they ate their meal. Arman decided he would go with them further than the pass. He wasn't sure he'd be a lot of use, but he offered whatever help he could give.

To Ayra's relief, Edvin's attitude regarding finding Kelton seemed to have changed. While they had lost some time moving on foot, he assumed the company had stopped a time or two to replenish supplies. Also, he knew the road they would take through Tiseden wound to the west, moving toward their location instead of away.

"If we make good time, I think we can intercept them. I just hope the map in my head is accurate."

"What is the plan after you get Kelton?" Arman asked.

Edvin ran both hands through his hair and closed his eyes. "I don't know. I've been trying to figure that out."

Ayra's shoulders slumped. She had been so preoccupied with finding Kelton, she hadn't thought of anything after. Where would she and her brother go and what would happen to Edvin, she wondered. She felt foolish for being so shortsighted.

"You will be able to go back home, won't you?" she asked Edvin hopefully.

He kept his eyes on the fire. "No. I can't. I left my post in the prince's company. I'm a deserter. If we sabotage Prince Gibsen's plan, I'm sure he'll cover everything up." Arman's eyes widened at the mention of Prince Gibsen, but he didn't say anything. Edvin threw a stick into the fire. "No one will take my word above his and Rooney's. I can't go back to Midivard."

Ayra thought of the other men in the company. It was possible none of them were in on the plot, only selected to protect the prince like Edvin. And there was one Edvin had talked to. "What about Tress? He knows what you heard. He helped you with my...abduction." Now that they were friends, it didn't seem like the right word. "Or rescue rather."

Edvin smiled faintly. "Yeah, but Tress only carries an apple's weight more than I do. My father would probably believe him, but it's no small thing to accuse a prince of plotting against his father with a well-known warmonger. And anyway, Tress didn't hear anything himself. Only has my word. Honestly, he was skeptical of my whole *plan*. He wanted me to wait, but...I didn't. I don't know if he would risk ruining his family by making bold claims he couldn't prove or even be certain of. No, we're on our own that way."

She studied his drawn face. So these were the thoughts that had been smothering him. Frustration mingled with fear welled up inside of her once again. She almost wanted to go back to Darkwater where she knew what to expect from day to day. She never had to find food or worry about underhanded dealings. At that moment she finally understood why her grandmother had called it a sanctuary. Why she had been afraid to leave it.

She leaned back on her hands and looked up at the trees. With her eyes closed, she listened to them whisper to her.

Breathed deeply the smell of the forest. Felt the persistent, mild tingle in her fingers. The quarry may have been a sanctuary, but this was where she belonged. In the world outside of rocks and dust. She imagined Tanna's face, confident as she pulled the rain clouds over Mihtengard. Ayra determined she would set everything right. She just needed to figure out how.

16

THE sun was setting on the travelers for the fifth time since entering the new country. The thick forest and many flowing waters of Tiseden slowed their progress more than the woods of Mihtengard had. After two days of grappling with the terrain, they decided to travel by road when possible.

Edvin still felt confident they could find the company before it reached the coast—before Prince Gibsen reached Covalt's island.

They had passed through a couple villages, the first being the same one Arman had lived in before he ran away to the mountains. The second they had passed through only the day before, buying some flatbread and apples with coins Arman had brought. Aside from a few curious looks, the fair-haired residents of the villages had not paid them much attention.

Edvin maintained his merry demeanor for much of the time, but Ayra could tell he didn't feel as lighthearted as he projected. Sometimes he walked behind her instead of beside her and didn't always look her in the face. She dreaded stretches of time when he remained quiet, aside from a few words here and there, and worried when he stayed in the forest longer than what typically took him to find food. She always noticed when his jaw flexed and his movements became fidgety.

It was difficult not to think of Kelton, but she did her best to set her own worries aside and tend to Edvin's. She found he relaxed when she talked, so she made a conscious effort to tell stories from the quarry or mention anything interesting she thought or saw. She sat near him when they rested and laid her head near his at night.

As the daylight thinned, Edvin suggested they move off the road a good distance to camp for the night, and Ayra readily agreed. Walking on a road always made her feel skittish. She looked forward to the evenings when they moved back into the shelter of the trees.

In less than a week, Ayra had fallen in love with the forests of Tiseden. She had no idea there were so many shades of green. Staring up into the tall, thick pines left her feeling awestruck. Despite their heavy purpose here, the green leafy curls that littered the ground made her smile, and she felt delighted every time she spotted a fat, yellow slug or discovered a colony of unique mushrooms.

The only thing she disliked about the forest was the way it

hushed everything. Sounds were not clear and cheerful here like they were in the open woods of Mihtengard. The songs of the birds and chatter of the squirrels were muffled by the dampness. Even footsteps were quiet. If she were alone, the forest would not be so full of wonder, especially in the dark.

They came upon a slight clearing and deemed it a fair campsite. Then each of them set to the self-assigned evening tasks—Arman gathered wood for a fire, Edvin disappeared to hunt supper, and Ayra collected the water pouches to refill. She always tried to locate a spring first and settled for a stream if she had to.

Passing over one large stream and wandering a little further, she found a smaller one that she traced to its source out of the ground. Not far away she could hear the roar of a river. She sat down and placed the first water pouch in the little pool to fill.

This time in the day, when she was alone, was when she opened herself up to feel her worry. Her thoughts always wandered to Kelton first. She hoped Prince Gibsen was still treating him well and that he wasn't too afraid for her. She tried to imagine he was still enjoying himself—eating Arty's delicious food, sparring with the other soldiers, sleeping soundly on a cot under the cover of canvas. It felt like years since she had seen her brother. She wiped a few stray tears from her cheeks, replaced the cork on the full pouch, and put the other in to fill.

Gradually, her thoughts rebelliously turned to where she was heading—near Covalt. She imagined him looking similar to King Ivar, big and robust with an ugly, scraggly beard and menacing eyes. She felt her stomach tighten and her mouth go dry at the sight of the man in her mind and forced the dark thoughts from her head to focus on her task.

When two swollen pouches rested beside her, she stared into the clear, cold water at her knees. She lifted her hand and gently curved her fingers. Ripples formed and faded. She traced her finger in a circle creating a whirlpool. As the tiny water tornado grew, her thoughts drifted to Edvin. Once again, a voice in the back of her mind told her he was hiding something from her. She hushed the voice, hoping for the final time, and pictured his lively, brown-eyed, grinning face and dark swooping hair. She couldn't prevent the smile that formed on her lips.

Suddenly two hands grabbed her around the waist. Her heart sank from her throat to its proper place when the hands slipped away and a familiar laugh rumbled in her ears.

"Edvin, I…you…one of these times I'm going to…"

"You're going to what? I've seen you fight with a makeshift knife. I'm not afraid of you…yet."

She laughed despite her pounding heart and shaking hands. She turned and looked at him crouching behind her. His features had lost the heaviness she had noticed a half hour before. She patted the ground beside her. He dropped his bow and three cleaned fish and took the offered seat.

"I've been watching you do your little tricks like you do when you're alone." He gestured at the pool. "I've noticed you're more relaxed. It looks like you aren't even trying."

Ayra wasn't sure if she felt pleased or embarrassed he had been spying on her. She thought about his observation for a moment.

"It is easier when I'm alone. Like it happens more freely. I don't feel as…distracted, I guess."

He cockily leaned back on his hands and raised his eyebrows. "Distracted, huh?"

Ayra felt her cheeks warm as she realized he might have determined *he* was a distraction. She hurried to add, "Yes, I just feel like I can think better when you…when I'm alone." She silently cursed herself because that addition didn't clear anything up. She looked deeper into the water.

"Does it bother your arm as much when you practice by yourself?"

Ayra rolled her right shoulder. "No, I guess not. But I also do just little bits."

He sat forward again. "Pretend I'm not here. Do something big."

She looked sideways at him. "It's kind of hard for me to pretend you're not here."

"Is it?" He grinned playfully.

She rolled her eyes, but her mouth twitched into a half smile. She looked downstream. Just to take him down a peg, she successfully pretended he was not sitting next to her with his knee touching hers. She closed her eyes and drew in a deep breath and exhaled to clear her thoughts.

Then focusing on the babbling stream, she put out her right hand, with her thumb pointing up to the sky, and gradually pulled her hand toward the spring source. Water about ten paces away stopped and slowly pushed back upstream creating a swell.

She continued to pull just until the newly created pool touched the toe of Edvin's boot. Then she released it and watched it flood into its regular bed.

His face snapped back to hers. "How did that feel?"

Ayra said nothing and returned to swirling the water.

He nudged his shoulder into hers. "All right. Well done. You can stop pretending I'm not here, now. Did that make your arm ache?"

Ayra shrugged. "I don't know. No, I guess not."

He lifted a finger and poked her in the forehead. "It's in your head."

"What?"

"Your arms and hands. They're just secondary. Your ability is in your head. When you focus on physically doing the work— on that rope you said you feel—it strains your muscles. You can't handle as much." He poked her head again. "When you focus on the task with your mind, it's easier."

She thought about it for a minute. It made sense. The more she concentrated on the water the less she thought about the pull. Images of the women she had seen in the memories Wil retrieved flashed through her mind. Though physically fit from doing quarry work, none of them looked notably strong. But in their faces—in their eyes—there was a fierceness she had instinctively noticed but had not paid attention to. A quiet but undeniable confidence in their ability.

"Ayra," Edvin called her back to where she sat. "You are stronger than you think. You just need to get it in your head."

She looked at him. She could see in his eyes he was not teasing her. He meant it. They stared at each other for a moment, the happy, little stream babbling to itself the only sound. She watched his eyes quickly search over her face, then he shifted and placed his hand on the ground behind her and leaned his face into hers.

Her heart gave a strange, quick beat at the sudden nearness and panic swelled inside her chest. She grabbed the water pouches, scrambled to her feet, and began hastily walking in the direction she had come.

"We should probably get back to Arman. I'm sure he's soured on us by now for leaving him so long," she hurriedly called back. It was the first excuse she could think of for fleeing from him. Her stomach buzzed with a mysterious warmth.

Edvin caught up to her with just a few easy strides, adjusting his bow on his shoulder.

When she felt like her voice would come out more evenly, she cleared her throat and said, "I think you're right. I think I've been focusing too much on using my arm strength. Thank you for helping me figure this out."

His hand rubbed over the back of his neck. "Yeah, sure," he said simply, humor dancing in his eyes. She couldn't tell if he was laughing inwardly at her or at himself. He took the full water pouches from off her shoulder and slid them onto his.

Ayra expected to find poor Arman pouting at the campsite. When they walked up, he was sitting by the fire, flicking scraps of bark into the flames. But he looked up at them with a smirk instead of a scowl. "Well, well, well. Here are my friends. Can't say I'm a bit surprised you are together. What have you two been doing out there in the forest...alone?" He closed his eyes and puckered his lips.

Ayra narrowed her eyes at his fish face, but the embarrassment that sprung from his nearly true accusation made her tongue tied.

"We decided to leave you here and got a few miles away before we realized you'd probably starve to death." Edvin said casually. "Since we've grown to love you like a puppy, we came back." He dropped the slimy fish in Arman's lap.

"Hey!" he shouted, but his deep-throated laugh bubbled out. "I could find my own food if need be."

The evening proved to be a lighter one. They continued to joke with one another, and Edvin told some more of his stories. It always amazed Ayra he still had stories he hadn't told her. It was like he had an endless bucket of tricks. When the sun completely retired for the day and the blue light of the moon passed through the canopy, they tucked up under the trees for shelter. Ayra's fingers tingled constantly in this environment, varying in degree. Rain wasn't as easy to predict when water was everywhere. It had rained in the night or early morning each day since they arrived in the damp country, and they had learned their lesson after only one rude and wet awakening.

The cool night air was still except for the distant sound of rushing waters and the comforting crackle of fire. Ayra picked through the thoughts and realizations of the day. If Edvin's theory proved correct, maybe she would be able to do more than splashes and ripples—things of more importance. She hoped with time and practice she would be able to obtain the same level of power as those before her, though the idea still didn't come without the taint of anxiety.

A lone owl asked its question somewhere overhead. She listened to Arman's gruff snores from the tree over, then tuned her ears to hear the nearer, softer snores from the head less than three handbreadths from hers. A peculiar, new tickle of nervousness dripped its way into her stomach and a smile tugged at her lips.

17

AYRA startled out of a light sleep when her name was whispered in the dim light between night and dawn. She pushed up on one arm to look at Edvin. His finger was pressed to his lips, and he motioned for her to lie back down.

He pulled himself closer until his head was so close his hair brushed her forehead. "There's someone in the trees, coming this way," he said in a low whisper.

Ayra felt her heartbeat quicken. "What should we do?"

He glanced over at Arman. "Whoever it is will probably find us soon, with the smoke from the embers and that snoring. We should try to move." He looked around again, keeping his head near the ground. "Or maybe it would be better to just stay put. I don't know. Whoever it is, they're on a straight course to us."

Ayra looked at the trees. Thick fog lingered around them,

making her hair and blanket feel damp. The forest seemed to fade away into the mist.

The earth could drop off just through those trees, Ayra thought. Out of the corner of her eye, she saw Edvin reach for his bow and quiver.

Ayra's fingers tingled, reminding her of the power she possessed. Still on her side, she motioned her hand as if she were parting a curtain and concentrated on the fog obscuring the trees where Edvin had indicated. A rift appeared and slowly stretched away from them, like earth being separated by a plow.

Nothing appeared.

"Push it all away," Edvin whispered.

With one broad sweep of her hand, a wave of fog rolled through the trees, creating a clear semicircle before them. Then Ayra heard it. A whistled melody. It stopped. A twig snapped somewhere just beyond the open air.

Edvin propped himself up on his elbow. He felt around the dirt before he found a small stone and tossed it at Arman.

With a snort, Arman's eyes popped open. "What?" He looked at Edvin and then at Ayra. The alarm she felt must have been clearly on her face. Without a word, he grabbed his hatchet and glanced around, searching for a threat.

Another twig snapped and a dark figure emerged from the fog. Ayra could not see his face but could tell it was a man. A very large man. She sat up as Edvin and Arman simultaneously shot to their feet. Edvin nocked an arrow but kept the tip ponting down.

The man strolled toward them, clearly not intimidated by the girl and two boys.

"Good morning, sir." Edvin called out. Ayra was amazed how casual his voice sounded, as if they were meeting on the street. "Something we can help you with?"

The man stopped and crossed his arms. "I'm searching for a boy and a girl. Of Mihtengard." His accent sounded similar to Arman's but heavier. "The boy would be 'bout your height. Probably 'bout as scrawny. The girl with long brown hair and freckles. Been searching the area for 'em for days. Got word from a local two days ago they had been through and tracked 'em this far. Have you seen 'em?"

Ayra held her breath.

Edvin stepped in front of her. "No sir, haven't seen them. What is it you want with them?"

"Me? Nothin'. Other than I'd just like to ask the boy why he killed my dogs. And perhaps what made him think I'd tolerate a cut in my pay. He knows there's someone who has particular interest in the girl."

Ayra tried to swallow but her throat spasmed making her nearly gag. She peered at the man from behind Edvin's legs. His hair was frizzy and dark blond, roughly tied back behind his thick neck. He had on a dark leather tunic over a shirt that appeared a size too small. A set of sheathed knives lined the belt around his waist.

No one spoke. Ayra could hear her heart pounding in her ears. She searched with her eyes for something she could use for protection and grasped a sharp rock she found near her leg. She glanced at Arman and could see the hatchet shaking in his hand. She wished she hadn't dragged him into this.

The man sneered. He took a few steps closer. "I'll be takin' the girl now."

Edvin raised his bow. "No, I don't think you will. Stay where you are or I'll release. And I don't miss."

The man laughed—a raspy, awful sound. "You think I'm afraid of one of your little sticks? And anyway, it'll be pretty hard to shoot with your hands tied."

"What?" Ayra heard Edvin mutter as he spun around and released an arrow just as a man leaped from behind a fallen tree. The arrow grazed his shoulder and soared into the trees. Unfazed, he crashed into Edvin and wrestled him to the ground. Ayra's head jerked back as a third man grabbed her by the hair and wrapped a solid arm around her neck. Her grip on the rock loosened, and it fell from her hand.

Edvin continued to struggle, nearly getting the best of his opponent. But the man caught hold of him in a lucky moment and pinned him with his arm twisted behind his back. Arman stood frozen in place, looking back and forth from his pinned friends to the brutish talker.

The man strode up and crouched an arm's length away from Edvin, whose face was pushed sideways into the dirt.

"You ain't so good with your ears when you're distracted. What's your pa going to say when he hears your throat was slit 'cause you was stupid?"

Ayra felt her captor's hot breath across her cheek and instinctively tried to raise her shoulder to her ear to block it. His thick arm tightened, constricting her airflow. Her hands flew up and clawed at his arm.

The talker looked up from Edvin. "Ease up, Kenrick! She's to be unharmed."

"Only a little squirm, Oswine," Kenrick said as he loosened his hold.

"What should I do with this one?" asked the bald man who had Edvin pinned. Ayra couldn't see his face, but he had a thick scar across the back of his head.

"Kill him," Oswine said coldly as he rose to his feet.

The bald man pulled a knife from his bootstrap. Edvin jerked his shoulders but couldn't get free from the man's vice-like grip.

"Stop!" a young voice boomed.

All three men turned to Arman as if suddenly remembering he was there. Ayra couldn't turn her head all the way, but she could turn it enough to see Arman's hatchet pointing at the scarred man.

"Let my friends go."

The men exchanged looks and burst into laughter. "What do you think you're going to do, rat?" Oswine took a few steps toward Arman.

Ayra frantically glanced around for anything she could do to get them free. She reached for her rock, her fingertips barely brushing the edge. The mist she had disrupted had already settled back in. She didn't know if she could gather enough to

183

disorient the men, but it was the only thing she could think to do. Slowly she curled her fingers and gathered fog, holding it in a ring around the group, and waited for Arman to make a move.

"I...I..."

In a flash Arman dived forward and kicked the smoldering log from last night's fire. Glowing hot embers burst into the bald man's face. His hands covered his eyes as he cursed in agony, his bulky body falling backward into the dirt. Edvin rolled away and scooped up the knife the scarred man had dropped. Oswine lunged at Arman with his hands outstretched reaching for his neck. Arman swung his hatchet wildly, and the large man ducked back when the blade sliced across his palm.

Kenrick tightened his hold again and stood, pulling Ayra up with him. She kicked her heel into his shin, but he only tightened his grip. Edvin whirled around and threw the knife, sinking it into Kenrick's side. He cried out and released her to clutch his wound.

"Run!" Edvin shouted as he snatched up his bow.

With a soft swoosh, fog flooded the little campsite. Oswine lunged at Arman again just as Edvin released an arrow. It made contact with a sickening sound, but Ayra didn't turn around to see where it had hit. Arman and Edvin caught up to her in seconds and fell into stride. Ducking and weaving, time seemed to slow as they struggled over the thick forest terrain.

Ayra continued to direct the mist behind them, hoping to obscure them from the men's view. The roar of the river grew louder and louder until it was at their feet.

It was as large as it sounded. Wide and deep, churning angry in its course over and around large rocks. Downstream, a fallen tree stretched across the river. Ayra and Edvin spotted it the same moment, and Arman followed. When they reached it, the trunk was clearly too narrow and rotten to hold more than one of them at a time.

"Go first," Edvin said as he grabbed Ayra by the waist and swiftly lifted her onto the log.

She held her arms out for balance and moved as lightly as she could across the weak, slippery bridge. The very tip of the tree had been washed away, but the remnant end rested on a raised bed of smooth stones. She barely noticed the cold that seeped into her boots when she splashed into the shallow water. She turned to see Arman awkwardly begin making his way across and, upriver, two ugly figures racing toward them.

"Arman hurry!" she screamed.

Edvin turned to see the men coming, each with a knife drawn. He reached for an arrow, swiping his hand through air. His quiver was gone. Without waiting for Arman to be completely across, he stepped onto the log. He had only placed his feet several times when the wood shifted, dropping several inches. Arman's arms flailed, his boots slipped, and his body fell hard on the log, snapping it in two. Edvin jumped back to the bank as his side sank into the water and Arman and the other half of the bridge hurled downriver.

Ayra swiped her hand and commanded the water around Arman to push toward the bank, his body narrowly missing several of the flooded boulders. When he grasped the brush on the bank, she turned her attention to Edvin. The men were almost to him.

Across the raging water their eyes locked.

And for the first time since their journey began, there was fear in Edvin's eyes.

She closed her eyes and forced a deep breath. When she exhaled, she pushed the chaos swarming in her mind out with the air. She put her hands out and opened her eyes. With all the concentration she could summon, she pushed against the current, fighting to keep the water from spilling out the sides. An unseen dam halted the flow, and the riverbed, covered only by inches of water, appeared between them. In seconds, the wall of water doubled in height.

Edvin leaped down the sloping bank and splashed across the rocky floor, darting over and around bare boulders. The men reached the bank just as Edvin left it and after a pause of trepidation, slipped down after him with wide eyes and outstretched arms. Ayra felt her hold on the water slipping.

"Jump!" she screamed.

Edvin launched himself toward the bank. He caught arms with Arman, just as the wall of water broke from the base. The force of its collapse pushed the men's feet out from under them, and the furious river swept them out of sight.

Ayra did not know when Arman had come to her side. Her head pounded, and everything began to swirl. She kept her eyes open only long enough to watch him pull Edvin completely out of the water. She felt a cold sweat overtake her body and a wave of nausea as her knees gave out from under her. In a fog, she felt her body lift out of the pool of water and heard Edvin's far away voice, only able to make out her name. And then nothing.

18

THE gleeful trill of a bird pulled Ayra from the far reaches of sleep. The warm glow of sunlight leeched through her eyelids, and slowly, she forced them to open.

She was sitting with her legs tucked up toward her chest and her head resting on something solid and warm. When she realized it was Edvin's chest, she popped her head up to look at his face. He was sound asleep with his head leaned back against a large fallen tree. She looked around herself and discovered his tunic and arm were both wrapped protectively around her.

"He tried to stay awake, but I told him I'd keep watch," Arman whispered. "He's worn out like an old man's teeth."

Ayra turned her head to see him sitting on the other side of her, his hip against hers, his face edged with fatigue. He gave her a half smile.

She looked up to find the sun high in the sky. "How long have I been asleep?" she roughly whispered back.

"Oh, a while. We—Edvin carried you, you see—we got as far from the river as we could until neither of us could run any further. I don't know how soldiers do it. Fight and march. Fight and march. Something like that takes the spit right out of you." He paused and looked at his hatchet. "Oh, your dresses were both wet around the bottom and up one side from when you passed out. You were all chilled, and I...well, I thought maybe you'd get too cold in those damp layers so I—it sounds bad now but—anyway, Edvin insisted we leave them on you. So he put his tunic around you and we sat like this to keep you warm."

Ayra was grateful Edvin had the sense to keep her clothed and simultaneously felt amused by Arman's awkward ways. She followed his eyes down to his hatchet. "Are the men...gone?"

He looked at her and then at his hatchet again. "I think so, yes. Edvin stuck that Oswine fellow twice—once in the neck and the other in the chest. We're pretty sure he's gone for good. The other two, well, you pretty much took care of them."

Ayra hadn't seen Edvin shoot a second arrow. She hated to feel glad someone was dead, but knowing Edvin had given him two death blows gave her a twisted feeling of relief.

She didn't want to think about her role in ending the other two men's lives.

"Thank you, Arman. For staying with us. If you hadn't been there, Edvin would be...and I'd be..." She couldn't bring herself to finish either thought.

Arman looked at her and smiled. "That's what Edvin said." He shrugged. "I did what I could."

It was a simple response, but she didn't mistake the pride in his words. She smiled back at him.

Edvin stirred and opened his eyes. When he looked down and found Ayra awake, he quickly pulled his arm from around her and sat up straight. She nearly fell over when her support pulled away so suddenly.

"You're awake," he said with a hoarse voice. "I...or you...are you all right? Do you hurt anywhere?"

Ayra *felt* her body and stretched her arms. "My arms hurt a little. And my head hurts quite a lot. But I think I'm fine. You?"

He relaxed his shoulders and bobbed his head. "Fine. I'm fine." He looked back at her. "That thing you did—with the river—was pretty wild. You saved me."

Ayra smiled and felt a glow spread from her chest to her face. She pulled his tunic from around her shoulders to hand it back to him. He insisted she keep it until she was sure she was warm. She felt mostly warm and dry aside from some dampness in her skirts but wrapped his tunic back around herself again anyway.

Edvin and Arman worked out their course again, this time deciding to avoid all roads and all villages. Edvin cursed himself for making those careless mistakes and promised to be more cautious.

As they hiked through the trees and down short slopes, Edvin frequently stopped to listen to their surroundings. With only his bow slung across his shoulder, Ayra felt a piece of him was missing. Without their supplies and tools, she felt a creeping sense of vulnerability. The way Edvin's shoulders stayed tensed, she knew he felt it, too.

When the sun dipped low in the sky, they searched for a sheltered place to sleep. Ayra wished for some of the rocks that littered Mihtengard. The stony guards felt more protective than soft, rotted trees and bushes. Arman found a fallen tree that was partially hollowed enough for the three of them to tuck into. At least it would hide them from one side.

They agreed a fire would be too risky, so to keep warm, they huddled inside the wooden cave with Ayra in the middle. Arman was the first to fall asleep. His snores worsened when his head fell forward, so Ayra periodically had to push his head back. It would have been funny if they were not trying to go through the night undetected. She hugged her legs to her chest and looked out into the darkening forest. Without a fire, the night was not as welcome to her. Her body felt tired, but her mind continued to work through the events of the morning. Edvin had been quiet all day, and she guessed he had been trying to do the same.

She looked sideways at him to see if he was asleep yet. He sat with his long legs stretched out, his arms folded across his chest, and his head tipped back against the crumbly, decomposing wood. His eyes were closed but his breathing was shallow, unlike the deep breaths of sleep.

"What are you thinking?" she asked just above a whisper.

"That this was a terrible idea," he replied without opening his eyes.

She knew what he meant, but she wanted to see him smile. "I don't think it's so bad. It's a little cramped, but we would be cold if we weren't packed in. And I kind of like the smell of dead wood mingled with skunk and sweaty boys."

He didn't move, but his mouth twitched into a crooked smile. "For the last time, I am not a boy. And I'm glad to hear you have developed an appreciation for the fine musk."

She nudged her shoulder into his. "We're doing all right, aren't we? In a few days we'll find my brother. And then we can figure everything else out."

They both were quiet for a time. Darkness had completely overtaken the forest. The creatures of the night began to stir, and there was no crackling fire to cover all the mysterious sounds. Ayra tried to focus her thoughts on Kelton. She missed his face and rolling her eyes at his antics. She thought of the times he had helped her dig in her pit because she was so far behind. She missed him more than she ever thought she would.

"I've never killed a man before," Edvin said suddenly. Ayra snapped her attention to him. "I've trained to be a soldier for much of my life. And have hunted for even more of it. An animal's life has value, too, and I'm never reckless in my hunting. But it's not the same. A man versus an animal."

"Edvin, you had no other choice. He would have killed you *and* Arman."

"I know." He opened his eyes and raised his head. "I know. I'm just surprised it's not the same. And that it's bothering me. My father trains all his soldiers to take a life only when necessary.

When that life is a threat to what is right. It was necessary. So I guess my father would approve my decision."

"I think he will be proud of a lot of your decisions."

"Maybe." He fiddled with the leather strap around his wrist. "This leather is a scrap from when his saddle was made. I wear it to remind myself to always do him honor. I'm glad I won't be around when he's told what I've done." He folded his arms and laid his head back again.

Ayra hugged his tunic tighter around her shoulders and leaned back. She wanted to say something that would prove he was doing good things. "Thank you for protecting me."

A small, cynical laugh came from his throat. "Protecting you? Look where I've brought you. No, I'm no protector."

That had not worked as she had hoped. There was nothing she could say to refute his words. They were heading closer to the coast. Closer to danger. Closer to Covalt. If they were lucky, they would intercept the company miles away from the sea. But they were quickly losing time.

She could not think of anything else to say that might make him feel differently. His body looked relaxed, but his face was taut. His jaw flexed off and on. Arman's snoring grew louder, and she pushed his head back for the umpteenth time. A wolf howled far in the distance sending a chill down Ayra's back.

She remembered how comfortable she had felt that morning. Safe even. Hesitantly, she laid her head on Edvin's shoulder. He kept his arms folded and his head back, but gradually his breathing deepened and slowed.

She relaxed into him a little more and aligned her breaths with his, and in the morning could not remember exactly when she had fallen asleep.

19

AYRA cupped her hand and scooped up the cold spring water. It was fortunate Tiseden was such a wet land since they no longer had water pouches. She sipped slowly, hoping it would feel more satisfying that way. Her stomach growled, but there was nothing to offer it but water. Last night's meal had been light with only a handful of mushrooms each.

The last five days had passed as quietly as their footsteps on the soft earth—speaking little as they walked through the daylight hours and huddled together through fireless nights. The forest itself was quiet but as a result of the attack the other day, Ayra no longer trusted the quiet. The sensation she was being pursued by a predator was now a very real thing in her mind.

Edvin estimated they should come upon the company soon, but he told them honestly he was not certain where they were or which road the other group would be traveling. He kept their path pointed north, northeast, following the veins of main roads, and said they should come out where they needed to.

The quiet travel left Ayra largely to her thoughts—menacing men who attacked her family and her friends, a defenseless brother somewhere without her, a friend who had lost his home because of her, the need for counsel from a grandmother who no longer walked the soil. She swiped at water and pulled dew from tree branches to distract herself, but nothing worked for long.

"Here," Arman said, offering his hand as Ayra readied to hop down off a log.

"Thanks." She felt a tug as her skirt caught on a branch and yanked to pull it free. "What I wouldn't give to have trousers."

Arman laughed. "I'd offer to trade, but I don't think your dress would fit me."

She smiled. Arman had held onto his genial ways as they cleared their own path through the forest. A few times she had sensed an underlying feeling of strained effort in his actions, though. She could see in his eyes he didn't always feel the smiles he gave. But he pressed on with them, never complaining.

They were quiet again. The drill of a woodpecker echoed through the damp. Ayra watched Edvin as he walked ahead of them. His shoulders seemed broader without the tunic she now wore, and even though his posture looked rigid, there was still an easiness in the way he moved. Each step was sure, every leap over a fallen tree effortless. She liked the way he frequently glanced back, as if making sure she was still behind him. She knew he was listening constantly, focused on moving forward while keeping their distance from villages and people.

The number of roads and groups of travelers were increasing. He felt this was a good indication they were on the right track. Tiseden Crown City was near.

It hadn't occurred to Ayra before, but with the number of people they had avoided, she had begun to wonder how Prince Gibsen planned to move through the country. Surely citizens would notice the royal company on their roads. It would be difficult to get to Covalt without anyone asking questions. If that really was where he was heading. Edvin had just shrugged when she had asked him what he thought.

"It's strange for me," Arman said suddenly without prompting. "Being back in this forest. It doesn't feel like I ever belonged anywhere but in Mihtengard, but at the same time, it feels familiar. I don't have any memories of Prashura, but I've been wondering if it would feel familiar, too. Maybe we never leave a place all the way behind."

Ayra thought of the quarry. The color of the rock. The pounding of the mallets. She could still see and hear everything in her mind. She never thought she'd miss the smell of cooking cabbage, but she was hungry enough, if she could just catch a whiff, she might be satisfied.

"Almost all my memories are in Darkwater. Everywhere feels unfamiliar to me."

Arman pulled a branch out of her way.

"Where are you going to go after you get Kelton?"

Ayra shrugged. It was a question she had asked herself many times. The plan she had worked out in her head to rescue Kelton was a weak one, she knew, but she ran through it over and over anyway. When they found the company, she would slip in—unnoticed of course—while Edvin and Arman waited in the trees. She would tell him to come with her, which he would. Then the four of them would get as far away from everyone as they could. Arman would go back to Wil, and she, Kelton, and Edvin would…that's where the plan halted.

What would they do then? Every scenario ended with them hiding. But she did not want to be on the run for all of her days. And as beautiful as the forests of Tiseden were, she missed the warm woods of Mihtengard. The white barked trees and the smell of brush. Deep down she knew she was a stranger here and would be a stranger in any country but her own.

"Ayra," Arman said hesitantly. "I've been thinking about what you asked yesterday. How the prince is going to move through the country unnoticed? It does seem like a squirrelly thing to try. Maybe you really do have a relative here."

She looked ahead at Edvin, noticing an almost imperceptible change in his posture. She shifted the orange tunic that draped over her shoulders. "My family is from Mihtengard." Even as she said the words, she knew that didn't really matter. Families could spread. In a flash of memory, she again saw a man with a pack walking away.

Arman nodded and looked into the forest.

Within a few minutes Edvin stopped and waited for them to catch up. "I don't know about you two, but yesterday's mushrooms aren't going to hold me over until tomorrow. I can hear something, maybe a homestead off this way. Chickens. A dog. Should we try for it?"

"You mean steal?" Ayra asked.

"Yes, the whole cellar. Do you think you can run with a ham in your skirts? Arman how much can you carry?"

"Well, I—"

Ayra caught the gleam in Edvin's eyes. "He's joking, Arman. If you aren't saying we steal, how do you plan to get anything without being seen?"

"Honestly every idea escapes me but one. And I'm starving. We're just going to have to risk it. Arman? I think you're going to have to go in for us."

"I don't have any more money."

"I know. How good are you at sweet talking?"

Arman was silent.

"Begging then?"

"About as good as last month's milk."

"Let me see your begging face."

Arman tried to alter his expression, but whatever face he was trying to pull was ruined by his lurking smile.

Edvin rolled his tongue over his teeth. "Sure. Good enough. I could give you a good punch to the lip and you can claim you've been robbed."

"Edvin!" Ayra exclaimed near a laugh.

As they neared the homestead, Ayra could hear the pounding of an ax, the hits strong and clean. "I don't know about this," she whispered. "What if—?"

Edvin shook his head. "You and me, they've got thorough descriptions of. I doubt they looked at Arman long enough to do the same, if they survived."

Their eyes met. They hadn't talked about the attack for days. Neither of them wanted to think about it.

"I'll be fine," Arman said. "I'm not afraid. Tisedenians are known for their hospitality."

They crept toward the home and soon it was in full view. A large man was outside chopping wood as smoke drifted from the chimney. Chickens pecked at the ground and a dog sat on the porch. It appeared just as Edvin had said.

"I'll be quicker than a rabbit through a fox den," Arman said with a wink before he trotted off toward the home.

Ayra peeked over their blind just as Arman entered the clearing. The man swung his ax up onto his shoulder.

"What are they saying?"

"Sh." Edvin tilted his head.

Ayra watched as the man shifted his weight. He looked into the forest with a searching eye but not directly at them. He shook his head and turned his grip on the ax. Arman had his arms crossed over his chest and his back to them. Ayra couldn't see whether his face was happy or nervous or what. She watched Edvin's expression, hoping to get a better idea how the conversation was going. The man turned for the house and Arman followed. Before he went through the door, he gave a little wave to his friends.

Edvin sat back. "I'm surprised that worked. He told him that he was just passing through, said something about the breed of the man's chickens, then asked if he could have a meal. And now he's in the house."

"You're just annoyed you're not the only one who can talk his way into what he wants."

Edvin grinned. "I hope he's good enough to walk out that door with a roasted chicken filled with gravy for each of us."

They waited for a good amount of time before Arman reappeared, a bundle under his arm. He jauntily returned to the hiding place, and the three of them moved some distance away from the homestead before Edvin couldn't wait any longer and Arman untied his bundle of bread, cheese, salt fish, and apples. Arman had eaten while in the house, so the spoils were for Edvin and Ayra to split.

The picnic wasn't large but did much to restore the spirits of all three of them. With a full stomach Ayra felt hope budding again that their quest would soon be over and they could begin figuring out the next step.

Hours after they resumed their journey, a small, sloping meadow opened before them. The afternoon was warm, and the clouds had cleared aside from a few traveling billows. Moss-like plants with tiny white flowers blanketed the ground.

Ayra stopped and bounced her heels on the soft, spongy rug. It looked like an inviting place to rest. She had voiced only the first few words of her idea when Edvin froze and lifted his hand to quiet her. He tilted his head.

"I think I hear them!" he said, surprise ringing in his tone. "This way, we need to get closer."

He pushed their direction east and picked up his pace. Ayra felt like she was crashing through the forest trying to keep up. She stumbled over logs and recklessly slipped down small slopes.

He stopped and listened again. "Yes, I'm quite certain now. I recognize the sound of the horse reigns and some of the voices. I can't believe we found them!"

"What do we do now?" asked Arman, huffing from the quicker pace.

Edvin looked at Ayra even though Arman had asked the question. "We'll have better luck getting Kelton at night. We'll follow them—they're maybe a couple miles away, I think—until they camp for the night. Hopefully that's before they reach the coast. I guess we need to make a plan."

Ayra was stunned. He didn't have a plan thought out. He really hadn't thought they would find the company. But he had seemed so sure.

They followed the company from a mile or so away until the sun was well past its afternoon placement. When the company stopped to set up camp, they moved in a little closer and sat down to rest and formulate a plan.

Edvin leaned back on his hands. "I think the easiest way to go about this is you two stay here and I'll go get Kelton."

"That's not going to work," Ayra scoffed. "The last time my

brother saw you, you had a knife to my throat." Arman's head snapped toward Edvin, his eyes wide. Ayra's mouth twitched, but she went on without explaining. "He may only be fourteen, but he is *not* stupid. He won't go with you. He'll resist like he did before, and you'll be caught. Then Arman and I will be out here without you…and then we'll all be in trouble."

Arman's shoulders slumped. Ayra felt a small stab of guilt for his hurt feelings, especially since he had just procured a good meal for them, but knew her words were true.

"Well, what do you propose then?" Edvin asked.

Ayra looked him in the eye. "You and Arman will stay here, and *I* will go get my brother. He will come with me. Quietly. I'm certain."

"No," Edvin said as he sat forward. "Nope, that's a bad plan. I don't like that one."

"Why?"

"Because if *you* get caught, then this will all be for naught. And who knows what will happen to you. I'm running a big risk bringing you here in the first place."

He had a point. And her water talent was nowhere near advanced. Covalt might not let her live. Or he would keep her until she was useful. She couldn't decide which would be worse.

She thought about the company and wondered if the men knew they were in danger. She wondered again how they had moved through Tiseden. It didn't make sense to think they could stealthily move through a well-populated area. Or that they would be so near Tiseden Crown City.

"Why are they on the road to the city if Covalt is out on an island somewhere at sea? Wouldn't they need to sneak around? I'm starting to wonder if Prince Gibsen really isn't heading to Covalt. Edvin, maybe you heard wrong. Or misunderstood something."

His jaw flexed. "After all the trouble I've taken for you," he said coolly, "you still doubt me?"

Arman shifted uncomfortably and looked around at nothing in particular.

Ayra looked down at her hands. "I just know it will be best if I go get Kelton alone. I'm going and you're staying. You can argue all you want, but I won't stay here. If I get caught…then you'll just have to come get me."

She hoped he would laugh or at least smile, but he didn't. He laid back on the ground with one arm draped over his face. Either he knew she would do as she said or he knew she was right. One person sneaking into a camp of soldiers would be hard enough, but two would be a disaster. She would rescue her brother alone.

20

THE evening dragged itself into night, and the shy moon showed only half its face in the cloudy sky.

Edvin had spent his time listening to the conversations of the men to see if he could pick up any useful information. It was difficult for him to hear a whole conversation at a time with so much chatter. He heard Kelton a few times, and Ayra breathed a sigh of relief when Edvin told her he sounded fine.

He also pieced together that there had been an accident a few days ago with a couple of the horses and the wagon. Three men, including Tress, had been injured. Unable to travel, the injured men and four others were left in a little camp along the roadside to supposedly be picked up on the way back.

Prince Gibsen's camp grew quiet a couple hours after dark, and they waited a few more hours to make sure the soldiers were settled. Edvin tried for the fifth time to convince Ayra he should go, but she stood firm. Her plan would be best.

As she readied herself, she looked into the thick forest, each tall tree resembling its neighbor. It had looked more friendly some hours before. A knot formed in her gut, and she realized she might not be able to keep her direction in the dark. When she voiced her fear, Edvin readily offered to walk her to the camp, and she consented, feeling the knot partially untwist. After an awkward half-hug from Arman, Ayra stepped into the mess of trees with Edvin.

They walked noiselessly side by side, stopping periodically for Edvin to listen to the camp. Before she knew it, Ayra could see the foreign outlines of canvas tents. They crept up to the tree line about ten paces from the back of the camp. Edvin narrowed Kelton's tent down to three possibilities.

"Does your brother snore?" he whispered. Ayra shook her head. He pointed to the one in the middle. "I think that one. It's the quietest. And I'm pretty sure he's alone." He listened again and craned his neck to get a good look. "There are two night guards. They are supposed to be on either side and moving periodically. Lucky for you, it's Ox and Hadar. They aren't much for protocol and are both on the road side playing Pegs. I can't see or hear anyone else awake. I'll be here waiting for you." He looked like he was going to say more. Ayra hesitated, waiting, before he simply added, "Hurry."

She nodded, took one step before slipping off his tunic to give back to him, then forced her legs to move the rest of herself out into the clearing, keeping her head and shoulders low. When she reached the tent, she peered around the corner.

The little city of tents was tightly packed, most likely for safety. But it actually made her feel like she had cover and could move more freely. She couldn't see anyone, so she proceeded between two tents, keeping close to the wall of the middle one. She peeked around the second corner and upon finding it clear, sucked in a breath and slipped in through the tent opening.

Inside the tent was pitch black. She couldn't see cots, bodies, or anything. She stood lamely at the opening, looking at the darkness, unsure what to do.

After a few minutes she decided to pull the flap back to let in whatever moonlight would enter. She breathed a sigh of relief when the silvery light allowed her to make out a single cot with a small figure stretched out on it. She moved closer and knelt beside the little bed. She stared at the face of the brother she loved so much. It had only been weeks since she last saw him, but he looked older somehow.

"Kelton," she whispered. He didn't even stir. She poked him in the shoulder. "Kelton, wake up." He rolled onto his back and blinked his eyes. "Wake up. It's me."

His head jerked in her direction. "Ayra! You're alive!" he whispered loudly.

She hushed him and smiled. "Yes, obviously. You have to come with me. I don't have time to explain. Get your boots on."

"What? Why? Where are we going?" he asked more quietly.

"Edvin is waiting for us. He's—"

"Edvin? Ayra, you're still with Edvin? Where is he? We have to tell Prince Gibsen—"

"No, Kelton listen to me. Edvin is good. He's my friend. Prince Gibsen lied to us. Come on, I don't have time to explain it all now."

"No. Listen to *me*. We have three soldiers from Tiseden accompanying us to Crown City. We're going where Prince Gibsen said. But Edvin. Edvin comes from a family of traitors, Ayra. Prince Gibsen, the other soldiers. They all said so. We searched after he took you. I'm sorry we didn't find you. I'm so glad to know you're not dead. Rooney said Edvin probably took you hoping to get the money from our relative. You know, for a ransom."

"What?" She paused for just a moment. "But he said…"

"Rooney said Edvin's father was certainly in on the plot. They sent Ox back to Midivard to alert the king. He caught up with us again and said the king sent scouts to continue searching in both countries. He—"

Kelton immediately hushed when the flap of the tent pulled back further, and Edvin stepped in. Ayra froze, and Kelton shot up on his cot. She put her hand on Kelton's leg hoping to keep him calm while she sorted everything out. She could only see half of Edvin's face, but she recognized the angry glint in his eye and tight jaw. He had been listening.

He stepped toward her with his hand held out and whispered, "Ayra, we have to go. Now." Anger mixed with foreign panic laced his words.

"No, wait. I know you heard. Is it true?"

He quickly glanced over his shoulder as he moved closer and grabbed her by the arm. "Someone's coming. Come on."

She felt heat flare up in her chest that he wouldn't just answer her. "Edvin?"

He tensed but before he could speak, Kelton let out a shout. "In here! Edvin! He's in here!"

Edvin released her arm and bolted out of the tent. Like a wasp nest thrown to the ground, the sleepy camp erupted with shouts, clanging metal, and whipping fabric.

"Here! We have him!" one of the men yelled.

Ayra couldn't move. *What just happened?* Edvin was from a family of traitors, Kelton had said. And Edvin didn't deny it. If it wasn't true, he would have said something. But his father was a commander in the army. Or so he had said. And he was angry. She remembered the time she saw a camp worker try to return home with gold tucked in his shoes. When the guards confronted him, he cursed and swung at them. A guilty person is angry when caught, Tanna had said.

Kelton grabbed her hand. "Come on." He led her out of the tent to the huddle of soldiers near the tree line. Two men had Edvin pinned to the ground on his stomach, his mouth already gagged with a rope.

"Ayra!" Prince Gibsen came up from behind. He took her by the hand and looked her over. "I'm so relieved to see you. Are you all right? Did he hurt you?"

She looked at Edvin and felt a sharp twist of her stomach

when he lifted his head to look at her. "No! No. He didn't hurt me. I…"

"Get him to his feet," ordered Rooney.

Edvin's eyes held Ayra's gaze as the men tied his hands and lifted their knees off his back. He jerked his shoulders as they pulled him up, fighting their grip. Kelton stepped protectively in front of Ayra. She still felt like she couldn't breathe. She reached forward and grabbed her brother's hand again.

"You are a filthy traitor and a deserter just like your grandfather." Rooney exclaimed as he stepped closer to Edvin. "King Leofric was a fool to trust your family again!" He put his face near Edvin's. "You should never have been assigned to this company. You have betrayed our prince, our noble king, and all who are present. And what of the girl? What torments and confusions you have put her through." He signaled his hand to one of the men holding Edvin. "Traitors deserve execution."

Ayra's heart jumped as the soldier drew a knife from his belt and raised it toward Edvin's throat. She didn't want to watch but couldn't look away. Edvin closed his eyes. There was no fear in his face. Only shame.

"Wait!" shouted Prince Gibsen. "Rooney, you forget your place here. Traitors deserve trial before execution. There will be no Mihtengardian blood spilt on Tiseden soil. We will have two men escort him to Midivard in the morning."

"Forgive me your highness, but we are already low in numbers. Would not it be…"

"I *said* he will be escorted to Midivard in the morning. I will not have his blood on my head, though it surely will be spilt. Just not here."

"Very well," Rooney said with a bow. He turned to the two men flanking Edvin. "Erik and Ox. You will take him in the morning as the prince has commanded. Tie him well—make no mistakes—and put him in your tent."

The two men pushed Edvin toward the camp. He jerked out of their grip and walked on his own in the appointed direction. Ayra looked at the ground as they passed. The crowd began to disperse, mutterings of accusation and surprise drifting to her ears. Her feet felt like rocks pressed into the ground.

With some prodding, Kelton took her back to his tent and gave her his cot. A soldier brought them extra blankets, and Kelton made a bed for himself on the ground. He asked about the past few weeks—where she had been and what she had been told—but after receiving only short replies, he got the hint and fell quiet.

It felt strange to be under the shelter of a tent. She could not see the stars or clouds or treetops. She was where she was supposed to be but felt lost. *There is a darkness that follows those we least expect.* She wondered how she could have been so blind. Edvin had been so easy to trust. She had believed every word he said. She understood now why he had been irritable. Why he hadn't wanted to bring her here. Why he wanted her to stay back with Arman.

She shot up on the cot. *Arman.* He was still out there. He was waiting for them to come back. She threw her legs over the side.

"Ayra, what are you doing?" Kelton asked.

"My friend. He's out there in the forest waiting for us to come back. I have to go get him."

"Are you joking? They aren't going to let you go into the forest in the dark. *I'm* not going to let you go into the forest in the dark. Your friend will be fine until morning."

"No, I have to go get him and tell him what's happened." She was glad she hadn't even taken off her boots and hurried to the tent flap. An arm crossed her path and blocked her from stepping out into the open.

"Where are you going, miss?" A soldier whose face she recognized but name she could not remember stood guard at the tent door. "I have orders not to allow you to leave this tent."

"I...I have...I need to use the privy, please."

The man shook his head. "Sorry miss. You are not to leave this tent. For any reason. Orders are orders. And I follow mine."

Her shoulders slumped, and she returned to her cot.

For the second time in his life, Arman had been left to wait in vain for someone to come get him. He probably would realize something had gone wrong and begin making his way home before light.

In less time than it took her to skin a hare, she had lost both of her friends. One through no fault of his own, and the other had never actually existed.

21

LIGHT flooded into the canvas tent when Ayra opened her eyes. She sat up and glanced around. Kelton was not in his bed. *It must be late morning,* she thought.

The night hours had been long, and she had tossed and turned. She felt she would still be awake when the sun came up, but now that time had passed. She needed to sort everything out—where they were going, who they would see, and everything that had to do with Edvin. She had not wanted to speak to him last night but needed to now. She needed answers.

She ran her fingers through her hair and adjusted her extra dress layer. She looked down at the torn and muddied skirt. She had been sleeping under trees and stomping through the mud for weeks. Though she washed her hands and face in creeks every day, she was neither tidy nor groomed.

Hesitating only seconds, she decided she did not care if she looked bedraggled and walked through the open tent flap.

On the far side of camp she noticed a tent different than the others. It was dark green instead of brown and round instead of rectangular. The Tisedenian soldiers' tent. So the company did have an escort.

On the other side of camp she could see Arty cleaning up from the morning meal. A few other men were beginning to pack up tents. The tent she thought Edvin had been taken to was already down. She spotted Kelton helping take down Prince Gibsen's tent. She made her way to him, trying to avoid eye contact with the other men.

Kelton looked up and moved to meet her. He gave her a hug. "Didn't do that last night. I'm so relieved you're here, Ayra. I've been so worried. Are you truly all right?"

She did not feel all right. Not right at all. Her head throbbed between her eyes, her back felt stiff, and her stomach felt heavy and sickish. "Yes, I'm fine," she said, forcing a quick smile. "I'm relieved to be with you again, too. I bet I've worried about you more than you worried about me."

"I doubt that. I thought you were dead."

She smiled weakly again and gave him another hug. She had so much to tell him but now was not the right time. She glanced around the camp again. "Where's Edvin? I need to talk to him."

"Edvin?" Kelton looked at her with his eyebrows pinched together. "Not sure why you would want to talk to him. But you can't anyway. They already took him. On his way back to

Mihtengard to get what he deserves."

Ayra looked around again, hoping Kelton was mistaken. "He's gone? Are you sure?"

"Yeah, I'm sure. They left early this morning just when it became light. I was up," he proudly added. He had picked up some of the soldiers' habits, evidently.

Ayra put her hands up to her face and pressed on her closed eyes. She couldn't think straight with her head pounding so hard. She dropped her hands and looked around at the soldiers again. "Come here."

She grabbed Kelton's hand just like she used to when they were children and dragged him to the back of the camp near the tree line. When she was certain they were out of earshot she took him by the shoulders.

"What did the other men say about Edvin's family? How are they traitors? I need you to tell me everything you can remember."

He shrugged. "No one really told me exactly what happened. But his grandfather was accused of treachery against the king. He disappeared before he could face trial. Why?"

"His grandfather. Has anyone told you about his father?"

"Oh yeah, they talk about him. Vanfir or Vanper…"

"Vansar?"

"Yeah, that's it. Vansar. He—you're hurting me, Ayra."

She dropped her hands and nodded for him to continue.

He gave her an odd look and rolled his shoulders once before continuing. "He's lead commander of the army. Or I should say was. Probably won't be anymore. Most of the men seemed pretty surprised he would be involved. And that Edvin would do something so risky. Some were pretty upset for a while."

All night Ayra had doubted everything Edvin had ever told her. Her stomach relaxed a little now that she knew at least not everything was a lie. She ached to talk to him, to sort everything out. "Kelton, I don't know what to think about everything. Edvin thinks we are in danger—or at least that's what he said—and...other stuff." She glanced around and lowered her voice to a soft whisper. "Have you heard anyone mention the name Covalt?"

Kelton looked up and poked out his bottom lip. "No. I've never heard—wait, yes I have. Covalt. Yeah, the other night by the fire Rim said, 'I'm glad Covalt is dead or else I'd hate this forest.' Or something like that. No one said anything so I didn't ask. Who is it?"

"Dead," she whispered to herself. Covalt was dead. Her heart should have leaped for joy—there was no Covalt, no danger. But it sank. "Never mind." Ayra looked at the camp again. Each man looked preoccupied with his task. The tents were nearly packed. "Come with me. We need to go find my friend, Arman."

He folded his arms and dug in his heels. "No. Rooney told me this morning you and I are not to go wandering."

Ayra could see in eyes he wasn't going to budge, and she didn't have time to argue anyway. "Fine. I'll go myself. I'll be right back."

He protested, but she turned and walked into the forest. She had only just passed the tree line when she heard Gibsen call her name. The idea to run swept into her head, but she turned around to face him instead.

He jogged up next to Kelton. "Ayra. Where are you going?"

"I left a friend in the forest. He might still be waiting for me. I'm going to go find him."

She saw a flicker of something in his eyes. Concern? Or something else? "I am sorry, but I cannot let you go. You must stay here...we are nearly ready to leave. Come now."

Kelton turned with Gibsen toward camp. Without a word Ayra spun around toward the forest and broke into a run. As if fleeing from the wolves again, she weaved past rocks and trees and skipped down short drops in the forest floor. She could hear movement and calls from behind but didn't slow her pace.

Just ahead, a large, felled tree stretched across her path. There wasn't enough time to go around, so she prepared herself to jump it. A few paces away, she leaped, but before she cleared it, the front of her skirt caught on a thick, crooked branch. Her body lurched forward and landed hard on the moist earth. Kelton and Gibsen stood over her, puffing.

"Ayra, what is wrong with you?!" shouted her brother between breaths. "Why would you—"

Gibsen pushed Kelton aside and held out his hand. "You cannot leave the company again. I will not allow it."

She opened her mouth to protest, but something in the prince's expression made her close it again.

She looked at his extended hand and felt the urge to bite it. Catching a glimpse of Kelton's pleading face, she held back her teeth and instead batted away Gibsen's hand and got to her feet on her own. With one glance back into the forest she turned and limped back to camp with them.

"I am sorry to have been careless with your safety," said Gibsen. "I try to trust all my men. My father and his council hand select my company for every journey I take. Some individuals are just very deceptive. I am deeply sorry for any stress that has been thrust upon you."

Ayra nodded but said nothing. She couldn't make up her mind who was being deceptive. She found it was not as easy to talk to the prince as it had been in the beginning. She had not noticed before how stilted his manners were.

When the last tent was packed onto the wagon, the remaining men of the company mounted their horses. Kelton slipped up onto his as if he had done it all his life. She had not thought about riding a horse again. It seemed more appealing to just go on foot. She slipped off the stirrup once before she was able to put her foot in securely and pull herself onto the mare's back.

The Tisedenian soldiers rode at the head of the group with Prince Gibsen and Rooney directly behind them. Their tunics were a deep forest green, and they wore feathered brass helmets, just as Arman had mentioned when he told his story. She hoped her kind friend's feelings were not injured, and he would find his way back to Wil's safely.

But foremost on her mind was Edvin.

She couldn't stop wondering where he was every other minute. Though he had lied and tried to use her, she couldn't bring herself to wish him harm. It was possible she would be a citizen of Tiseden soon and might never know Edvin's fate. His carefree, brown-eyed face flashed before her. She quickly banished it but not before she felt a stab in her heart. Deep inside everything felt wrong.

As they rode forward, Ayra battled the urge to turn her horse and run the other way. *Covalt is dead. Everything is fine,* she repeated to herself over and over.

Hours passed as the company trotted onward to its destination. She heard one of the men behind her say they should reach Crown City soon. The tingling in her fingers intensified as they progressed, and she clenched and unclenched her fists to try to dispel some of the discomfort. She gazed up at the sky full of dark clouds. It had not rained this morning, but it appeared it would do so soon.

From the distance, a unique sound flowed into Ayra's ears. It reminded her of rapids on a river, but instead of constant, it was rhythmic, rising and hushing. A chilled wind picked up her hair and whipped her skirts against her mare. She breathed in and recognized the fishy smell of a lake.

She shifted in her saddle. "Crown City isn't on the sea, is it?" she asked the young soldier behind her. She thought his name was Rim.

"No, it's south of the sea. A couple hours ride, but that's just a guess from the map I remember."

She turned to face forward again. One of the Tisedenian soldiers looked over his shoulder at her but said nothing. No one around her seemed concerned, but she felt it again. Deep in her gut something was not right. Rain began to fall from above, but instead of sprinkling the promise of life, it seemed to drip with dread. A shiver slipped up her spine.

The trees thinned as they rode up a stiff hill. She watched the soldiers of Tiseden ride up and over the slope. When Prince Gibsen and Rooney reached the top, the prince's white horse halted. He glanced around and pulled his horse back. Rooney reached over and snatched the reigns from the prince's hands. The horse balked but quickly relented and followed the other horse, disappearing over the hill.

Ayra and Kelton exchanged puzzled looks. A soldier rode up next to him from behind. She turned to her left to see another one beside her. He smiled reassuringly, but his expression looked strained.

When they reached the top of the hill, there were no buildings or streets for her eyes to take in. Only the sea laid out before them, a cold and unwelcoming blue under gray sky. Waves smashed into cliffs to the east and rolled onto the sandy beach where six men stood waiting, a large rowboat behind them. Out on the horizon, a lone island rose out of the sea like a scar across the water.

"Kelton! Run!" Ayra screamed.

She tried to turn her horse, but the soldier to her side blocked her attempt. He grabbed her reigns and pulled her horse along down the hill. Kelton remained next to her, mute and anxiously looking out at the open waters.

When the group reached the men, Prince Gibsen was shouting angrily at Rooney. Rooney stared at the prince as if he were watching a small child throw a tantrum on the floor. With an air of superiority, he motioned his hand, and two of the men seized Gibsen.

Rim slid off his horse and drew his sword, pointing it at the men holding the prince captive. "In the name of King Leofric, release him!"

Another soldier dismounted and drew his sword as well, his eyes franticly shifting from face to face. A third Mihtengardian alighted, drew his sword, and in one swift motion, pushed it into Rim's back. When he withdrew it, Rim dropped to the ground. The other soldier who had been ready to defend the prince glanced around to see unarmed Arty seated on the wagon with his hands up and no other loyal face among his comrades. He dropped his sword and raised his hands.

The men proceeded to tie the prince's hands behind his back. He shouted a few names, but no one came to his defense.

The Tiseden guards slid off their horses. From their smiles and familiar greeting to the six men on the beach, Ayra knew they were going to be no help.

As the men conversed, Ayra looked at Kelton again. He sat as if in a trance. They were surrounded and far outnumbered. She looked at the water and remembered the burning in her fingers. She put out her hands and concentrated on the water, pushing the waves sideways. The water sloshed against the side of the boat. She pushed again and again, inching the boat the rest of the way into the water. One of the men turned to see the boat drifting away from the beach.

"What under the stars?!" he exclaimed.

"The girl! Grab the girl!" Rooney shouted.

Ayra's concentration broke, and she felt the mounted soldier next to her grasp at her waist. She scrambled out of her saddle, but just as her feet hit the ground, a body slammed into her, knocking her onto the wet, hard-packed sand. She writhed and clawed and tried to pull out from under him, but he held her firm. A damp rag covered her mouth and nose. A bitter taste filled her mouth. She jerked again to get free but felt her limbs go limp and watched the beach grow dark.

22

OUT of the darkness, voices drifted into Ayra's ears. She tried to make out words, but the sounds only garbled and sloshed in her head. A moan escaped before she gave her throat permission to release it. The voices stopped. She could hear the measured sound of the sea somewhere nearby.

When the voices picked up again, she sensed harshness in one of them. Slowly, her eyelids lifted and allowed the dim light of the room in.

Four forms stood before her, but she couldn't make her eyes focus on any of them. She tried to use her hand to rub the blurriness from her eyes, but her hand wouldn't come out from behind her back.

When she leaned forward to tug it free, her stomach retched, and the contents emptied onto the floor at her feet.

The heaving stopped, and she lifted herself back into an upright position. Most of the fog in her head seemed to have cleared. She was seated in a worn, purple-cushioned chair with low armrests, her hands bound behind her back. The walls and floor were made of a dark gray stone that diminished the late afternoon light filtering in through two windows.

Prince Gibsen was before her with his arms crossed, and his expression a boiling mixture of anger and fear. A thickset man she faintly recognized stood to his side. Opposite them, Rooney stood with another man, but one she had never seen before. He was shorter than Rooney and was neither bulky nor slight. His head and jaw showed no trace of stubble. His thin lips curved with amusement as she studied him.

"Welcome, Ayra of the House of Regnan," he said with a slight bow. His voice was low and refined. "I am delighted you are awake. I have awaited your acquaintance for some time."

Memories of the beach crashed into her mind like the waves against the rocks outside. A vile feeling of panic rose up in her chest, and she felt her breaths quicken. Though she had never before seen his face, she knew this man.

Covalt.

She searched the room for Kelton. "Where is my brother?" Her voice sounded foreign to her ears.

Covalt cocked his head to the side. "He is well. You need not worry about him…at the present. You have given us quite a little run, my dear. Cost me two of my good men." He glanced at the man next to Gibsen.

It was the man with the large scar from the river attack.

"But it was fortunate your brother was left behind. It made things a little simpler for me for you and your friend to predictably try to fetch him. Has the boy with the ears been disposed of?" he asked without looking away from her.

"Yes, my lord," Rooney said with a nod. "Two of my—your—men took him this morning. I'm certain all has been resolved by now."

Edvin. He had been right about everything. If she had left with him the night before he would still be safe. She shut her eyes and tried not to imagine him—unarmed, bound, and gagged—meeting a horrid fate.

"Rooney, this is not…my father will…this is not what we discussed," Gibsen stammered. He had attempted to make his tone authoritative, but it faded to near whimpers. He looked at Ayra. "I truly believed we were bringing you to a relative. The letter my father received. Rooney convinced me it would be well. That you would be safe, and I would receive…something to help Mihtengard in return."

Covalt chuckled and shook his head. "Oh, yes. I nearly forgot." He drew up a pouch tied around his waist, reached in, and produced a large, round safner. The same gem Ayra had seen in Wil's vision. "He would like his reward, Rooney. I think that is fair. The Azure Stone. For you, my prince," he said patronizingly and tossed the ball to Gibsen.

Gibsen startled as the stone bounced off his chest, and he fumbled to cup his hands around it. Cruel laughter filled the room. He looked at the other men, his face red and laden with confusion. Covalt turned his attention back to Ayra. His garish blue eyes shone with an awful glint like polished ice.

"Why do you laugh?" Gibsen demanded. "What is so amusing?" He examined the stone in his hands and looked questioningly at Ayra.

"Shall I let him in on the joke?" Covalt said to Ayra. "I think it best if I relate the whole of it, hm? Nearly two centuries ago, in a dungeon cell, Henride Regnan placed a safner ball in a pouch and charged a kitchen boy to take it far, far away while other prisoners looked on. He told the boy that it possessed *special* power and that it had brought great misery to his family. Now, this common boy knew more than Henride perceived, for he knew the Regnan family worked water and sky."

"So it is true. Whoever holds the stone can command the skies," Gibsen interjected, excitement ringing in his voice.

"Silence!" Covalt barked without removing his gaze from Ayra. Gibsen shrank at the command and tightened his jaw. Covalt straightened, clasped his hands behind his back, and in a cool tone admonished, "I have a distaste for interruption. The young man took the stone and fled to the southern countries to roam for the remainder of his life, seeking sages and seers to unlock the mysteries of the stone. He failed. His son brought the stone to Tiseden with the hope that an abundance of water would induce the stone to work. It failed to impress. When he was charged with several severe crimes, he presented the valuable safner piece and its unique history to the royal family in exchange for clemency. It was accepted and my ancestor named it the Azure Stone."

He paused and slowly glanced around the hushed room, pleased with his captive audience. "My favorite tale as a boy. The stone fascinated me, and I hoped to make it useful someday. Unlike the rest of my family, I believe in mystical powers. But like it had the kitchen boy, the stone's power eluded me. I have had much time to ponder this history in recent years. It occurred to me that perhaps what I really needed was a member of the Regnan family to teach me its secrets. So I sent a scout to Mihtengard to make friends for me and make friends for me he did." He glanced at Rooney, then turned to Gibsen. "Kings by birth rarely are well suited to reign, as you well know Prince Gibsen. You have felt the order of your birth an error on the side of destiny, have you not?"

Gibsen flinched and looked on the verge of speaking but held his tongue.

"Of course you have or you would not have taken such a risk as sneaking behind your father's back and smuggling his prisoners out of the country. All to prove your own heroism." Covalt turned back to Ayra. "Among other bits, Rooney discovered a small portion of your family was sent to the labor camp in case the stone was recovered and your people could be useful again. Mysteriously, Mihtengard never seemed to struggle without the water stone. But now I think I understand. It is a bit of a disappointment to learn the stone holds no significance, and I cannot, myself, gain any real ability. But I think we can make this situation work." He lowered his face to Ayra's, and his icy eyes shone with desire. "I will have power one way or another. And now, from what Rouden tells me of river witchcraft, I have my water Regnan. What a delight to find you are young."

"The deal is off!" Gibsen cut in, his eyes burning. The fire flickered when Covalt turned toward him, but he pressed on. "The deal was I get a gem that can bring water to my country. Not a worthless stone. You cannot keep us here! My father will come searching for me. You cannot form an army big enough to defeat Mihtengard's. You have no time and no chance."

Another round of laughter filled the room.

Covalt smirked at the young prince and held his arms out to his sides. "My army is already formed. And it will grow rapidly. It is not as difficult as one might suppose to collect a following. People just need the right motivation. For some, to be on the side of power is effective." He twitched his head in Rooney's direction. "Others the promise of wealth. For the rest, terror works very well." He glanced at Ayra.

Gibsen's thin composure snapped. He lunged at Covalt with a guttural cry and outstretched arms. In one solid, swift swing of his cudgel, Rouden clubbed the prince on the side of the head. He slumped to the ground, blood pooling onto the stone beneath his head.

Ayra felt numb. The cracking sound echoed in her ears. She leaned forward heaved again, her empty stomach attempting to squeeze out any stray bits. A cold hand covered her forehead and pushed her head back. She shuddered at his touch.

"You have made a mess on my floor. But there will be forgiveness. This will be much easier if we are friends. I could have escaped years ago, but I do not want to *escape*. I do not want to *run*. Can you imagine the power a man could obtain if he controlled the sea and sky? If he could topple every navy, wash away every army, and dry up entire countries? I can. I live it in my thoughts daily. I took quite a gamble to get you here, not positively knowing you could help me. But I have no regrets."

"I can't do what you think I can," she croaked. "I will be no use to you. Please, let us go."

He chuckled mirthlessly and crouched down in front of her, his face a handsbreadth from hers. "Your family is not only gifted with water. You, evidently, are also gifted with your tongues. Do not lie to me. I know you halted a river to save that boy. And I know with the right motivation, you will do much more." His mouth twisted into a thoughtful pose. "Your brother. He seems to be a frail child. I would wager those bones under his skin do not bend much before they break."

"If you touch him…"

His lips curled into a knowing grin. "I knew you would see things my way. And what about revenge on Mihtengard? Surely you have thought about it. The country that has abused your family." His grin widened as he studied her eyes. "Yes, I see it. But I think the boy locked in a cold cell three floors below us will serve as a motive…for now."

Ayra gathered the saliva in her mouth and spit in his face.

He flinched and wiped his face against his shoulder. She defiantly held his gaze as he slowly stood. For a moment neither moved, and Ayra felt her nerve weaken the longer she looked into his eyes. If he had reacted immediately the worst would already be over, but he stood motionless before her.

Dread filled her veins, and she knew it flowed into her eyes, despite efforts to keep it hidden. Without warning, the back of his hand struck her jaw and sent her out of the chair. She hit the cold stone floor before she even felt the pain in her face. Fear kept her pinned to the stone.

"You will obey, Ayra. You will see. I have a way with people." He motioned to her. "Take her to join her brother. Remind her just how precious he is."

Without a word, Rouden grabbed her by the shoulders and lifted her to her feet. He gave her a shove and followed her out of the room and down a crumbling, spiraled staircase. She tried to look straight ahead as he forced her to step over the bodies of two guards in green tunics, all the while wobbling without the use of her arms for balance.

A short passageway at the bottom revealed four doors. He opened the second one on the right, and as soon as she entered the room, two arms flew around her neck.

"Ayra!" Kelton cried out. "I thought you were dead again, and this time was worse than the first."

She laid her head on his thin shoulder only a moment before Rouden tore him from her. One thick hand gripped Kelton's shoulder as the other fisted hand slammed into his gut.

Kelton grunted and hunched forward.

"Stop! Stop!" Ayra screamed.

She kicked at the man's legs, but his elbow swung back and knocked her across her already bruised jaw. She stumbled backward and, without free arms to slow her fall, hit the stone hard. He released Kelton, who dropped to the ground clutching his gut.

"You would do well to respect the master," the man sneered as he left the room and shut the door with a clank of the lock.

Ayra squirmed to her brother's side. "Kelton?"

He didn't lift himself from the floor. She listened to his uneven breaths until they normalized. "What do they want from us? Where is Prince Gibsen? And the others?"

She pictured Gibsen lying in his own blood. Words rushed out like water over a cliff. "I can't do it! I can't do what he wants. He's going to..." Her body began to shake against the damp stone floor.

Kelton sat up and pulled her into a sitting position, keeping his arms wrapped tightly around her. He didn't speak, but Ayra could feel his fear.

With a prick against her heart, she remembered the comfort she had taken from Edvin's confidence. Even when he had doubted, he'd acted with confidence to help her feel unafraid.

Taking deep, steady breaths, she gathered herself again. She made Kelton look at her. "But I will figure it out. We'll get out of here. We're going to get out."

He nodded.

They sat side by side in silence for a long while. Ayra's wrists were beginning to burn from the rubbing of the rope, and her arms ached from being in an unnatural position for so long. She circled her thoughts around what kind of clever plan Edvin would come up with. Looking around the dim room, she noticed a small cut out in the stone above their heads that led to the world outside and provided the only source of light. The afternoon was fading and within hours the little cell would be dark. There was no way out for now.

They would have to sit and wait.

23

THE gilded glow of twilight seeped through the hole in their cell wall. With each passing minute Ayra's dread increased and her sham confidence waned. Her bound wrists throbbed, and her throat begged for something wet.

She had passed the first hour telling Kelton everything—her journey with Edvin, meeting Wil and Arman, the visions she was shown, and the newfound talent she possessed. Kelton listened intently to every detail. The cell had been silent since she finished her story.

Suddenly a faint scraping sound echoed in the still cell. Ayra sat up straight and looked around for the source. The sound grew louder and louder until a rectangle on the far wall wiggled and partially pushed out of formation. Kelton and Ayra's eyes met just as the stone fell to the ground.

"Anyone there?" a voice whispered through the new hole. Ayra recognized the voice immediately.

"Arty!" Kelton rushed to the hole and peered through.

"Shh. Kelton. Are you alone? Hurt?"

"No, we're both here and mostly fine. Ayra and me."

"Good. Cecil is in here with me." Ayra remembered the young soldier who had dropped his sword. "And two Tiseden guards. We're all unharmed. But Prince Gibsen is here and is in a bad way. We've dressed a wound on his head and only just now got him to wake, but he's not making any sense yet. Mumbling nonsense."

Even though he was badly hurt, Ayra exhaled a breath of relief that Gibsen was still alive. And the sound of Arty's voice swept away the isolated feeling that haunted their cell.

"What do you suppose they want with us?" Kelton asked, pretending to not know Covalt's plan to use his sister and fishing for how much Arty knew.

"I imagine has to do with a ransom for young Prince Gibsen. Or revenge on King Leofric. We're in a fine mess, ain't we. Why we're all still alive, don't know. Just hope he finds reasons to continue to keep the rest of us around."

A reason to keep them around. As she listened to Arty, Ayra realized Covalt could use any one of their lives to persuade her to do his bidding. The sudden weight was as heavy as the cell walls collapsing on top of her.

Ayra jumped as boots scuffing on the stairs echoed through the hallway. At Arty's quick instruction, Kelton replaced the stone in the wall. He scrambled back to Ayra's side and settled just as the latch on the other side of the door lifted. The door opened, and Rouden lumbered into the room. The bright light of his torch startled Ayra's eyes.

"Both of you. Come with me."

Ayra slipped on her skirt as she tried to get up without the use of her arms. Kelton noticed her struggle, reached under one of her arms, and helped her to her feet. He did not let go as they followed Rouden into the hallway and up the stairs. Laughter and voices from somewhere in the tower bounced around the stairwell. The bodies of the slain guards had been removed, but dark stains on the stone steps remained as a warning.

Rouden led them into the same room Ayra had awakened in. Now that her mind was more alert, she noted the furnishings in the room—an ornate table stacked with books, accompanied by one high-backed chair, and a neatly made bed adorned with colorful pillows. A painting of a crowned, noble-looking man with blue eyes and a short beard hung on one wall, as well as several other paintings depicting stormy sea nights. An easel loaded with a canvas and brushes and paints was tucked in one corner. Rooney lounged in the purple cushioned chair she had sat in hours before.

Covalt stood at the larger of the two glassless windows, staring fixedly out at the sea with his uncommonly thick hands clasped behind his back. He reminded Ayra of a hawk scouting for its prey from a perch.

A few minutes after they entered the room, he turned to them with a sincere smile. "I hope you found your room comfortable." He bounced on his heels and walked across the room. "I'm sure you are in need of more respite, but we haven't much time. You see, the *king's* guards take week-long shifts with me." He gestured toward the portrait on the wall. "My brother likes to ensure I am well cared for, of course. Fortunately, he has grown quite at ease and no longer keeps all the rigid procedures, so we only have a handful of soldiers to worry about. The current set of guards seem to have disappeared, but a new set will arrive promptly at sunrise five days from now. My army is poised to assemble shortly after sunrise and prepare for my arrival. Before any alarm can be raised by the failure of the current set to return, we need to be ready. I need *you* ready, Ayra."

A shiver ran up her spine. His words and demeanor confused her instincts. His warmth and friendliness, as if they had known one another for years, was simultaneously disarming and chilling. The odd mix of feelings unsettled her guts, and she felt Kelton's grip on her arm tighten.

Covalt picked up a wooden bucket of water and set it in front of her. He pulled a knife from his belt and stepped behind her, closer than necessary. He pressed the cold blade against her skin for just a moment before expertly cutting the twine that bound her wrists.

With knife still in hand, he stepped around to face her again. His pale, smooth skin marked the years of pampering he had received as a youth.

"Show me," he said softly.

Ayra shook her head.

In one quick motion his knife slashed across Kelton's upper arm. He cried out and covered the wound with his other hand. Ayra's chest filled with heat, and her fists tightened.

"Show me…please," Covalt said again. His cold stare burned into hers.

She squeezed her eyes shut.

"Give in, Ayra."

She wished she could shut her ears to his voice, too. If she refused, everything could be over quickly. Finished. But something inside her prevented her from resisting again. She opened her eyes to the little bucket and swooped her hand. Water sloshed out, leaving it empty.

Covalt grinned and looked at Rooney. "Wonderful!" He turned back to her and stepped closer. "You say you cannot do much, but I can see in your eyes you are capable of a great deal." The smell of hunger tainted his breath. "Shall we see what else you can do, my dear?"

He took her by the hand, and his baritone laugh filled the room when she jerked it away. Rouden stepped behind her and gave her a push toward a metal door on the opposite side of the room. She glanced back to see Covalt grab Kelton by the arm, his fingers squeezing into the open knife wound. Kelton grimaced and paled, and Ayra had to look away from his pleading, tear-filled eyes.

With a dirty sneer, Rooney unlatched and opened the heavy door revealing a bridge wide enough for three men to stand shoulder to shoulder, spanning the distance to a twin tower.

As Rouden pushed her to the middle of the narrow walkway, Ayra took in her surroundings. Under the arched bridge, the water heaved up and down in a little cove carved out of the curved island. Low, weathered walls on both sides of the walkway served as barriers from a plunging fall into the foamy water or—for the unlucky—the rocks below. The dark sea, open and foreboding, stretched out before them with a thick golden light lining the western horizon as the setting sun fought violently to keep control of the sky. Clouds streaked the space overhead and beyond in gray, purple, and pink.

Covalt released Kelton's arm. The boy was pale as death as he protectively clutched his arm again. Looking into his face Ayra knew neither of them could endure this for long. She looked out over the water again searching for a way out.

"Do something," Covalt coaxed in a soothing voice. "The tide is moving out, and the water is calm. It should not be difficult to show me something worth seeing."

Ayra eyed the three men who held them prisoner. She glanced at the knife Covalt turned in his hand. If she got a hold of the knife, she would only get one jab or two before the other men grabbed her. There wasn't any way she could physically overpower any of them. A clumsy attempt would only put them on edge. And if she did manage to do something, surely there were other of Covalt's men standing guard elsewhere on the small island.

She glanced at Kelton again. His eyes were closed, and deep

red blood oozed between the fingers covering his arm. Out of the corner of her eye she saw Covalt move again. The knife sliced over Kelton's forearm.

He dropped to the ground and began to sob.

"No! No more. Please, no more," Ayra begged, looking at her brother. "I will do something. Just give me time to gather the strength. Please."

Covalt nodded and stepped away from Kelton. She couldn't see him when she looked out over the mass of water, but she could feel him hovering behind her like a hungry vulture.

They were all too alert. She needed them to develop some trust in her—to relax—and she needed time to think. She and the others had a slim chance of surviving, and she did not want to be careless with anyone's life, especially Kelton's.

She put her hands up to her chest with palms facing out. Slowly she pushed, concentrating on moving as much water as she could. A swell formed and pushed its way out to sea, against the incoming waves.

"Again. More," the voice behind her commanded.

She pushed, and another swell formed, slightly larger. Over and over he made her push large swells away.

"Make it rain," he commanded.

"I can't. I've never done that."

He held up the knife. "Try."

She took a deep breath and exhaled slowly. Kelton's sobs had subsided, but he still knelt pitifully on the ground with his eyes closed. She did not want to see him hurt again.

Looking up at the sky, she focused on a section of clouds and brought her hands together, hoping the wisps would gather. A small section pulled together but nothing came of it. She could tell her strength was fading. She tried once more, managing to gather in a little more.

Her hands dropped to her sides. "I'm too tired. And hungry. I can't do it for very long even when rested and full."

Covalt moved near her and placed his hand under her chin, turning her face to his. He studied her eyes for a few seconds.

"Get them some food and let her rest in her room. A blanket, too. I want her strong in the morning."

"I mean no offense, your highness," Rooney said. "But I do not think we can spare anything to feed captives. We have little food as it is."

"Then you will miss your meals. I want her fed."

Rooney straightened his back and scowled at Ayra. It struck her how well he had hidden his ugliness. Rouden grabbed her by the arm and pushed her toward the door. He bumped the barrier with his leg, and a small wall stone toppled into the sea below.

Kelton and Rooney followed closely behind. When Ayra glanced back, Covalt stood serenely staring south at the land that would soon be his.

24

TO Ayra's relief, Rouden did not tie her wrists again, which allowed her to dress Kelton's wounds with strips of fabric torn from her skirt. The one near his shoulder was deep and needed more care than she could provide. He could not lift his arm without excruciating pain.

Rooney brought a bowl of potatoes and salted fish and spit in it before setting it on the ground. Despite that, Ayra and Kelton shared the meal. Her bruised jaw made it painful to chew, and the amount was only enough to take the edge off their hunger.

Ayra removed the loose stone to see how the other men were faring. Arty reported Gibsen was not improving. If he didn't get care from a healer and into better conditions soon, he would surely take a turn for the worse.

After replacing the stone, the two siblings sat in dark quiet while Ayra sifted through plans. Other than the one Arty had found, they could find no loose stones, and the hole in their cell was too high and too small for them to climb through. They would have to go through the door. If she had anticipated Rooney bringing their meal, they might have been successful in pushing past him. But that time had passed, and it was likely Rouden would be next to open the door. Whether they attempted to get past him or tried ramming down the door with their heads, the result would be the same.

For a while Ayra considered the possibility of the two of them jumping off the bridge. Neither could swim, but she could keep them afloat and push toward the shore. But she eventually dismissed the idea, unsure they could clear the rocks when they jumped or that she could keep them above water over such a distance. And what about the men next door who were only alive because she sat in a cell? If she escaped and left them behind, what would be their fate?

She worked through possible scenarios until her ideas became irrational. With Kelton's good shoulder leaning against her and a blanket to share, they huddled together in a corner and fell into a fitful sleep.

When the sky outside the window changed from black to gray, Ayra heard boots on the stairs. She slouched lower, hoping the latch on their door wouldn't lift. But it did, and Rouden's frame filled the doorway when the door opened. He followed Ayra and Kelton up the stairs, through the room, and out onto the walkway like the evening before.

The raw, morning sea air blew around her, making her dress heavy and damp. A sliver of sun crowned in pink peeked above the eastern horizon.

Covalt stood with his arms folded, Rooney lingering petulantly behind him. When she neared, he turned to greet her.

"I trust your night passed pleasantly," he said cordially. "I, myself, did not sleep well. Your gift has given me much to be excited over. I hope you are prepared to impress me with more than little splashes and ripples." He flipped the knife in his hand as his eyes flicked to Kelton.

Ayra stepped up to the low wall. Kelton gingerly sat down in a corner by the door, his hand shielding his deep cut. His eyes were squeezed shut and his mouth contorted as if he had just been stricken across the face.

"You will stand in the presence of greatness, boy!" Rooney barked at him. "You wretched little…"

Covalt lifted his hand to silence him. "Ayra. Please."

Ayra glanced at Rouden standing behind her on her left. He was built like a bear, tall with thick shoulders and chest, but his movements were stiff and awkward. The protective wall met him mid-thigh. *One solid push and he'd be over*, she told herself. He had a knife in his belt that she could grab when she pushed. But she needed more than her own strength, and Covalt was twitching with impatience. She needed to act quickly.

She closed her eyes and with a few deep breaths, isolated herself from everything happening around her. Then, looking up at the sky, she brought her cupped hands together. As she concentrated, the clouds miraculously gathered and darkened. The sound of raindrops patting the stone gave her a push, and she continued to gather clouds until the sky opened into a downpour. Ayra smiled despite herself as rain soaked through her dress and puddles began to form on the mossy stone at their feet.

Covalt laughed and exchanged looks with his men. Rooney seemed unimpressed, but Rouden shifted his weight and looked uneasily at Ayra.

The water below was too tame to be lethal. Ayra hoped she had enough strength left to change that. She lifted her hand and waved it in a circular motion just as she had frequently done before. Never had she created a whirlpool larger than a couple feet across, but the river attack and the current downpour gave her new confidence. Gradually, the swirl grew wider, faster, and deeper below them as water obeyed the guidance of her hand.

"More!" the deep voice commanded as he stepped closer.

She continued to make it grow, not because of his command but for her own purpose. Mentally, she moved it faster and faster, ignoring the slowly increasing ache of her head. She hoped if she made it move fast enough it would take on a life of its own and not collapse as soon as she pulled her concentration away.

Now that Covalt was beside her, she studied him out of the corner of her eye. He was smaller than Rouden. It would be easier to move him than the large man, but his stance was more centered. It was likely she would only knock him off balance, not send him over the edge. And she had to think past pushing one man off.

Keeping her hand moving in a circle, she flicked her eyes to Rouden. He had stepped out from behind her to peer over the wall and stood mesmerized by the spinning funnel below, his lips frowning at the sight. Rooney also stood as if in a trance, a trace of a smile on his pointed face.

Ayra could feel her mind tiring and knew she needed to act. As the men stared at the water, she discreetly stepped back, placing herself almost behind Rouden. With all the force she could muster, she threw her body forward and slammed her shoulder into his back. His relaxed body lurched forward, and his arms flailed out to the sides. His thighs hit the stone wall, but he did not topple over the edge like Ayra had hoped. She drew a sharp breath as he steadied himself. Just as he became still, the weakened stones gave way against his legs, and his boots slipped on the wet moss. He whirled around, terror covering his stoic face. His hand failed to find a hold, and he disappeared from the walkway. Splashes and cracks sounded as body and stone hit the surfaces below.

A thick hand seized Ayra by the throat. With an awful realization she had forgotten to snatch Rouden's knife, she clawed with her fingernails at Covalt's hand. His grip held fast.

"That was a mistake," he said calmly, water dripping down his face.

Kelton jumped from his place on the ground and dove at Covalt's waist. Before he could touch the hem of the man's tunic, Covalt's boot hit him solidly in the gut and sent him sprawling backward into the stone wall. His body was too small to cause it to crumble, but the blow left him dazed against the stone.

"You kill him or me, your plan fails," Ayra choked out.

He lifted her a little, forcing her onto her toes. "If I can't gain complete compliance my plan fails as well. I have no use for a devious water rat. Or her pathetic brother." His grip tightened.

She kept her eyes wide as the air in her lungs diminished, fearing they wouldn't open again if she closed them. The swirling water below was beginning to slow. She kicked at him, but he stood firm. The edges of her vision began to blur.

As rain continued to fall, Ayra's focus fell on Rooney standing behind Covalt. She didn't want his face to be the last she ever saw but couldn't look away. Suddenly, a *thump* sounded, and his cruel face grimaced before dropping out of sight. Covalt turned his head. His hold loosened, allowing Ayra to draw in enough air to gather her senses. Her heart leaped as Edvin, bow in hand, sprinted toward them from the opposite tower.

Covalt shoved her to the ground and drew his knife.

"The water!" Ayra rasped.

Edvin didn't slow or acknowledge he had heard her. Just before reaching them, he threw his bow into Covalt's face, catching him by surprise, then ducked low, slamming his shoulder into the shorter man's middle. Their bodies crashed against the wall, the stones gave way, and both disappeared over the edge.

Ayra scrambled to the gaping hole and looked down as both men hit the water, tumbled stones just missing them. Covalt surfaced first, and Ayra circled her hand again and again to speed up the still spinning water. Edvin surfaced near Covalt and grabbed him around the neck. The men thrashed and shoved, alternately being held under, drifting together toward the whirlpool.

"Get away from him!" Ayra screamed. If they separated, she could push Covalt to the whirlpool herself.

Edvin tucked his legs and pushed off Covalt's chest with both feet, but Covalt's strong hands caught him by the ankle and yanked him back, pulling him underwater. Ayra put out her other hand and tried to separate them herself. Waves washed over their heads, and she struggled to decipher what was her doing and what wasn't.

The water swirled furiously as the men neared its gaping mouth. Ayra pushed at Edvin harder, but Covalt's iron grip didn't slacken. Before she could try again, the swirling current caught hold of them, and both heads disappeared.

"Where's Edvin?!" Arman shouted as he ran onto the walkway from the opposite side Edvin had rushed in from.

"In the water! I can't see him."

He looked down at the whirlpool and bolted back through the door. Ayra spun her hand in the opposite direction once, and the spinning slowed. Seconds later the tip of the funnel rose to the surface. Ayra watched the empty water as it began to heave up and down again in its natural rhythm.

Arman appeared on the rocky water's edge, searching up and down for any sign of their friend. The rain around the island reduced to a drizzle.

A darkly clothed body surfaced for just a glimpse before it sank again into the deep waters. Off to the far side another body surfaced, the burnt orange color catching Ayra's eye.

"There!" she shouted and pointed for Arman.

He dashed across the rocks as she pushed Edvin toward him. When Arman jumped in and caught Edvin around the chest, Ayra looked at Kelton.

"I'm all right. Go. Hurry!"

She stumbled to the tower and ran down the steps, leaping over several unconscious Covaltmen. By the time she reached them, Arman had Edvin all the way out of the water and on his side.

"He's not breathing," Arman panted. "Do something!"

Ayra's heart pounded as she knelt next to her lifeless friend. Red seeped through his soaked shirt where Covalt's blade had sliced across his side. "I don't know what to do. What do I do?"

"The water. Get it out! Get it out of his chest."

She placed her trembling hand over his chest and imagined his lungs filled with water. If she did not pull enough, he would surely die, but she didn't know what would happen if she pulled too much. She looked at his pale face once more before putting all her focus on the foreign water inside his chest. With a slow and gentle swipe up his breastbone, a gurgle erupted from his throat and seawater spewed from his mouth. His reflex to breathe sparked to life, and he raked in a scraggly breath before he began heaving and coughing.

"That'll do it!" Arman whooped.

Ayra grabbed Edvin's cold hand with both of hers and inhaled a deep breath as if she had been underwater for days.

25

EDVIN finished coughing and sputtering and rolled onto his back, breathing raggedly with his eyes closed. Ayra watched his chest rise and fall to make certain he really was all right.

"You fish scum!" Arman said. "What were you thinking flying into the water with him like that? Stars and rivers." Arman got to his feet and looked out over the water. "Are we sure he's dead?"

"Yes, I think so," breathed Ayra with her eyes still watching the rhythm of Edvin's breaths, his hand held tightly in hers. "How are you here?"

"Well, it's quite a story," Arman began. "I'll tell it to you now that he's shut up for a minute. After you two didn't come back, I went after you as soon as the sun gave enough light. Saw our friend here being led away all bound up and followed them some distance. When they were fixing to slice his throat, I rescued him. Didn't I?" He nodded and looked to Edvin for validation. Edvin nodded his head without opening his eyes. "Well, you did a lot of the fighting once I got your hands free. Scrappy, this one. Anyway, we took their horses and stuff—I got a sword—and made our way through the forest and came to some cliffs and spotted a crowd on the beach—just as some man grabbed you up. Edvin about lost his head, but I helped him keep it."

Ayra looked at Edvin and saw his mouth twitch almost into a smile.

"Anyway, we waited until dark, then ran up the beach 'til we found a boat turned upside down in the sand. I imagine some poor fisherman is scratching his head and cursing us. We should make sure we return that. Right. Anyway, we rowed out in the dark, sneaked up onto the rocks, and Edvin here listened to get an idea where everyone was and the general set up of the place. Are we sure Covalt is dead? Yeah, good.

"Well, bless the stars, the men were having a celebration of sorts and got themselves plum drunk and passed out early this morning. They're locked in that room now. We were just coming to get you when that big fellow beat us to it, so we freed the men with the prince. Edvin heard a few men in the other tower, and we split up. Took out as many as we could. And then...well you know what happened next. Hero here scrapped the sane plan to take on Covalt together and flung himself over the edge with the madman. I wanted to get my own hands on him." He clucked his tongue and looked at Ayra as if he were looking at her for the first time since he ran out onto the bridge. He glanced nervously at the water. "Ayra, you're all right, then? You've got some awful colors under your skin."

Edvin opened his eyes and looked questioningly at her, too.

She touched one hand to her bruised jaw. "I'm all right." Her head throbbed, but she felt no pain that wouldn't heal.

"Edvin!" Cecil came running from a tower, reminding them the three of them were not alone on the island.

They limped Edvin back to the old fortress and found Arty and the Tisedenian guards with three Covaltmen unconscious and restrained with ropes. Kelton was just reaching the bottom of the tower stairs. Ayra grabbed him up in an embrace. When he winced, she remembered his injured arm and quickly let him go but held onto his hand.

"What do we do now?" asked Arman.

Everyone looked from face to face. When no one spoke, Ayra cleared her throat.

"Arman, you and I will go with…" She looked at the most experienced looking of the two men in green.

"Bries," he said.

"Right. Bries. Arman and I will go with Bries to get help. The rest of you stay here and make sure the prince is safe."

Edvin shook his head. "No, I'll come with you. We don't know how many of Covalt's men might be on the beach." His voice was raspy from the water burns in his throat, and he was clutching one hand to his side.

From his bloodshot eyes and pale skin, Ayra was certain he

was not well. If he went ashore with her and ran into trouble, he would be too weak to fight. Even though she felt safer with him, he needed to stay. For the past two days she had thought him dead. Now that she knew he was alive, she planned to keep him that way.

"I need you to stay here and protect Kelton...and everyone else. Keep the doors locked until we return. Please?"

He looked at her for a moment and reluctantly nodded his head. Less than a half-hour later, a small rowboat with three passengers made its way toward the beach.

The sea of green tunics bustled around Ayra as she sat alone near a campfire. Eight days had passed since they left the island.

After she, Arman, and Bries made it ashore, Bries led them to a military camp not far outside Tiseden Crown City, where he alerted the commanders. The Tiseden military was mobilized to meet the gathering of Covaltmen on the beach four days later and a battle ensued. Realizing they were a body without a head, some Covaltmen fled while others stayed to fight to the death in honor of their master.

Military posts were now being set up in villages to protect the people against any rogue men. Ayra wondered if Covalt would have been surprised by the advancements his brother's army had made since the previous uprising. She couldn't help feeling she would have been key to his success. The notion made her feel both sick and powerful.

King Tobian had offered the Mihtengardians shelter in one of his military camps to recover and wait for word to be sent to Mihtengard. Bries and the other guard verified Covalt's revolt in the tower, giving credit to the Mihtengardians' claim they had been attacked by Covalt's men. All but those who knew the truth assumed, as Arty had, that Covalt was after Prince Gibsen. None supposed the man had actually been after the girl.

Prince Gibsen came around several days after being attended to by a healer and requested Ayra to his tent as soon as he was able to comprehend the situation. He apologized to her for being careless once again. His father had dismissed the letter from a man claiming to be her relative. But Rooney had approached Gibsen in private saying he could take the remaining members of the Regnan family and claim the promised fortune—a powerful water stone that had originally belonged to Mihtengard. Rooney had convinced him he would be a hero among his people and in the eyes of his father if he brought rain back to the land. Under the guise of a trade mission, Rooney had been able to select some of the soldiers to accompany them.

It had been a carefully orchestrated plan that had fortunately failed. But Ayra could tell it had changed the confident prince. Though he sat erect on his cot, something about him sagged. He was hesitant to return home and answer to his father, but she knew he would realize there was nothing else for him to do. Ayra had tried her best to reassure him that she held no ill will toward him, though she couldn't deny the inward disdain she felt for him and his family.

"Here you are, Ayra." Her brother's voice broke through her rambling thoughts. A bandage was wrapped around his head to cover a gash from the rocks. Though his other wounds were concealed under his shirt, Ayra still saw them in her mind and felt a twinge of guilt that he had taken the brunt of the pain inflicted by Covalt. The deep purple bruises on her jaw and neck had already faded into yellow, and she had not a scratch on her. He dropped himself next to her. "How long do you think before we return to Mihtengard?"

Ayra had asked herself that question many times. With the greatest threat to their well-being now gone, the thought of returning to her country had been forefront on her mind. She tried to picture herself in the city Edvin and Gibsen had described. High walls and tall towers. Winding streets. And people. Hordes of people. The images made her stomach tighten. She knew she would not fit in. She would be shunned just as she had been in Darkwater. And the thought of seeing Gibsen's royal family left a bitter taste in her mouth.

"When the prince is well enough, I suppose. Might be a few days, could be weeks."

He flicked a stick into the fire. "I think he'll heal quickly. He's strong, you know."

Ayra bobbed her head but said nothing.

"Tress seems to be all right, too, don't you think?" Kelton added after a pause. "His head wound doesn't seem as bad as before. I was sure glad to see him and the others ride into camp this morning."

"I was, too," Ayra agreed. "And I think he seemed well."

A couple days after leaving the island, Edvin and Cecil had gone with a troop of Tisedenian soldiers to find Tress and the other six soldiers left behind. First, they found the remnants of their burned camp. They continued to the closest village and learned, after an ambush that had cost two soldiers their lives, the men had obtained refuge with a farmer and his wife. No doubt Rooney had staged the horse accident to minimize opposition on the beach, then organized the ambush.

Ayra glanced around the camp, searching for a particular dark head among the crowds of corn-silk colored hair. She and Edvin had not spoken alone since her arrival in camp, and she hoped to before supper. She caught a glimpse of his tall, orange-clad figure just as it disappeared into the trees, a bow and quiver over his shoulder. She excused herself from Kelton and followed after Edvin.

She felt at ease ducking under pine boughs, leaping over narrow creeks, and padding through the soft soil. She smiled to herself as she realized just how quietly she could move if she kept her movements slow and deliberate. Soon she spotted him. He was stopped, half-hidden, a little ahead of her.

He didn't turn toward her, and her smile widened as she crept closer to him. She knew she wouldn't be able to get too close to him without being heard, so she picked up a pinecone and threw it. The missile hurled toward its target and bounced off his back. He startled and whirled around to face her.

Ayra grinned. "I didn't think there was any way I'd ever be

able to sneak up on you," she said as she closed the distance between them.

He smiled sheepishly and rubbed his hand over the back of his neck. "I wasn't even listening. I guess I was thinking about too many things. Want to stay with me while I shoot?" he asked, removing his bow from his shoulder.

She nodded and sat down on a fallen tree, swinging her legs under her skirts. He released arrow after arrow into the soft, rooty bottom of a fallen tree in the distance. As she watched and they joked and laughed, Ayra pretended there wasn't an army camp nearby, and it was just the two of them again.

She had not breathed this easily in days, and she could tell Edvin had surfaced from the depths of dark water as well. His movements were light, except for a few winces when the healing wound on his side twinged, and his laughter came easily, though he was not exactly the same Edvin she had come out of Mightengard with. She couldn't place what was new about him, but he was changed somehow. She supposed they both were. After he emptied his quiver several times, he sat down at her feet and leaned his back against a nearby rock.

As she studied his face and watched him fiddle with the leather around his wrist, heavier thoughts entered her head. She thought about what he had experienced and remembered the young soldier on the beach. "Edvin, I'm sorry about your friend, Rim. He was very kind to Kelton. And the other soldiers, too. I'm sure they were good men."

Edvin nodded and continued to look at his hands.

They sat in silence for a few minutes, a nearby stream softly murmuring and the treetops swishing to the rhythm of the wind. Ayra continued to recount events and for the hundredth time, recalled his panicked face the night they had tried to get Kelton. His look of shame when Rooney accused him. She needed to get the words that had been burning in her throat out.

"And I'm sorry I doubted you that night. I—"

"No," he shook his head. "I should have told you…about my grandfather. My father was born six months after he left, and my grandmother raised him and my uncle on her own. My father had worked hard to gain King Leofric's trust, but my grandfather's life still plagued him. That's why my mother took me to Wil. We didn't know if the rumors were true. There was no real proof except that he had disappeared." He drew a deep breath. "But the visions didn't prove his innocence. The rumors—all of them—were true. He was a traitor. For years he sold military secrets, stole from the crown, you name it, he did it. And I was too ashamed to tell you. I thought…I thought you would mistrust me like you did before. But if I had just told you, you probably would not have questioned. Hearing Kelton tell you what the others had said—accusing me *and* my father— and hearing your confusion…I got mad. It was stupid, but it burned me. And then I didn't have time to explain."

Ayra nodded. She wondered for a moment how differently things would have turned out if they hadn't been separated. They would have fled into the forest with Kelton and avoided all the terror of being on that wretched island. But then what?

Edvin's name would have remained tainted, and he certainly would not be returning home to Mihtengard. And what would have happened to Prince Gibsen and the others?

For another fleeting, frightening moment she wondered how her life would look right now if he and Arman had not gone after them. Even though Prince Gibsen, who Edvin was entrusted to serve and protect, was also a prisoner on the island, her stomach fluttered at the idea that maybe he had really gone just for her. "Thank you for fetching me...us...from the island."

He smiled. "Well, I certainly couldn't leave Arty out there. He's got some recipes in that head that I would sure miss. It was fortunate for you he was there, or I might not have come." He batted her foot. "And I suppose I should thank *you* for not letting me drown. We make quite a pair, you and I."

She smiled and lightly kicked his shoulder with her foot. "I hope I never have to save your life again. Twice is enough."

He looked at his hands for a minute. "Ayra, what are you planning to do once we get back home?"

Home. Is that where she was going? "I don't know yet. I thought of going back to Darkwater, but I don't think I want to. Maybe Kelton and I can find work in a village. Or maybe there is somewhere in the East countries we can be safe."

"So you won't stay in Mihtengard for sure? You won't come to Midivard?"

Ayra shrugged. "I don't really know. Probably not."

"Huh." He threw a pinecone. It cracked against a rock and fell into a bed of rusty pine needles. "Have you thought about carrying on your grandmother's work?"

"What do you mean?"

He looked up at her with his head cocked sideways. "Miht-engard is drying up, Ayra. We're fine for now, but in a few years, we won't have enough water to support our farms and gardens. You could help with that. Don't you feel a sense of duty to your king and people?"

Ayra narrowed her eyes. "To *my* king and people?" she scoffed. "The people who came to the quarry looked down on my family. We had been there for decades. None of them did anything to help us. I don't owe them anything. And as for King Leofric, the thought of him makes me sick."

"Ayra, how can you say that? You know very little of him and what he's done for the people of Mihtengard."

Ayra felt heat rise from her chest to her cheeks. The jumbled thoughts that had been floating in her head took shape and formed into words. "He is the descendant of the man who *murdered* my family, Edvin. He murdered them. And then king after king left us out there. For what? For their own wealth. They were never going to let us go."

"A person should not be held accountable for the actions of his predecessors," he said defensively. He launched another pinecone to an unseen destination.

Ayra felt a stab of guilt for insinuating such now that she knew his family history and given what she had previously thought was her own.

He leaned back again. "And think of it. All that time, the

women of your family continued to do what they could from where they were. They helped our country for two centuries. Without being given anything. Without being told."

Ayra remembered Tanna telling her she had an important purpose, but the idea left her feeling a bitterness she could not swallow. She folded her arms and lifted her chin. "Well, I am not going to! All my life I've hated the wrong people. Maybe the right ones should suffer a bit."

She could not bring herself to look at him, but out of the corner of her eye she saw him stiffen and his gaze trained on her profile. She swallowed and took a deep breath, but the flame inside was only fanned.

He stood, scooped up his bow, and walked away to collect his arrows. When he returned from his crude target, he said, "I see now that we view things very differently." He turned away from her and headed back in the direction of the camp.

Ayra looked the other way, into the deep, damp forest. Her eyes began to sting, and a few drops slipped down her cheek. She swiped her sleeve roughly across her face and refused to let any more fall. *I've no reason to feel guilty, and he has no right to make me,* she thought. But his rebuke lingered, and she could not wring it from her conscience. Reluctantly, she slid off the log and traipsed back toward camp.

26

THE Wolfjaw Mountains grew as the company neared the Tiseden-Mihtengard border. After less than two weeks of rest and recovery, Prince Gibsen was anxious to return to his home and had declared himself ready for travel. Against the healer's advice, the remaining eleven members of the Mihtengard party and Arman, along with twenty soldiers in green, had begun the trek toward the mountains. The prince had fared well on the journey, only having three dizzy spells that nearly dropped him from his horse.

At the foot of the north-facing mountains, the Tisedenian soldiers turned to make their way back to their stations. A company dressed in orange supposedly awaited the smaller group's arrival just on the other side of the narrow canyon that cut through the Wolfjaw Range. The United River flowed swiftly beside them, anxious for its final destination.

As they entered the canyon, Ayra stole a glance over her shoulder at her friend. His shoulder was occupied by a bow, just as it should be. She hoped she would remember exactly how the cowlick in his hair swooped. Their eyes met, and he gave her a smile before she turned to face forward again. She couldn't help feeling behind that smile was disappointment. Over the course of their travel, she and Kelton had decided to return to Wil's homestead with Arman until they were able to make better arrangements for themselves. Out of the corner of her eye, she had often noticed Edvin watching her, but he had not spoken to her much since their decision.

Arman was happy about the plan. He mentioned one evening around a campfire how he had not minded his and Wil's isolation before, but now he felt life would be incredibly boring without anyone else around. Edvin invited him to come to the head city sometime, and he'd show him the sights. Arman had grinned at the idea and repeated the words 'come to the head city' as if he had received an exclusive invitation to the heavens.

The horses rounded the last bend and ahead, along the tree line made of small pine and tall white-bark, leafy trees, Ayra spotted the warm-color clad camp. She surprised herself by feeling a wave of relief wash over her. They had made it back to Mihtengard. What surprised her more was to realize she was relieved for the sake of Prince Gibsen. He would be safe now, along with her other friends.

The men at the camp stood at attention as the prince

approached. Ayra felt the curious sets of eyes staring at her, her horse directly behind Prince Gibsen's. The knots that had come undone thread themselves anew, and she fought the urge to kick her heels into her mare and ride out of sight of them all. She glanced at Kelton's face, glowing with pride at the reception they were receiving.

The captain of the new company approached Gibsen's horse and asked him to dismount for a rest from travel. Ayra frowned when Gibsen agreed and clumsily dismounted his horse. The other riders alighted as well. She was hoping to keep moving and not spend time among the soldiers. She noticed the crowd that gathered around Edvin as his friends in the camp greeted him.

"Ayra," Arman called, as he approached her and Kelton. "The company is going to continue down this road, but my…our homestead is that direction. If you and Kelton agree, I think we should head that way on foot. If we leave now, it being early in the afternoon and all, we can cover some distance before it gets dark. We are looking at about four, maybe five, days of walking, I think."

Ayra looked at Kelton. He shrugged, leaving the choice to her, just as he had all the other decisions since arriving on the island. "Yes, all right. No sense in waiting until the company moves again."

Arman grinned. "Excellent. Let's scrounge up a few supplies and be on our way. I'm sure Wil's got worry maggots in her gut. I've been gone longer than ever before."

Ayra informed Gibsen they were going to depart and travel

the rest of their journey on foot. He had one of his men prepare three small satchels with food rations and a knife for each of them. He offered them an escort, but Ayra declined.

"Are you sure you will not come with us to Midivard, Ayra? I am certain my father would be honored to have you join his house. I cannot promise he will not send for you anyway. Please consider continuing with us."

Though her hostility toward the humbled prince had thinned in the last week or so, she still could not feel any desire to go and serve any king of Mihtengard. She politely refused again and thanked him for releasing them from the quarry and for the satchels. With a sincere bow to her and a handshake with Kelton, he returned to his tent.

They then bid Arty and Tress goodbye. Arty gave Ayra a gruff hug and told her how sorry he was they weren't able to locate her and Kelton's kin. She assured him she was happy just as things were. He patted Kelton's back and told him to come get a meat pie if ever he came to Midivard. Tress gave each of them a handshake and wished them luck. When Ayra and Kelton returned to Arman, Edvin was standing with him.

Arman slipped his hatchet into a satchel and slung it over his shoulder. "Well, let's say our goodbyes and get a move on."

"Actually, I'll walk with you a bit," Edvin said. Then looked at Ayra and hurriedly added, "If that's all right."

"I don't know," Ayra replied. Secretly her insides jumped at the idea. "The last walk I took with you started with a knife and you throwing me into a river."

He grinned. "My mother has always said I'm good at making friends. But I promise I'll keep my knife in my pocket this time. Can't promise about the river, though."

"All right then. You can come. Just for a little bit."

The four of them set off around the base of the mountain in search of the road that led to Gowen, moving at a pace with no hurry in it. Edvin was once again full of stories, and Ayra never tired of hearing them. She even requested a few he had told her before so Kelton and Arman could hear them.

When the sun perched itself atop the western mountains, they reached the road they sought, and Edvin declared it was time for him to turn back. He shook hands with Arman and Kelton and wished them safe travel. When he turned to Ayra, each just stood and stared at the other for a moment. As if suddenly remembering himself, Edvin pulled something from around his neck.

"This is for you." He held out a loop of leather with a pretty-colored rock intricately tied in the center. She noticed for the first time the absence of the leather from his wrist. He smiled sheepishly. "I made it…for you. It's one of the rocks you picked up and then dropped when we crossed over the mountain."

She took it from his hand with a warm thrill in her stomach, put it over her head, and pulled her long hair out from under it. "Thank you."

He stuck his hand out for a handshake.

A laugh bubbled out Ayra's throat at his awkward gesture, and instead of taking his hand, she quickly wrapped her arms around him before she lost her nerve. He easily returned the embrace.

"Take care of yourself, all right?"

She nodded, her face still buried in his chest, and felt him kiss the top of her head before he pulled away and turned to walk in the direction they had come. He gave one more nod to Kelton and Arman as he passed them.

The two boys began to walk again, but Ayra's feet wouldn't move. She stood there stupidly, with a wrapped rock clutched in her hand and a warm spot on top of her head, and watched Edvin walk away from her. She waited for him to turn around— to wave or give her one more smile—but he disappeared into the trees, swinging a stick at the tall grass, without even a glance.

She almost called him back—she knew he would hear. But she did not know what she would say or do if he came. She did not want to go to Midivard and that was his home. That was where he belonged. She could not ask him to stay with her on a mountain away from everything he loved. The deep hollowness in her heart seemed to expand more than she thought possible. She ached to find where she belonged.

When she was sure he was not going to reemerge from the trees, she turned to follow the dusty, crooked road ahead.

27

THE old woman cried tears of joy when her boy came home and warmly welcomed her two new children. "I can see the past, not the future. I was sick with worry when you did not come home as you should have," she said reproachfully to Arman. "But all is well now. We shall have a fine warm season."

She claimed not to see the future, but her prediction for the warm season proved true. The months passed quickly, the four of them working through each day together.

Arman and Kelton spent much of their days harvesting and breaking down trees for cold season fires, trapping small game, and occasionally finding temporary work in the fishing village in exchange for supplies they could not produce on their own. The two boys were similar by nature, prone to be content with life and happy to have busy hands, and had become like brothers. Kelton had been so withdrawn and unmotivated the last four years, Ayra worried the Kelton she knew before Tanna passed away would never come back. But she was pleased that this new life brought out the best in him. He worked hard and never complained.

Wil spent her days teaching Ayra everything she knew about preparing a home for the cold season. They worked side by side, tending the garden, cutting and fermenting cabbages, salting and drying the game and fish the boys brought home, making soap, harvesting wild honey. Ayra had become proficient in milking Nanny, the goat, and she was delighted when her first tiny batch of cheese turned out well.

Sometimes in the afternoon Ayra practiced drawing clouds from the other side of the mountain, gathering them together, and making it rain over the immediate part of the valley. Wil told her the garden had never produced so much, which she was not sure she believed since she was also told the well had never gone dry in all the years it has been used. Working for her own keep and learning new skills brought Ayra much satisfaction, though. She almost felt happy.

But in the evenings, she climbed up the rocky barrier protecting the little home and looked out over the world below. As she gazed at the tops of the woods and the patchwork fields far in the distance, she wondered what kind of people were out there. What would they do when their little farms ran out of irrigation water? What would they eat when crops failed to produce enough for family stores?

After turning over those type of thoughts for a time, her mind always wandered to what the people did aside from farming and working, what kinds of games they play in the warm season when it's hot, what it's like to have a crowd of friends and family.

She had quickly realized after returning to Mihtengard that she had no desire to find a home on the other side of any of its mountains. But the hollowness in her heart had only been filled enough by the little homestead to not be a deep ache. She felt restless as soon as her body stopped working—like at any moment she would break into a run and never stop.

The moon was beginning to battle the sun for more time in the sky, and the crisp feeling of harvest season made its appearance in the evenings. With her chores done, Ayra climbed up onto her perch. Her mind wove through thoughts like it always did, as she rubbed the mark on her shoulder.

One question in particular had been on her mind throughout the day, and she allowed herself to dwell on it now. What do the dances of the people down there look like? Some evenings in the quarry, music from the village floated over the pit to her ears. She had loved to hear it but remembered its sweet sound always came with a bitterness. She was never invited to listen, it was only by happenstance she could hear it. But as she pulled a memory of the music and hummed the tune, all bitterness seemed to have abated. It was only sweet to her.

Surprised by this, she reflected on other things about the village or the quarry that had always bothered her. The blankets and clothes they had been given always seemed to have pity woven into their threads. But as she thought of them now, it was kindness they were made of, not pity. Guards were placed to ensure people completed their work but also to protect them from predators or those who would do harm. Her family had been given a little home, modest as it was, and it had shielded them from rain and the cold of night.

Nothing had been perfect. If she could go back and change her family's circumstances, she would. But she found she wanted to let go of what had passed. She wanted to look forward to the future. With all its beauty and wonder, all its uncertainties and challenges, she wanted to look it in the eye and hold her ground.

She looked out across the valley, inhaled a long, cool breath—holding it just for a moment—and released. A peace she had never known before settled over her like warm rays from the sun.

She remained on her thinking rock until darkness completely overshadowed the valley. When she walked through the little door, Wil was in her rocker with a small fire burning before her. The door to the boys' room was already closed, which meant they had retired for the night. Not feeling sleepy yet, Ayra crossed the room and knelt next to the old, creaking chair, hoping Wil would stay and keep her company a while. Wil stroked her hair a few times, which always reminded Ayra of Tanna's nurturing touch.

They sat for a time in silence, and Ayra found herself staring into the fire. The crackle and wave of flames always made her think of Edvin and the time they spent sitting across from one another laughing and talking, the way the swoop in his dark hair reflected the orange glow. She wrapped her fingers around the rock that hung from her neck. Even though she thought about him daily, even hourly if she was really being honest, she had only recently let herself admit she missed him. And not in the same way she had missed Kelton. She didn't like when her heart wondered what kept him from coming to visit.

"Something troubles you, Ayra." It was not a question. Ayra looked up at Wil. The ancient woman chuckled. "I see by the look on your face you think you hide it well. But I see you up on your own little mountain. Like you are looking for a way down and cannot find it."

Ayra turned away from Wil's searching eyes to look at the fire again. She smiled a little at the mountain comparison. She had put Ayra's exact feelings into words. "Yes. And it feels like either I will tumble down it before I find the path or..." She swallowed hard. "Or I might never even get down it at all."

Wil stopped rocking and was quiet for a moment. "I have not made the best use of my gift," she said reflectively. "While I am fond of being a recluse, I know I could have done more good with my years if I had made myself more accessible to my people." Motioning her hand toward the door. "All the people down there in our valley. I know I have used my gift here, but it's not the same as being out there. Among them. Knowing them. And doing more for them than just answering their questions. The past holds many lessons, Ayra. Lessons of happiness, of grief and pain. Folly and triumph. Friendship and animosity. We can learn so many things from those who came before us. And years ago I determined to learn those lessons *through* others, never really learning them for myself. Never experiencing them firsthand."

The rocker creaked into motion again. She took a tired deep breath and exhaled slowly. Ayra looked up at her and saw dullness in her typically spry eyes. "The gift of my ancestors from the Creator will die with me. I have spent all my life here. Hiding in the mountains. And because of that, a gift to Miht-engard will be forever lost." She turned her eyes to meet Ayra's. "Do not make the same mistake, my child. Do not hide all your lifetime in the shadows of a mountain fearing the people you were meant to help."

Ayra slept fitfully through the night on her bed by the fire. She had recurring nightmares from the events during the re-newal season, but tonight she tossed for a different reason. She felt pulled in so many directions and ideas came disjointedly.

When the first morning bird began to sing outside the little window she woke enough to think clearly. She knew she *could* help the people of Mihtengard from the mountain. Tanna had done it from the quarry. But Wil meant she could do more than just bring rain to the valley.

She needed to be involved, working with the people and the Crown. A part of her country. The way her family had been in the beginning.

She thought of the ancestors she had come to know through

memory and flitted through some of her favorite images. It was odd to feel she knew these people, though she had never seen them in body.

A week passed and chores continued as usual. Ayra told no one of her thoughts of leaving until one sunny afternoon, when a company from Midivard arrived bearing a letter from the king. The Regnan siblings' presence was requested at the castle.

28

THE buckskin horse balked at the main city gate. It seemed to feel as suspicious of the towering, stone city wall as Ayra did. She gripped the reins tighter, fearing the dampness of her palms would make the leather slip out of her hands. She gave the animal a gentle kick with her heels and rocked her body forward, but it didn't move. Cecil, one of the six soldiers who were sent for her and Kelton, rode up beside her and grabbed the reins.

"Come on, Benoff, you beast." The young soldier looked at Ayra apologetically. "He does this every time." With a sharp tug, Benoff followed Cecil's horse through the gate.

Ayra gasped at the sight that was a far cry from the woods, fields, and villages she had passed in the last week. Two and three story buildings made of wood and stone lined a long, wide street, packed in like mouse pups in a burrow. Instead of the dirt she was accustomed to, the road was laid with rectangular, gray stone that created a unique clacking sound under the horses' hooves. Arches that seemed to appear randomly opened to alleys, creating veins between the buildings. And each street and alley seemed to be pulsing with industry.

Prim women and girls near her age, all with thick, brown braids, were pulling laundry from lines strung between taller buildings, carrying baskets of bread or eggs, brushing down horses, consoling crying babes. Men were sweeping stoops, pounding mallets against hot metal, herding small flocks of sheep, repairing masonry, unloading goods from carts. Children ran through the streets in troops, laughing and gaming with one another. It seemed to Ayra everyone had a purpose—working or otherwise—and if one didn't, he or she was skilled at pretending.

More than once Ayra chided herself for searching the crowd for a familiar face accompanied by dark, swooping hair.

After what she thought to be endless turns of populated streets, they came to another tall wall, though not as tall as the first. An iron gate, flanked by two enormous bears carved in stone, barred them from the castle grounds on the other side. Cecil exchanged words with two men on the inside of the wall, and a lever was pulled. The portcullis lurched and slowly opened, accompanied by a loud clanking sound. As soon as they were through, the soldiers alighted and led their horses up the road. Ayra and Kelton exchanged glances and did the same.

The short road up to the castle cut through a patchy, brown

lawn that Ayra supposed was once soft and green. Thin hedges, tipped with the golden colors of harvest season, lined parts of the lawn in a simple design.

The castle itself was immense—much larger than it had appeared when the city had come into view while traveling. Ayra had no idea men were capable of building something of this measure. Three squared towers lined the front of the castle with three mirroring hind towers, all joined by lower walls and made up of precisely cut and placed light gray stone that Ayra recognized as the same stone found in Darkwater Quarry. Glass and shuttered windows sporadically dotted the stone like knotholes in an old tree. The castle had a simple yet refined appearance. Ayra smiled as she took it all in.

When they reached the steps leading up to the large doors, stable hands took the horses. Directly on the other side of the door was a large, wide hall, with eight columns lining either side and a guard dressed in brown standing at each column. An orange flag with the red bear hung over the empty throne at the head of the room.

Aside from the guards, the room was unoccupied. The six soldiers they had entered with stood just before the rough floor turned to polished stone. Ayra glanced at Kelton whose face hinted only a trace of nervousness. Ayra felt as though her heart was going to gallop right out of her chest and was certain the walls of the room were drawing closer together.

The scrape of a door echoed through the throne room.

"Ayra! Kelton!" called a warm voice. Gibsen confidently

walked toward them with his arms outstretched, a group of men and women following after him. "I am so pleased to see you again." He shook each of their hands. "May I introduce my father, King Leofric Yofreid of Mihtengard. Father, these are my friends, Ayra and Kelton."

A man stepped forward from the small cluster with his hand extended. Ayra was taken aback by his warm, gentle expression that was nothing like the repulsive sneer of his horrid ancestor. He had a long, well-groomed beard with a mouth that looked prone to smile peeking from under the peppered whiskers. He was only set apart from the other by a gold bear on his red tunic and an unadorned crown upon his head.

"The pleasure is mine." He shook Kelton's hand first and then took Ayra's, grasping it with both of his hands. "I have heard much about you both. Thank you for accepting my invitation. I have a proposition for you I would like to discuss privately. If you are not too weary and would be willing to follow me, we will get right to it."

Ayra tried to remember if Edvin had told her about conduct before the king. She felt like she should have curtsied or bowed when they were introduced and found she did not know how to address him. Your Majesty or Highness like in the fairy tales Tanna had read? Or King Sir or Sir King? She couldn't even remember if she could use his name. So she just nodded her head and tried to find comfort in the squeeze from his warm hands.

In the group behind him, whispers echoed from the finely

dressed ladies with long, intricate braids down their backs. Ayra's hand almost reached up to grab a strand of hair, suddenly conscious of her loose mane and dusty dress. But she caught herself and straightened her shoulders, keeping her arms to her sides.

The king led them to a smaller, high-ceiling room furnished with a long, stout table with smooth benches running the length of the sides. A large map with Mihtengard in the center and all the surrounding countries was hung on the wall, and Ayra stared for a moment, tracing her journey from the quarry to Tiseden and now to Midivard. Only Gibsen and four others she did not know joined them in the room. Once all were inside, the king closed the door.

"Now, please, be seated. Gibsen tells me...Oh, I quite forgot. This is my elder son, Crown Prince Leoson."

The crown prince bowed his head. "Pleasure to make your acquaintance." He was dressed the same as the king only wore no crown. Gibsen looked at his brother admiringly, and Ayra sensed the same goodness from Prince Leoson as she did from his father and brother.

"My loyal chief adviser, Lady Harriet," continued the king gesturing to a woman seated beside Prince Leoson. "Marium, our head of agriculture." Then referring to the tall man with dark, serious eyes, "And High Commander Vansar."

Ayra about choked and felt her face grow hot. She wasn't prepared to meet Edvin's father. She almost laughed at herself for feeling more nervous having him in the room than she did the king. They nodded at each other, and she wondered what, if anything, Edvin had said about her. For a fleeting second, she thought about inquiring how Edvin was and where he was but in the end said nothing.

"There. Now all are acquainted. First, I would like to thank you for aiding my son though he behaved poorly toward you." He must have noticed Ayra's questioning glance to Gibsen, as he hastily continued, "He has told me all, and Vansar's son has verified his story, along with the other surviving men as much as they know. I understand you have been through a great deal, and I heartily apologize for the risk Gibsen took with your lives. I assure you he has felt a proper amount of guilt and has been justly dealt with." Gibsen's face reddened as he looked down at his hands. "You have saved many, Ayra. Though your efforts cannot be made general knowledge for several reasons, know you have the never-ending gratitude of the Crowns of both countries.

"And now I must also apologize for the treatment of your family. We keep so many records that sometimes things are...lost, for lack of a better word. And much of King Ivar's reign remains concealed in the folds of history. In all my life I had never heard of the Regnan family—there are many hands that handle my debtor camp affairs, you see—until I received the letter requesting you both in Tiseden, which I found suspicious from the start." He quickly eyed his humbled son. "Lady Harriet?"

"Yes," Lady Harriet continued. "We requested our historians

to look into the matter and found loose documentation of your family being in Darkwater, but not the original records, if they were ever made. What we found, Ayra, Kelton, was a release for your family from the camp."

"But we were never told…" Ayra looked around the table.

Lady Harriet spread a yellowed parchment across the table. "The document is dated long ago. After King Ivar's death. And was supposedly signed by a member of the House of Regnan. The name Regnan does not appear on our records afterward, but evidently your family never left. We may never know who was working within the castle, or perhaps the camp, to conceal your family or how they remained undetected so long. Rooney may have found more about your family, but if he did, I'm afraid those records are now lost. We found none searching his chambers. But it must have been mere chance that he followed a series of names and found the two of you."

Ayra could not understand. She held out her hand, and Lady Harriet slid the document across the table to her. As she looked over the paper, a memory flashed. She had seen the signature before. Kneeling on the floor at Wil's feet that dark night that felt so long ago.

"In any case," King Leofric continued, "since learning of your situation, we have sifted through the other two debtor camps to ensure there are no other forgotten families. We found none and have taken measures to ensure there will be none in the future. I hope that is resolved satisfactorily to you."

Kelton looked to Ayra, and she nodded her head.

"Good. Now that things of the past are settled, on to the present. Gibsen and young Edvin tell me you have a gift that would be useful to the country, Ayra. I understand your family has been responsible for our rainfall for quite some time. True?"

"Yes," she said, finally finding her voice. "That is true, Your High...you...sir."

The king smiled at her graciously. "You must know we are in great need of that rainfall to return—we get so little naturally it turns out. Our farms and people are beginning to suffer, and I cannot tell you the weight that has been on my chest the last several years as I have beheld a constant clear sky. I would like to offer you a position on my staff. I will provide housing, food, and wages for you and your brother in exchange for rain, and in time, after you have properly developed your knowledge of our water system, service on the Water Affairs Board so you may learn where water is needed most and assist in its management."

Ayra was at a loss. She had expected him to ask her for rain but not to offer housing and an adviser position.

"Also," he continued, "it has occurred to me that not one of the advisers on the Debtor Camp Board has ever lived in a camp. I would like you to attend some of their meetings. I like to be sure things are running properly and my people are being fairly treated while working off debts. Your life experience will be of great help in rectifying any issues my current board members are unable to detect. Kelton, you may assume a position on the board when you come of age, if you so desire. Until then, we will find other suitable work for a boy your age." He paused to wait for a response.

Ayra stared at the table trying to quickly sort everything out. She could provide Kelton with a permanent home and protection. But there was always a chance the next king could turn to darkness. She stole a glance at Gibsen and Crown Prince Leoson.

The other issue foremost on her mind was her ability. She had been able to make it rain on the mountain, but she had not pulled the clouds from very far. What if she failed?

Kelton nudged her with his elbow. She looked at his face and could plainly see he wanted her to accept. She tried to think what Tanna would want her to do. Her family had hid for so long, afraid of being hurt again. Afraid to leave the safety of the quarry.

She deliberated a moment more and selected her words carefully. "I thank you for the opportunity, but I want to make it clear I have not developed my gift as those before me. I'm not certain I can bring the rain you need."

The king leaned back in his chair, keeping his eyes on her, and placed his hand thoughtfully up to his mouth.

"From what Edvin tells me, Your Highness, she is fully capable," Vansar offered from across the table. His voice was smooth like his son's.

Ayra's mouth twitched as she fought a smile.

King Leofric nodded. "Well, Ayra? Will you try it?"

The path forward cleared before her. She was not going to hide in the shadows anymore.

"Yes, Your Maj—er High-ness...I will work to meet your expectations."

King Leofric beamed at her as he stood. "I have no doubt you will. I cannot thank you enough, Ayra. We will have your quarters prepared at once."

29

AYRA and Kelton were given a comfortable, two-room apartment in the staff quarters of the castle. They sent word of their new situation to Wil and Arman and assured them they would visit after the cold season. Ayra tucked a pressed wildflower into the letter hoping it would reach the old woman intact.

Small meetings and private education classes kept her and Kelton busy. The king wanted to ensure they were educated in the history of their region, as well as obtain a basic understanding of arithmetic, economics, and the water systems that had been developed. She was grateful Tanna had taken the time to teach both of them to read or they would have been woefully behind.

Kelton quickly made friends with the other staff members his age, but Ayra found it more difficult. She was beginning to learn some names and had even been invited to sit with the same group of girls twice. But conversation didn't come easily to her, and she found it hard to relate. She was always relieved to retreat to her and Kelton's quarters.

Her bedroom window faced the distant East Wolfjaw Mountains, and in her spare time she focused her efforts on pulling clouds into the valley. Though she was anxious to strengthen her skill and wanted to please the king, she had ulterior reasons for spending her free time working.

Hours and days passed without any sign of Edvin, and it felt as if some of her happiness in the castle had been prematurely snuffed out. Surely her friend had heard from his father that she was in the head city. His name was mentioned several times by girls in the dining hall, with sly smiles and giggles, but she did not dare ask anyone about him.

After eating supper, two weeks from the day they had arrived, Ayra walked alone back to their room. Following his new daily routine, Kelton had gone out to the courtyard for a game with his friends. As she ambled through the maze of corridors, people bustled past her carrying armfuls of rich fabric or baskets of fruits and vegetables. The Harvest Holiday was next week, and no doubt preparations were already beginning. Ayra smiled to herself knowing she'd be invited to *this* Harvest celebration.

She arrived at their door and entered the small apartment. With an exaggerated exhale, she loosened the tie at the end of her braid and ran her fingers through her tresses. Out of respect for her king and adviser positions, she had voluntarily taken on the custom of braiding her hair. But only for official meetings. On her own time, she left it loose and free.

As was her habit, she moved toward the window, but something on the little table caught her eye. The butterflies in her stomach stirred to life as she gently lifted a small raspberry tart with a perfectly fluted, golden brown crust. Under it she found a note written in scrawly black ink.

Welcome to Midivard, Pit Girl.

With an irrepressible smile, she set the tart down and with the note in hand, skipped to the window and flung it open. She searched the grounds immediately below her and then the royal stables a little further off, and as she hoped, her eyes found a tall, dark-haired soldier in an orange tunic. He was casually talking to the stable boy with his hands in his pockets and his head cocked to the side.

"Hello," she said, hoping he was listening for her.

His head snapped up to her fourth-story window and a grin overtook his face.

"Meet me at the west gate?"

He nodded and immediately turned to make his way to the gate, leaving the stable hand baffled by his abrupt departure. By the time Ayra made it through the staff quarters and down the three flights of stairs—proud she only got lost once—and talked her way past the sentinels at the door who couldn't remember seeing her before, nearly ten minutes had passed. Her excitement to tell Edvin everything that had happened during the warm season and since arriving in Midivard buzzed in her stomach. It spiked when she spotted him leaning against the stone wall with his arms folded across his chest. When he saw her nearing, he shot away from the wall and smiled.

"Hi," he eloquently said, rubbing his hand across the back of his neck.

"Hi," she returned, relieved she was not the only one who was nervous.

"There's an orchard a little distance outside the city that way. Want to see it?" His shoulders seemed broader than she remembered.

"Yes, I would love to. I have been cooped up in these walls waiting for…" She trailed off, deciding to spare him the mopey details of why she had not ventured out.

After an easy exit through the small, guarded castle gate, Edvin guided her through the noisy city streets, then out beyond the main city wall. As they strolled down the well-worn dirt road, occasionally moving to the side for carts rolling past, they chatted about the city and the king.

It only took minutes for the mood to lighten and both of them to relax. He told her he had tried to go in the company sent for her, but he had already been assigned to a military training in the East Mountains. He had just returned late last night.

"My father has kept me nearly smothered under his boot

since hearing everything that happened. And his ears hear *everything*."

"Why should you be punished? If it weren't for you, Kelton and I would be in Covalt's hands and Prince Gibsen would be…well, probably not safe here. He should herald you a hero."

He laughed lightly. "That's the way I see it, too. But my father is a man of precision and planning. He sees my actions as reckless. Says I need more training. He's probably right, though. My plan worked but honestly wasn't well thought out."

"Really? I hadn't noticed," she said in mock surprise.

She told him the skills she had learned from Wil—that she could milk a goat and make cheese—and about the work she had done with Kelton and Arman. He inquired after Arman, and she reported he was well when she left him. He asked her if she regretted leaving the little home behind. She admitted that she missed Arman's happy ways and odd sayings.

When she saw a shadow cross over Edvin's face, she quickly added, "He's become like another brother to me. I miss Wil, too. She was so kind to us. But I don't regret coming here."

His countenance cleared, and he looked out toward the mountains, clearing his throat. "My mother asked me to invite you to supper the night after tomorrow. If you want to come. She's anxious to meet you, but I can't say I'm excited to take you around my brothers." He squinted one eye. "They're kind of obnoxious. So if you…"

She readily accepted the invitation and wondered if his brothers were any more obnoxious than he could be.

When they hadn't been disturbed by any passing for some time, Edvin asked how her talent with water was developing. She pointed to the feathery clouds overhead.

"I pulled those from the other side of the mountains. I was worried I wouldn't be able to pull them from this far. I didn't know if King Leofric would keep Kelton and me if I failed to be useful. So it's a relief to know I can. And now it's almost like water—on the ground or in the sky—wants to obey me. Like it listens for me. It's getting easier, just like you said it would."

He looked up. "Is there enough up there to make it rain?"

She smiled. "I've found I don't have to gather them. If I can just get enough pulled over the mountains, they gather themselves. But…"

She looked up with her hands out in front of her, palms up. As she slowly curled her fingers into fists the clouds gathered directly over their heads and slightly darkened. Within minutes small droplets sprinkled their faces. Edvin's boyish delight made her laugh. The clouds opened up in a downpour, and the two sprinted for cover under the orchard trees. The sweet smell of ripe apples clung to the air.

When she had caught her breath, she acknowledged, "It isn't much and won't last long. But I am getting stronger and pulling more and more."

"That was amazing!" he replied. Out of the corner of her eye she saw him look at her. "You are amazing."

She felt her cheeks warm and turned her head away from him. The rain around them was already fading into a drizzle.

"It's no surprise," he added haughtily. "You did take lessons from Master Edvin."

Ayra rolled her eyes and turned to march out of the orchard.

"Now, wait a minute," he said, catching her by the hand and pulling her back to him. Her heart began to pound when he did not let go. "I want to tell you something."

"You do?" she said staring at his chest. She searched herself but could not find the courage to look up.

"Yeah, I do." He shifted his weight. "I thought of you the past four months."

She swallowed hard, hoping to swallow the heat from her cheeks. "You did? How much?"

"Oh, you know, a little bit. Every time I gutted a fish or saw someone trip over a rock."

He was only teasing her. She tried to pull her hand away, but he held it firmly. His thumb moved over the back of her hand, and her heart skipped a beat.

"And every time I saw a girl with brown hair, which is only most of them. Or heard even a drop of water. Every time the sun went down at night and when it came up each morning and all the time in between."

He paused, and a smile found its way to her lips. He seemed to take heart from the little smile and reached up to tuck a strand of hair behind her ear.

"Guess I thought of you a lot. I missed you, Ayra. I missed seeing your hair down and loose. I missed hearing your thoughts and trying to make you laugh. It nearly drove me crazy not knowing for sure you were safe. I was a fool to let you stay on that mountain."

"Let me? You couldn't have made me leave."

"I know." She could hear the smile in his voice. "That's why I didn't even try. But I was hoping…well, I hope the king's request and a promised raspberry tart weren't the only reasons you came."

She bit her lip and bounced lightly on her toes. "They weren't."

Courage to look up seeped into her bones and before it leeched out again, she raised her eyes to his. The usual sparkling humor in his brown eyes had been replaced with a soft, beautiful seriousness. He wasn't teasing her now. He cupped her face gently in his warm, calloused hands, his thumb brushing her cheek, and when she didn't flinch—didn't shy away—he bent his head and kissed her. And for a moment her active mind stilled to listen to her brimming, bounding heart.

When he pulled away, her mind took over again, and she scrunched her nose. "Guess this means you're going to have to teach me how to dance."

His mouth twitched into that perfect crooked grin, and he put his forehead to hers. "Prepare to be dazzled."

She was pretty certain she already was.

The following morning, Edvin took Ayra and Kelton to the market. Ayra was nervous about the whole idea, but when Edvin laced his fingers with hers she felt nothing but excitement. From a few blocks away, hints of roasting meats, frying yeast breads, and fragrant perfumes twisted through the air to Ayra's nose and muffled shouts from peddlers attempting to clear their carts of goods could be heard.

When the trio rounded the corner and entered the market district the sight almost overwhelmed Ayra's eyes. It was larger than she had envisioned. Much larger. The gray stone that covered the city was hidden by vibrant colors in every direction. Painted wooden carts and stands lined both sides of the street. Orange, blue, and red flags, some emblazoned with the red bear, flapped in the light breeze. The people moved and shifted like waves on the sea. Within minutes Kelton spotted his friends. He and Ayra made plans to meet later, and she watched her brother wander off with the group. She was sure she had never seen him so happy.

Edvin took her to his favorite fry bread cart first, where the vendor knew him by name. The bread was perfectly golden and drenched in freshly churned butter and wild honey. It was the second best thing she had ever eaten, coming second only to the 'I've-not-forgotten-you' raspberry tart. She tried not to be embarrassed when Edvin reached up with his thumb and wiped away the melted butter running down her chin.

With full bellies, they wandered through the labyrinth of goods. Frequently, Edvin was stopped by people he knew. He introduced her to every single one. Ayra was puzzled how he could keep so many names straight. And many appeared to be good friends. She was not at all surprised he was so well liked.

As they neared a vendor selling various ropes, Edvin quickly steered her in a wide circle around the cart. A blocky young man with curly, auburn hair was examining the merchandise.

"See that fellow?"

She had noticed him even before Edvin pointed him out and nodded. With a feigned look of dread, he pointed to the scar near his eye. Ayra looked back at the man and saw the next stand over was selling live eels contained in a barrel of water. With a flick of her hand, water sloshed out of the barrel and drenched the burly brute.

"Hey! Watch it!" he growled, glaring at the fish merchant, as two snickering pranksters hurried away. Evidently not everyone liked Edvin.

By late afternoon, after hours of browsing and eating, Edvin and Ayra found seats by the round stage. The actors were busy setting up their props.

"Oh, good. This one's a comedy," Edvin said. "You'll like it."

She spotted Kelton and his friends nearby, laughing at their own jokes. An outsider would never guess the small, jubilant boy had been raised in Darkwater Quarry, away from crowds and fun.

As the play began, Ayra scanned the crowd. All around her were people of Mihtengard. Her people. Couples holding hands—some smooth skinned and others wrinkled and weathered. Mothers bouncing their precious babes in their arms. Fathers standing in the back rows with wide-eyed children on their shoulders. Musicians filling the air with joy and actors filling it with laughter. She did not understand the strong, suddenly formed bond she felt with so many people she did not know. With people who had no inkling the freckled girl with long, wavy brown hair sitting among them was charged with providing them with an essential element to their way of life. But deep inside she felt the shift of responsibility.

And she, Ayra of Mihtengard, would not let them down.

Acknowledgments

Special thanks to Jana and Megan, for braving my first full draft ever when it was nothing but kitty litter and liking it anyway. You gave me hope. Thank you Melissa, Tara, Niki, John, LeeAnn, and Roger. Your enthusiasm for my writing was much appreciated. And an extra thank you to Niki for your time in creating the beautiful cover art.

Thank you to my children for taking naps, playing together, and making it easy for me to find time to write.

And last but not least, thank you, thank you, thank you to my husband, Travis. Your unfailing support makes all the difference in my endeavors.

Other Books by the Author

The Falcon Princess

A Pretty Game